Home Runner

MILLIE PEREZ

Copyright © 2026 Milagros Perez

All rights reserved. No part of this book may be reproducedor used in any manner without the prior written permission of the copyright owner, except for the use of brief quotations in a book review.

To request permissions, contact the publisher at millieperez.author@gmail.com

Edited by Beth Lawton @vbedits

Cover art by Buero Sued @buerosued

Formatting by Sandra Maldo @smaldo.designs

For my people pleasers
And those who'd love to be pleased
by a burly MLB coach, too

AUTHOR'S NOTE

Hello lovely readers and welcome back to the world of the New York Monarchs.

This is the third book in an interconnected series, and I am so excited and cannot wait for you to dive into these new characters. I have included aspects of my personal journey of being a chronic people pleaser, something I still struggle with to this day. I've also included a storyline that heavily highlights the importance of our found families. As a daughter of immigrants, I wasn't able to grow up alongside my blood related family. And while I missed them dearly, and was able to form connections with most of them later on in life, I credit much of the love and support I was raised with to the other first-generation kids I grew up with, who I lovingly refer to as my "cousins."

With Daisy's story, I hope that we all learn to chase the life we've always dreamed of, without waiting for the permission to do so. And I hope some of you feel seen in her story, too.

If you can't get enough of Luke and Daisy or the New York Monarchs, I've added a special treat at the end of the book. A sneak peek of the next couple that come after Home Runner, which I'm super excited about!

Below are some content warnings. Please take them into account before reading this story to ensure an enjoyable experience.
Happy Reading!

xo,
Millie

CONTENT WARNINGS

Discussion of death of a parent (off page)
Brief mention of infidelity (not between main characters)
Mention of drug abuse (not by the main characters)
Microaggressions towards Afro-Latino hair
Brief mention of deaths due to drunk driving
Open door spice with explicit sex scenes

PROLOGUE

DAISY

I've always dreamed of my wedding day.

Not so much the decor or guest list, but the quiet moments in between the madness with my new husband.

Sneaking kisses during the endless toasts. Making funny faces when the photographer wasn't looking. Or whispering inappropriate jokes under our breath.

And at the end of the night, I'd get to stare at him while he ditched his tie as we left our wedding venue to start the rest of our lives together.

I look over to the man next to me in time to catch the silky noose around his neck loosening and a small smile threatening to break free.

His dark brown beard has been tamed for the occasion, and his wavy hair seems to have gotten a trim.

My dress is a comical white poof around me, leaving minimal room for movement. In search of comfort, I dig the veil out of my hair and release a sigh of relief.

This should be what I imagined when I dreamed about my wedding day.

Except… I've deviated from the plan in a few crucial ways.

Because the man beaming down at me as he grabs my discarded veil and tosses it out his open window *is not my husband*.

And instead of a limo, I'm in what many may consider a getaway car.

Because I, Daisy Stonehaven, am officially a runaway bride.

No, this is not what I dreamed of when I thought of my wedding day.

And it's clear as day, that my life as I know it has officially gone up in flames.

Chapter One

LUKE

THREE DAYS, TWO HOURS, AND FORTY-FIVE MINUTES BEFORE

I FORCE MYSELF TO look away from my watch and focus on my men warming up on the field.

The incessant countdown has taken over every crevice of my mind lately. I need to figure out how to shut it down before I end up doing something reckless.

Speaking of... I groan as I see the incoming call on my phone. Three poop emoji's stare back at me. I should have known better than to spill my guts to the one person who is like a dog with a bone. Especially when it comes to me talking about my feelings.

But I don't have time for this, especially right before a game. So I send the call straight to voicemail. Let it be a problem for another day.

I look up, intending to focus on work, but instead zero in on our team photographer as he makes a beeline toward me.

I silently curse as I pull down my baseball cap. Looks like it's going to be one of those days.

"Is today the day I'll finally get to photograph that dazzling smile you're hiding under that unruly beard, *Home Runner*?"

I cross my arms over my chest and grunt as I scan the field, making sure my guys are looking healthy and ready to go and ignoring the nickname I was given in little league, the one that somehow followed me throughout my major league career.

I may have grown to enjoy the limelight at the height of my playing career, but as a kid, I was easily overwhelmed by the attention that came after I hit a home run. To the point where I would continue running to *my* home after making sure to swing by home plate first. It was a funny story my mom told reporters after I got drafted to the MLB, but it stuck.

And it's not lost on me how little has changed. Because when that spotlight feels too harsh and blinding, I know exactly where to run and hide.

"Oh, c'mon, *Skipper*. Show off those pearly whites. Give the people what they want," he goads as he starts snapping away.

I pin him with a glare that has him straightening while dropping his camera to his side. "S-sorry about that. I forget you're not a fan of the term of endearment, *Coach*," he amends.

I sigh as I attempt to seem less surly and lift an unenthusiastic thumbs-up at Tom. He takes the photo quickly, although I'd be surprised if I was even in the frame since he didn't bother to bring the camera back up to his face.

But he's not in the wrong here. As the manager of the New York Monarchs, my team should call me Skipper or Weston. But when I was initially hired—after I spent five years keeping my distance from the sport—I was supposed to be the pitching coach. But our new general manager and now majority team owner, Luisa Álvarez, gave me a promotion before the ink on my *first* contract was barely dry.

I'd already become partial to the relationship I developed with the team as one of many coaches and didn't like the idea of having too much attention on me... once again. Something I should have thought through before I signed on the dotted line, because no matter what I tell them to call me, there's always going to be the murmured chatter behind my back.

I may try to convince myself that the attention is because I'm Luke Weston, the youngest manager in MLB history and not the former World Series champion who ran away from the sport after the unthinkable happened.

The headlines wouldn't stop, and people only cared about my personal life from that point on, no matter how many home runs I'd achieved during our pivotal game seven.

So I did what I do best. I ran.

I thought I'd never set foot on a field again. Yet here I am, like I never left, even though I look like a completely different person. Instead of the lean build that helped me steal bases faster than any player on my team, I've bulked up thanks to all the time I spent doing manual labor up north.

Alone.

I traded in the cleanly shaved face that regularly got invited to movie premieres for the overgrown beard that could probably use a trim and the ever-present scowl that apparently does nothing to keep people from invading my space.

"Damn, poor Tom is never going to get that shot of you smiling before he retires, is he?"

Here we go again. "I'm here to help you guys win, Martinez. Not pose and smile for the cameras. That's what they pay you the big bucks for."

He grins easily. "Yeah, they do. Although the strikeouts and shutout games don't hurt either." He winks as his eyes scan the crowd, his expression growing warmer when they settle on his daughter and fiancée.

I ignore the pang of jealousy that takes root in my chest. Mateo is a good guy and deserves all the happiness in the world. I sometimes need to remind myself that men like me are not meant to have someone waiting in the stands for them. Things are exactly as they should be.

Or so I tell myself.

I make a noncommittal sound. "Just make sure not to punch anyone on the field this season. Then maybe we'll snag that World Series win."

The jab doesn't land as my starting pitcher smirks. "Don't think I've forgotten you told Luisa that you'd have done worse had you been in my situation." I stare blandly at him as he raises his hands, backing away from me. "All right, all right, don't you worry. I'm back on my best behavior, promise." He chuckles. "Besides, have you seen the jersey Isabella is wearing today?"

I force myself to hold in another sigh. "Can't say I have."

"It says 'Future Mrs. Martinez.'" He fucking beams at me as if we're supposed to hold hands and jump around in a circle in excitement.

"Great. This game should be a sure win then. If I see you slipping, I'll have Luisa swap out Isa's jersey for Middlebrooks's and see if that keeps you in line."

He stops his retreat abruptly as his eyes narrow at me. "You wouldn't dare. And here I was about to ask you to be a groomsman."

I pinch the top of my nose while tilting my head down. "You're going to give me a headache today, aren't you?"

I can hear the smile in his voice. "So is that a yes?"

I mutter a curse under my breath. "If you want me there, then I'm there. You know that." I keep my eyes closed as I try to rub away the pressure building behind them at the mention of another wedding. Seems like they've taken over my life lately.

Nick Stonehaven, our team owner, and Luisa got hitched again last month in the Dominican Republic. Mateo and Isabella are planning something small in the summer since we'll be in the middle of the season. Then they'll have a big celebration during the winter holidays while we're in the offseason.

And then there's... *Three days, two hours, and thirty-five minutes.*

I shake my head as Mateo carries on. "Yeah, I kind of figured you'd be on board, but if Isabella asks, I'll say that you teared up a bit and I left you speechless."

I open my eyes and give him a bored look. He smiles as he continues to make his way toward the gate that will take him closer to Isabella's seat behind us. "Wow. Speechless, just like I said. Who knew coaches took directions so well?"

"Martinez."

"Yeah?"

"Fuck off."

"Love you too, Weston." He runs off.

Times like these make me think that I preferred when Mateo was quiet and kept to himself. But ever since he got with Isabella, his whole demeanor has changed.

It's great for him, but terrible for my lack of patience.

But I meant what I said. If he wants me standing there on his special day, then that's where I'll be. Because try as I might, I've unwillingly let a good portion of the Monarchs family get close to me. At least as close as I'll ever allow anyone to get.

Well, almost anyone.

"F-bombs don't make for family-friendly television, Luke." When the sweet voice carries over my back, I have to remind my muscles not to lock and remain seemingly calm. Something that I've come to master over the last year.

I turn only when I know I've mentally prepared myself to see her standing in my dugout.

It still doesn't stop the gut punch from hitting its mark.

Because there, standing before me with a wide smile, long dark hair clipped half up and half down, with warm brown skin I've spent one too many nights imagining feeling beneath my calloused hands, is Daisy Stonehaven.

She holds up a small mic pack with a teasing look on her face. "Going to have to save the potty mouth for the after-game interviews, Coach. Not on my channel if I can help it," she mock scolds.

I force the breath out of my chest and play along. "And exactly how many people are going to be listening to me while I'm mic'd up?" I raise a knowing brow.

She breaks out into a soft laugh that should be reserved for only the best humans to ever grace the earth and not tainted souls like mine, but I bottle up the sound every chance I get like a man starved.

"Luke, while I appreciate you being my very first guinea pig when it came to testing out Hot Mic, you no longer have to get wired up for every game."

My face scrunches. "Why the hell not?"

She does what she always does, which is bite the corner of her lip, and I do what I always do and act like it doesn't burn me from the inside out.

"First of all, you don't speak when you're mic'd up, which kind of defeats the purpose."

"I'm orchestrating the entire game, Daisy. I talk."

She considers my statement while tilting her head from side to side, clearly finding my answer unsatisfactory. "You point, huff, glare, and smack a few butts. A method that clearly works for you and the team but is kind of useless for a recording." She wiggles the mic pack.

A huff escapes my mouth. I don't realize my mistake until she points at my face and shouts a triumphant "Aha!"

"I'm not that bad," I mutter to myself, noticing that our media team looks ready to start with the national anthems and my guys are filing into the dugout.

Her face gentles as she hands me the pack and her fingers move swiftly to clip the small microphone to the inside of my Monarchs jacket. "Yeah, I guess you're all right." She pats just below the mic, keeping her hand there longer than necessary.

I clear my throat as I stuff the pack into my back pocket. "Channel?"

She rolls her eyes. "The usual. Seven."

The first day I mic'd up, she asked me what channel I wanted to broadcast from. I asked for her favorite number, then almost smacked myself upside the head when I realized how flirty my tone had gotten.

She'd blushed and said "seven."

I told myself it's many people's lucky number.

But it also happens to be the number I wore when I played.

And the thought that she was giving me a subtle nod was enough to send my simple crush into forbidden territory.

"And who has access to that channel?" I keep to the script we've said back and forth since I first volunteered to be her first test subject for the Monarchs online channel she runs.

She rolls her eyes playfully. "Only me."

"Good." My lips twitch with the urge to smile down at her.

That is, until the hand on my chest starts to slide off, the large diamond on her ring finger catching the sunlight, refusing to be ignored.

And there it is again.

The pinch in my chest. The low swoop in my stomach.

Her eyes follow my gaze, and I swear I see her slowly curving into herself. Her playfulness vanishes; her eyes dart around us, landing anywhere but on me; and her footsteps start to retreat. "Have a good game, guys," she says to the swarm of players around her.

They all nod and send a thanks her way.

She's about to step out into the clubhouse via the narrow hallway when she sends a weak smile my way, and suddenly it feels like we're no longer at Monarchs Stadium.

But rather a looming church as she finally turns and walks away.

Three days. Two hours. And twenty-five minutes.

That's how long until I have to watch Daisy walk down the aisle to another man.

And apparently how much time I have left before I lose my goddamn mind.

Chapter Two

DAISY

MY WEDDING DAY

I CAN'T BREATHE IN this damn dress.

I tried telling Vivian in so many ways that I thought it was too tight.

But my future mother-in-law never listens.

And I never stand my ground.

Maybe I need some air. I'm sure I'd be able to breathe better if I left this stuffy room that reeks of hairspray and burned split ends. Not sure if my hair will ever return to its natural curl after today's ordeal.

I push open the door that leads to the back of the church parking lot and leave it propped open so I don't get locked out.

I don't know why I was expecting a cool, calming spring breeze when I'm in the middle of downtown, where all I can feel is the heat from the building's air conditioning unit and all I can hear are the sirens of a nearby ambulance.

If I don't get a full breath in soon, they might have to circle back and pick me up.

I start pacing but stop when I realize my pointy shoes are giving me blisters. Because of course they are.

I look back into the room where my comfy Converses are calling my name. But I don't think it would be deemed appropriate for me to get married in my scuffed-up Chucks.

A startled laugh escapes me at the thought, and before I know it, I'm bent over with my hands on my knees, laughing uncontrollably.

How the flying fuck did I get here?

The laughter subsides as silent tears run down my face. I need to reel it in before it ruins my makeup, but I can't find the strength in me to care.

Gosh, I really need to catch my breath. I'm starting to feel lightheaded, and I can't handle a fainting spell on top of the mess I've made.

A wailing noise brings my attention back to the parking lot. Only to realize it's coming from me.

I cover my mouth with my hands. The last thing I need is the paparazzi to get a shot of me having a full-blown meltdown ten minutes before I walk down the aisle.

My father and Damien would never let me hear the end of it.

I close my eyes and knock my head back against the brick wall a few times.

I can't do this. I never should have let this go on this long.

I've had a healthy dose of doubts leading up to today, but last night, something broke inside me. Specifically, when Damien and my father cornered me at our rehearsal dinner and told me that I would be quitting my job with the Monarchs effective immediately.

Now that I'm to become Mrs. Fischer, the wife of a New York senator with clear goals of becoming the next governor and eventual president of the United States, I won't have time to entertain a "silly job in a sport meant for children."

They didn't ask. They informed me.

If they'd asked for anything else, I would have done it. I always have.

But the Monarchs are my family. The one place I feel truly at home. With people who love me unconditionally.

And I can't leave them. I won't. But I don't know what to do. The clock is ticking, and I'm running out of time.

I hear fast footsteps headed my way, and my eyes fly open. With my luck, I'll get mugged before meeting my groom.

For a second I consider that it might be a great excuse to postpone the wedding.

My thoughts snap back to the present as I realize that it's my best friend, Luke. He's here, and he's closing the distance between us.

"Y-you came. You actually made it." I hiccup.

"What's wrong? Did he do something to you?" His eyes scan my body, looking for the source of my distress.

"I'm okay. Just taking a little walk around the block. Apparently, it's my wedding day. Can you believe that?" My smile must look deranged.

"Daisy girl, talk to me. What do you want to do?" His warm, calloused hands squeeze my bare upper arms, and I sigh deeply.

I can breathe again.

"If only it were that easy."

"Try me. I'm going to ask you one more time. What. Do. You. Want?" he asks through gritted teeth.

I force my breathing to match his as silence surrounds us.

No longer can I make out the sounds of honking yellow cabs or pedestrians rushing their way back to work after lunch.

It's just Luke and me. And the answer to his question.

"I don't want to marry him," I say on an exhale.

"You don't want to marry him?" he parrots.

I manage to shake my head.

He steps back, releasing his hold on me. His warmth is gone, and the tightness in my chest returns.

He runs his hands over his thick beard and slowly starts to nod. "All right."

"What do you mean, all right? Everything is far from all right. I have five minutes to get my ass in there." I start to panic again.

He steps closer. "I'm going to make this real simple for you, Daisy." He cradles my face in his hands, his glacial blue eyes searing deep into my soul. "You're not getting married today."

"I'm not?"

He shakes his head.

"But—but what do I do now? There are over three hundred people waiting in the church. And I don't know if Nick can alert the media and tell them that I've fallen ill or have my father postpone—"

"Do you have any of your belongings in that room?" He nods at the propped door as he gently wipes away my tears.

"Uh… um, yeah. My phone and my weekend bag." I start stepping side to side, my feet now killing me.

Luke looks down at the pointy witch heels poking out from under my dress. "Okay, here's the plan. You're going to gather your things, ditch those shoes, and slip into the Chucks I'm sure you sneaked in here. I'll text your brother to prepare for what's about to go down. Then we're going to walk out, nice and calm, and you're going to sit your ass in my truck. Because you, Daisy, are not getting married today."

He smiles widely, and I freeze. I've never seen him smile like this, and now I'm glad I haven't, because it's downright devastating.

I shake the absurd thought from my head and try to grasp what Luke is trying to communicate with me.

"Okay, so toss the shoes and grab my phone and bag." I nod, the pieces slowly coming into focus. "I'm not getting married today." I smile my first real smile in what feels like forever.

"You're not getting married today." His smile now matches mine.

I go to move but stop to turn back to Luke. "Wait, and what are you going to do?"

He grins as he nods at the black truck in the mostly empty parking lot.

"Daisy girl, isn't it obvious? I'll be the one driving the getaway car."

Chapter Three

DAISY

"You know, if you wanted to take the crown for most dramatic sibling, all you had to do was ask, sis." I groan as my brother Nick makes light of the massive clusterfuck I've just caused. My sign of distress doesn't deter him as his voice carries from my cell that's on speakerphone. "And to think, there were so many ways I could have helped you really stick it to Damien, and you chose the route that didn't include a scenario in which I could have had my own moment to shine. Very bridezilla of you, if I do say so myself."

I don't tend to get carsick, but as the realization of what I've done starts to set in, I find it harder to keep the contents of my meager breakfast from making a reappearance.

There's rustling over the line, followed by a clear "ow" coming from my dear old brother. Before I can even muster the will to respond, my friend and now sister-in-law, Luisa takes over the line. "I swear, sometimes I wonder if your brother performed a spell on me, because why else would I be married to a guy who—"

"Because you love me!" Nick's muffled voice interrupts.

Any other day, I would be giggling up a storm at the thought of those two going back and forth between lovers and adversaries. But today is not that day.

"Guys, please." My voice unexpectedly breaks on the last word, and everything around me goes silent.

A warm, comforting hand finds my clamped ones and squeezes lightly.

I look to my left and find Luke's worried gaze locked on mine. "We need a plan," he says gruffly as he slowly directs his attention back to midtown traffic.

Nick is back on the line, and this time, I can tell he is in full business mode. "You're right. My apologies, Daisy. I know this couldn't have been easy for you to do, but please know that we are so damn proud of you and will handle the aftermath."

"Aftermath?"

"Yes, aftermath," he continues. "There are about three hundred guests plus staff in that church waiting for a bride who is currently tardy to walk down the aisle. It's only been fifteen minutes, so they're probably assuming you're fashionably late. But before long, someone will leak what has happened and we'll have a media firestorm on our hands."

I don't even realize I've made a distressed sound until I feel Luke squeezing my hands again. This time he unclenches my hands from one another and threads our fingers together until he's got a firm hold on me. "I'm not hearing any solutions, Stonehaven," he states in the same disapproving tone he uses while speaking to his baseball players when they're late to practice.

"Yes, I was getting to that, Coach. Which, by the way, good save today. Talk about right place, right time, huh?"

"Something like that," he mumbles.

"As I was saying, we need a plan. I've already texted all the heads of Stonehaven Media. They've already gotten a statement from me, which is better than any "unconfirmed sources" that I'm sure will be popping up throughout the week. It is set to go live as soon as you give me the green light, sis."

"A statement? From my brother? Isn't that, like, weird? And shouldn't I talk to Damien before going to the media?" I bite the nail of the thumb on my free hand, and for a second, I think Luke is trying to figure out a way to hold both of my hands at the same time.

Nick audibly sighs. "Daisy, I am the media. And unfortunately, you won't be able to talk to Damien before this goes live." His voice gentles. "You know why, don't you?"

I lean my head back and close my eyes.

How have I landed myself in such a dumpster fire?

I'm Daisy Stonehaven.

Certified people pleaser. Rule follower to a fault.

I would never cancel a dinner reservation, even weeks in advance. So how the hell did I end up running away from my very own wedding?

You know why, the voice inside my head whispers.

I was too much of a coward in the days and weeks—hell, even months—leading up to my wedding. I never spoke up. I waited up until the last second, until the walls were closing in on me. And even then, I think I might have still gone along with it. Walked toward a lifetime of unhappiness just so I could please the people who so badly wanted to see me at that altar. Unifying two prominent families whose last names were sure to leave a lasting mark on New York society.

If it weren't for Luke...

His thumb brushes over my knuckles softly, as if he knows the moment my thoughts have drifted to him.

I shake away my internal chatter and focus on the matter at hand.

Because I do know the reason why I won't be able to reach Damien before the news gets out. It's the same reason I haven't been able to get through to him for the last year of our barely there relationship.

He's not just Damien Fischer; he is *New York State Senator* Damien Fischer. And if he gets his way, come this November, he'll be crowned the youngest person to ever become governor of New York.

Meaning he's probably got his "fixer" lying in wait for any and every scenario possible today. And since I'm the one who left him, I wouldn't be surprised if his campaign chose to smear me in the media to help him save face and go up in the polls.

What a fucking mess.

"Listen, Daisy, we can tackle that in a minute. What we need this very moment is to get you to a safe place." He pauses, as if it pains him to continue. "I'm sorry, sis, but the paparazzi attention will be brutal. My instinct is to have you come stay with us, but it's already a media circus since we released our wedding photos, and to be honest, I think you deserve a break. To get as far away from this shit as possible. Which is why I need Coach to drive you to the private airstrip near LaGuardia Airport. My jet is waiting on standby, and the pilot already has the flight plans. You can stay at the house in the Dominican Republic. Some time on the island might do you good."

Luke's grip on my hand tightens momentarily. He quickly loosens it but keeps his eyes on the road as he asks, "Is that what you want, Daisy?"

"I-I don't know." I pause, trying to think through all the moving pieces. "I don't want to be anywhere near the public scrutiny, but I also don't want to get on a plane and flee. The last time we were at that house was for your wedding, Nick. And I don't think being in the place where I saw you and Luisa the happiest and most in love is the best spot to hunker down while I deal with whatever the hell is about to come my way."

"All right. Name a city and we'll get you there. Maybe you should go somewhere in Europe. I have a house in—"

The noise level around Nick increases suddenly.

New York City sidewalks would never be considered quiet, but now it sounds as though Nick is walking through Grand Central Station.

"Okay, change of plans, girl," Luisa starts, sounding slightly frazzled. "All the guests are making their way out of the church. They must have been notified. Which means..."

"I'm out of time." I finish.

"Daisy, we can—"

"Let's get you—"

Nick and Luisa are both interrupted mid-sentence by Luke. "I know a place where she can go." He stops at the red light and turns slightly to face me. His bright blue eyes bore into mine with an intensity I never knew possible. As if he's trying to communicate with me silently before he shares his thoughts with my brother and Luisa.

"Oh yeah? And where exactly is that?" Nick asks, unimpressed.

Luke's eyes never leave mine as he gives my hand one final squeeze. "With me."

Chapter Four

LUKE

This is a bad idea.

But what other choice do I have?

She needs a safe place to land until this all blows over, and I'll be damned if that place isn't with me.

I slowly move my hand out of her grasp and set it on the steering wheel. I immediately feel the loss of her hand in mine, but I fear that I may crush hers if I keep reacting every time the suggestion of her leaving my side gets brought up.

"Excuse me? With you?" Nick asks, most likely baffled by the change in plans. But if it hadn't already sunk in that I'm the man driving her away from that doomed marriage, then he hasn't really been paying attention to the lengths I'd go to for his sister.

"I've got a place we can go to." I hesitate for a moment.

I never intended on telling people where I go in the offseason and where I spent a few years in hiding after I unexpectedly retired from the MLB. The quiet place I desperately needed when grief consumed me. But if it means I get to keep Daisy safe and sound, I'll gladly hand over the information to her loved ones.

"It's in the Adirondack Mountains. It's about a five-hour drive. No one knows I have a home there. It doesn't even have an official address. It's just a large plot of land and a cabin. I've been able to keep a low profile when I go into town, so there's no way the media will track Daisy up there. She'll be safe."

"Five hours? Are you insane? Take the jet. It'll be faster and—"

"Flight plans are public and can be tracked. All it would take is a long-lensed camera snapping an image of her in a big white dress boarding your plane, and she would be followed. So how about we try not to kill the environment today and stick with my plan?"

"Seriously? You choose *now* of all times to speak more than a few stunted words and grunts? Unbelievable. Daisy? It's your call. What do you want to do?"

I chance a glance in her direction, and the sight still takes my breath away.

She's beautiful.

And she's sitting in my truck while we put miles between her and that damn wedding.

She's not marrying him, my mind chants.

I have to remind myself to take deep breaths and focus on the road more times than I care to admit. Especially because with Daisy riding shotgun, I'm carrying precious cargo.

Over the past year, my irresponsible crush on Daisy Stonehaven has remained in a secret compartment in my brain. But during the days leading up to her impending nuptials, I fear I may have done a shit job of hiding my true feelings for her. Feelings I had no business having for my boss's little sister, coworker, and, most of all, my closest friend.

Feelings that took me by surprise when she unexpectedly stirred my dead heart from a deep slumber and awoke protective instincts I never knew I possessed. Instincts so fierce that I found myself nearly growling over her anytime I felt her discomfort.

Feelings that she is clueless about.

I struggle with the selfish part of me that wants her to finally figure it out, then see how she reacts. To learn if those shared lunches at work meant as much to her as they did to me.

Or the time I drove her home after a girls' night got too rowdy and let her pick the music. Luckily she was too tipsy to notice that I circled midtown twice so she could listen to a song she loved on repeat.

Or Nick's wedding day, when she convinced me to spend the entire night dancing with her and didn't pay any mind when my players were most likely recording us with their phones. Something I would never allow because I value my privacy over everything.

Well, almost everything.

But that secret compartment in my mind was shattered to smithereens the second I saw her losing her goddamn mind behind that church. When she told me she didn't want to go through with the wedding.

She's not marrying him.

I suppress a groan of frustration. No matter how badly my body is vibrating with the knowledge that Daisy is here, in my truck, and no longer betrothed to that pathetic excuse for a man, I need to keep my head on straight.

Daisy is rattled. She needs stability. A moment to catch her breath.

She doesn't need an overly eager thirty-one-year-old man stepping up to bat for an opportunity with her when she's at her most vulnerable.

Unfortunately, when I became protective of Daisy, I knew I would have to include myself in the list of dangers as well. Daisy deserves more than a man who hides in the woods when the world shatters around him. She needs time to discover who she is now that she is no longer under her ex-fiancé's thumb. And I need to be the bystander who helps her get whatever it is she wants for her future. Even if that future doesn't include me standing by her side.

I steal a glance in her direction when I realize she has yet to answer her brother. And my heart does that thing where it overrides my brain and any prior logical thought along with it when I catch her already looking my way.

Her big, expressive brown eyes are incapable of hiding her thoughts, and right now, she's unsure.

Maybe that's why my friendship with her has always been easy. Apart from the fact that she might be the kindest person I've ever met, Daisy is an open book. I can tell when she doesn't enjoy something she's eating, even though she's too polite to say otherwise. Or when she's trying to tamp down her excitement with the events she's helped planned at Monarchs Stadium.

I can sit all day, staring at her, watching the way life blooms behind her irises as her attention shifts from person to person. As she offers everyone genuine smiles along with questions about their day.

Which is how it was easy to spot that something wasn't right when it came to her fiancé. Ex-fiancé.

Because anytime there was any mention of Damien, the light in her eyes diminished. For a while I told myself I was seeing what I wanted to see. That I selfishly came up with a narrative that fed my preposterous and unrequited crush.

But after meeting the guy and seeing the way he treated her as a pawn rather than the gentle soul that she is, I knew that look in her eye was not something my weak heart had conjured up for the sake of my ego.

I need to stop staring.

He's here. He's real. And this should be the final straw to these irrational feelings toward my coworker. My friend? I didn't think I was capable of having any of those again.

But Daisy is different.

She isn't a snake. She wouldn't put me through the hell I just crawled out of.

Although I fear that just her association with me would be enough to taint her pure soul.

Which is why instead of celebrating the end of a successful charity game with the rest of my team, I'm standing in the shadows, watching her with him and convincing myself that this is exactly the way things should be.

Her, with a stuffy but somewhat decent-looking guy. And me alone, with only the company of my demons.

But something is off.

Daisy can light up any room she is in with her sparkling brown eyes.

Instead, I can tell they're barely holding back tears.

What the fuck is he saying to her?

My fists clench as I force myself to stay put.

Daisy worked tirelessly organizing this event, and I won't make a scene and ruin it for her. She single-handedly managed to wrangle players from different teams to participate tonight and took care of every detail, even down to the catering. She also roped me into cake testing with her.

As expected, she kept pestering me about which flavors were my favorite. She's always asking others their preferences and opinions while keeping hers buried.

Little does she know she's not that hard to read. I saw her going back multiple times to take bites of the dulce de leche cake while she explained the décor for the afterparty.

So as her fiancé not so subtly taps her hips while removing the slice of untouched cake from in front of her and places it on an empty high table as he walks out of the private venue, I overflow with rage.

My body is begging me to follow him out and demand he tell me what he said to her so that I can do my best to scrub whatever hurtful words he used to cause her tears to form.

But my eyes won't leave Daisy. Haven't been able to since the moment I first saw her.

Isabella is standing by her side, but she's still struggling.

She has a good group of friends around her, and for that I'm thankful.

Friends.

The word doesn't feel right when it comes to Daisy. But nothing has felt right in a long time, so it's most likely that I'm just broken. After all, that is what everyone says behind my back.

I see one tiny tear escape, and before I've given my body permission to leave the shadows I've become so accustomed to, I'm on the move.

I don't break stride when I pick up two slices of dulce de leche cake from the dessert table.

I know it's her favorite. Which is why I told her it was mine.

I don't say a word as I place them in front of Daisy.

And I don't dare look back as I walk out of the room and into the night.

I blink until I find myself back in the present. I need to keep my head on straight, especially at a time like this, when Daisy needs me.

She's not marrying him. But maybe when she's ready, we could try and...

I knock the absurd thought from my head. Now isn't the time to worry about anything besides what Daisy wants. She took the first step, and I'm going to need her to keep being the one to call the shots here. Because if left to me...

"Daisy." My voice comes out gruffer than expected as I stop at a red light. I go to pull the tie around my neck only to realize I've already taken it off. Meaning the tight sensation around my throat is the anticipation that comes with waiting for Daisy to decide. And knowing I'll do whatever it is she asks of me.

"I-um. I don't want to get on a plane. Don't think I need to add my flying anxiety into the mix today."

I hold my breath as I nod, keeping my eyes locked on hers.

And like I knew I would, I see her answer before she speaks.

My hands loosen on the steering wheel as she says, "I want to go with you... if that's okay. I know you've already saved me by being there when I needed you. But, oh gosh, five hours, you say? Are you sure about that? That's a bit—"

"I was planning on going there today anyway." I nod to the back seat, where my small suitcase sits next to her weekender bag. "You'd just be tagging along. And you know I don't mind your company." In fact, I enjoy it more than I should.

I ignore the honks behind me as I hold up traffic. I'll wait as long as I have to for her final answer.

The nod comes before she speaks, and I slowly move my foot off the brake. "All right, then. Looks like we're going to the mountains."

Daisy keeps saying that she isn't hungry, but she's bound to crash soon, and I'd prefer if it happened after she had a little food in her system.

We're an hour outside of the city, and there are only gas stations and fast-food restaurants near our next exit. I decide to chance it and pull off the highway, hoping no one is loitering around the drive-thru and recognizes either of us.

"Why are we stopping?" she asks over the relentless buzzing of her phone. It's been going off nonstop since she gave Nick her approval to go ahead with the far too gracious statement. The one announcing that his sister and Damien would not be getting married today and would appreciate if the media could respect everyone's privacy during this time.

Surprisingly, Damien's campaign has yet to put out a press release.

And none of the calls or messages blowing up her phone are from him either.

If I never heard his name again, it would be too soon, but for Daisy's sake, I hoped he'd at least make contact to make sure she was okay.

I would move heaven and earth if I didn't know the whereabouts of my fiancée, but then again, I pride myself on not having too much in common with the senator.

Unsurprisingly, it's been her father doing most of the texting, and even though Daisy hasn't opened any of the messages, per her brother's advice, I could see a few of the previews when her phone sat in the console's cupholder. Needless to say, none of those messages screamed "concerned father."

She's confided in me a few times about her strained relationship with her dad. I've always tried to be a listening ear so that she knows she can come to me about anything. But her father and Damien might be neck and neck at winning the asshole of the century award.

I reach back and pull out a Monarchs hoodie and place it on Daisy's lap. "We're grabbing food to go. Flip the hoodie so the team logo isn't showing and drape it over yourself. I don't want to chance anyone recognizing you."

She chuckles. "Uh, hate to break it to you, but I'm not a major celebrity. Yeah, people may know of me in the city, but that's mostly because of Nick."

I do a shit job at suppressing my sigh as I pull into the lane with no line.

Her brows furrow. "I'm in denial, aren't I? Leaving the future governor of New York won't exactly go unnoticed, huh?" She chuckles dryly as she rubs her forehead.

"He doesn't have my vote," I mutter. "What are you in the mood for?" I nod toward the massive lit-up menu beside me, hoping to distract her from her thoughts.

She shrugs as she stares at her hands. "Not really hungry."

Her eyes meet mine briefly, and it's all the confirmation I need before turning to the intercom. "I'll have the number one with water." I don't need to scan the menu as I recite her usual order by heart. "And I'd also like to add the crispy chicken with no lettuce. Wedge fries and a large Coke. Oh, and the cookies and cream shake too, please." I drive forward before the total is repeated back to me.

With one quick look at Daisy, I know I've made the right move. The quiet glimmer in her eyes and the soft smile on her lips make me feel ten feet tall.

I pay, and we hop back on the highway without incident.

She polishes off every morsel of food.

The noise coming from her straw tells me that she's also finished her dessert. But the satisfaction in my chest only multiplies when she makes a show of shutting off her phone and tossing it in the center console.

"I'm in the mood for murder," she says as she picks up my phone, taps in my security code—the one she's had for longer than I can recall—and chooses a true crime podcast. "Feels extra dangerous since I'm going to a house in the mountains with a white man in his thirties. I'm practically murder bait."

I smile on the inside, because she sounds more like herself already. "It's actually more like a cabin in the woods. We're right on the lake but have views of the mountains, if that counts."

"Even creepier. That's perfect." She grins as she presses Play on an episode and settles into her seat.

She's asleep before we get to the first suspect. I pause where she left off so we can listen to it together when she wakes.

In silence, I let myself watch the only woman who has ever held my mind and heart captive sleeping peacefully next to me. And in that moment, I finally allow my thoughts to run wild.

She's not marrying him.
And she never will.
Because she's exactly where she needs to be.
Right here with me.

Chapter Five
DAISY

My eyelids feel like they weigh a million pounds.

I have zero desire to open them. Instead, I curl into the soft caress against my cheek.

I don't remember the last time I slept this well, and I'm doing everything I can to keep myself in this dreamlike state. Especially when the soothing voice I hear keeps lulling me into a deeper slumber.

"Time to wake up, Daze." I feel the caress one more time, right as I recognize Luke's voice.

Why is Luke in my room? Isn't it the middle of the night? Where—

My eyes snap open as my mind catches up with the events that transpired only hours ago.

I'm in Luke's truck.

And he's standing between the open door and my seat, wearing a poorly veiled look of concern. "We're here. Need help getting out?"

I rub my eyes, surely messing up whatever's left of my eye makeup. "No, I'm good," I say as I remain seated, blinking away the remnants of sleep.

I should probably make my way out of the car.

But I'm too distracted with how Luke's body is backlit by the full moon. His hair is usually combed back or hidden under a baseball hat, but tonight it's tousled, as if he spent the whole drive running his hands through it, allowing the strands to fall over his forehead. It looks so soft, and I feel the unusual need to run my fingers through it.

"You sure?" Luke's gaze slides over me tenderly.

I'm not blind. I knew Luke was an incredibly good-looking man the moment I met him. His kindness and soft-spoken words only added to his overall appeal. But I was engaged back then. And this girl believes in loyalty. Even if it's been blind and applied to the wrong people in my life.

I close my eyes and internally tell myself to get my shit together before any of my outrageous thoughts find a way to escape my lips.

I move to take off my seat belt, only to see I've already been unbuckled. Luke is still watching me, and if he doesn't give my muddled brain some space, I might do something stupid like ask what kind of conditioner he uses.

Instead of answering, I force myself to take fistfuls of my dress and slide out of the elevated passenger seat, landing as gracefully as possible while looking like an undercooked cupcake.

Luke doesn't move, which means we're standing too close to one another. Closer than two people who are "just friends" should be standing. He must have the same thought a moment after I do, because he takes a sizable step to the side. "I'll get our bags and meet you at the front door."

"Yep," I chirp as I grab my phone and his hoodie before turning back around and making my way to the quaint A-frame cabin.

Or so I think that's what I'm seeing. I can't really focus on my surroundings since I'm trying my best not to trip over my dress while also avoiding scattered rocks and acorns.

I'm glad I stepped out of the wedding shoes, the ones that should be advertised as torture mechanisms, before I left. Although it seems like the damage is already done, because not even my broken-in Converses can take away the pain of the fresh blisters on my pinky toes as they brush against the inside of my shoe.

I should be used to it by now.

Uncomfortable shoes, clothes, and the company I keep.

Kept.

Life with Damien meant a life of being scrutinized from head to toe, even when I wasn't standing in the same room as him. As if I were a walking billboard, representing the future of New York politics, and the campaign hinged on whether or not I was wearing shoes half a size too small and clothes better suited for someone with a deep love of buttoned-up tweed suit jackets.

I clutch my phone. I should turn it on. Surely Damien must have reached out by now. I don't know what exactly I plan on saying to him, but something, anything is better than leaving your fiancé at the altar in front of hundreds of guests and breaking up with him with a note written in lipstick on a mirror.

I hiss when I place my foot on the first step. These damn blisters are going to be a bitch for the next few days. I mentally tell myself to soften my footfall on the next step but never get the chance to.

One moment I'm wincing at the impending pain, and the next I'm being lifted up and carried the rest of the way in Luke's arms.

Correction, arm. Because he managed to swoop down and carry me with his right arm while his left still balanced our luggage.

I squeal in surprise, instinctively wrapping my arms around his neck, afraid I'm going to fall. "You know, you could warn a girl next time you're planning on sweeping her off her feet." I huff.

His lip twitches. "Oh yeah?" He glances down at me, then shrugs. "Guess I'll have to give you a two-second warning next time."

My jaw drops. Luke and I have always had an easy-going friendship. And while I've noticed that his jokes and smiles are hardly shared with anyone else around us, flirty banter is something we've never dabbled in, for obvious reasons.

It's mostly me making terrible jokes and him not throwing me out of his office like he does everyone else. Even when I not so slyly steal the fries off his plate after saying I don't want to order any.

I continue to stare in mild shock as his face returns to its usual stoic features. "Your feet hurt" is all he says, as if that is reason enough to short-circuit my brain on a day like this.

He barely has to shift me as he enters a code over a small scanner and unlocks the front door.

Thoughts of being cradled in Luke's arm take a back seat when I realize what we must look like.

I stiffen in his arm as he steps over the threshold, and his body instantly goes on alert. "What's wrong?"

I curse the man for being so goddamn perceptive. Can he not allow me to have one mini mental breakdown without noticing?

I shake my head and aim for levity. "Oh, you know. Me in a big white dress. You in a suit. Carrying the bride into the house. At least I can say I kept one tradition alive tonight, right?"

I swear he stops breathing, his eyes widening as the penny drops for him. "Daisy, I-I'm sorry. I shouldn't have... I didn't mean..."

I chuckle nervously. "While it's been mighty fun getting carried around and giving my battered feet a break, I think it's safe to put me down now. Um, how about a tour?" I pat his chest and instantly regret it. The man is built like a brick house and the last thing he needs is sad little Daisy pawing over him at the end of a long and exhausting day.

He quickly lowers me to the ground, not releasing his hold until I've lifted the hem of my dress out of my walking path.

He clears his throat. "Yeah. A tour. Sure. Uh, well. This is it." His hand gestures around us to the vast open floor plan that lets me see almost every inch of the home from where we stand. "It's spacious, but I built it like a studio, so there are no interior doors except the ones leading to the bathroom and closets. It's, uh, built it with only me in mind. I have a place in the city that has room for more guests. And more... doors."

I look over my shoulder as Luke shifts his weight from foot to foot. Why does he seem shy about showing me his place?

Yes, it is definitely not meant for entertaining a crowd, but it's beautiful. And so very Luke.

"No doors. Got it. That means I can snoop more easily." I smirk in his direction as I take in the place.

The walls are made up of smooth logs like the ones I used to see in picture books when I was a child, making me feel like we're in an adult version of a tree house. The kitchen is to our left. A small butcher block island stands in the middle of the space that houses beautiful dark green cabinets above and around a gas stove. It's tidy and no nonsense, like the man who must cook all his hearty meals in it.

To my right is a living room, with a plush brown couch that looks divine for mid-afternoon naps and movie nights.

And in front of us is a set of floor-to-ceiling windows and a sliding door that is currently giving us an unobstructed view of a lake and the moon shining in its reflection.

But my attention is drawn elsewhere.

To the one and only bed with views of the moonlit water.

Oh.

Now I understand the nervous look on Luke's face. He only has one bed, and it offers no privacy whatsoever. I could sit in that bed and easily throw a pillow that would land on the couch. Not that I'm going to sit on his bed. Or be in it in any capacity.

I may ask to steal a pillow off it so I can bring it to the couch, but besides that, there is no reason why I should be thinking about or looking at Luke's bed. None at all.

"Daisy, look," Luke starts.

I'm not sure what kind of conversation he's about to strike up, but what I do know is that I'm probably still blushing after staring at my friend's bed for longer than most would deem appropriate.

I'm about to make this awkward. I know it.

Luckily, the reminder of my full bladder seems like the perfect excuse to find one of those damn hard to find doors in this house and escape for a moment of reprieve.

"Um, where can I find the ladies' room? Or you know, the Luke room. Where you do your business. And wash yourself." I slap a hand across my forehead. "Jesus Christ, why does it keep getting worse the more I speak? How do I stop it? Luke, please put me out of my misery and point to a damn toilet before you come to your senses and kick me to the curb. Or in this case, serial killer wonderland."

The tension in his shoulders seems to melt as his eyes gleam with amusement.

"The Luke room with a toilet and where I wash myself." He points behind me. "First door on the right."

As he laughs, I scurry off, moving as fast as I can in the restrictive dress.

As soon as I close the door behind me, I rush to use the toilet. Something that proves to be difficult while holding up the heavy garment that feels more like a straitjacket than a designer gown. I kick off my shoes and wiggle my toes, silently promising myself that I'll never wear anything that causes physical pain to my body again.

I wash my hands and while I'm at it, start scrubbing at my caked-on makeup with the simple hand soap at my disposal. I have toiletries packed in my bag, but I can't stand the thought of looking like this any longer.

I stare back at my reflection, bare faced with a few streaks of stubborn mascara that I'll have to try to wash off with my actual skincare products later.

The person staring back at me shocks me to my core. Because I look... like someone else. Like the character I've been dutifully playing since Damien put a ring on my finger.

I glance down at the large diamond that shines tauntingly at me.

How did I get it all so wrong? Not just today, but the entire relationship?

All I wanted was a man who loved me. A person I could build a family with. Grow old with. Someone my dad, the only parent I've ever known, would approve of.

But somewhere along the way, our dates turned into business meetings.

Gentle suggestions became firm expectations.

And love was nowhere to be found.

He spent his days out on the campaign trail, and I spent mine alone in my room. Making myself useful to everyone around me so I wouldn't have to sit long enough to look around and see the condition in which my life currently stood.

It made me question if I was built for that kind of life, and if Damien and I were even compatible anymore.

Somehow, my father would always know when I was at my breaking point and would remind me that my future husband was working for the greater good. Not only for our state, but our home. And Damien always knew the right time to surprise me with flowers and dinner at a popular restaurant.

And even though he'd spend the entire meal standing up to shake hands and introduce himself to other prominent patrons, for those fleeting moments, it felt good to know I was with someone I could call my own. Someone I could be proud of, even though I don't believe he could say the same about me.

The woman who graduated with an MBA but turned down a job at my father's company to join my brother at the New York Monarchs and work alongside their social media team and community outreach.

I know I'm a total nepo baby.

Or a nepo sibling in this instance, since I wouldn't have a place in the Monarchs organization if it weren't for my brother unexpectedly inheriting the team from our estranged grandfather.

But regardless of how I got there, I found a little place in the world that I could claim as my own. I was excited about going to work every day. I finally had an amazing group of friends who actually liked me for who I was instead of what my last name could do for them.

And I found Luke.

A friend who I felt safe enough to be my true self with.

Not the stuffy twenty-four-year-old with pressed Chanel suits in muted colors, but the girl who goes out in comfy T-shirts, ripped jeans, and her emotional support Converses.

So how the hell did I get it so wrong?

How did I let this farce go on for so long?

I splash water across my face, hoping the cold bite will snap me out of my spiraling thoughts, but it's no use.

Somehow, the dress keeps getting tighter as the day drags on. It becomes harder to breathe, and I find myself clawing at my back, hoping to find the zipper and finally release myself from the cruel confinement.

Only to remember that my mother-in-law chose a dress that has tiny buttons running down the entire back.

I start to panic.

I need to get this dress off.

Right now.

I'm able to loosen two of the buttons near my upper back, but it takes forever, and the thought of wearing the physical reminder of today for another moment is enough to have me bursting out of the bathroom in search of Luke.

He sets my luggage on the kitchen island, his head snapping up. "Daisy, what happened?"

I dart for him. "I'm—the dress. I need it off. I need your help," I pant.

Luke's eyes widen as he looks around the room, as if he can call in an assist at a time like this. If I weren't in the middle of spiraling out of my mind, I might have found it amusing. "Please," I croak.

My broken voice seems to be the thing that springs Luke into action. He turns me by my shoulders to face away from him. "Careful, you've already scratched yourself here, Daze." He drags his thumb down an exposed piece of skin beneath my dress, and a shiver runs down my spine.

His fingers still momentarily. "I got you. It's going to be okay." And then they start to move, methodically releasing each button as his knuckles run down my back.

The panic starts to subside, but now I'm having trouble breathing for a completely different reason.

This can't honestly be happening right now.

I know it's been a long time since I've been touched by a man and even longer since I've been intimate with one, but this is not the time, and he is not the person I should be fantasizing about.

This is Luke. *My Luke*. And I can't risk ruining one of the very few real relationships in my life because my body doesn't know how to control its biological urges.

If Luke doesn't get me out of this dress in the next five seconds, I fear he's going to know why a small gasp escapes my lips every few seconds. Or how my shivers have nothing to do with the coolness in the air.

He's going to sense the illicit thoughts running through my head as his hands tease down my back like a lover's whisper.

I feel the warming sensation low in my belly and know it won't be long until there's physical evidence of my arousal.

"Luke, please. Just—rip it," I plead.

He speeds up the process, but he continues to remove each button carefully. "We're halfway there. I'll be done in no—"

"I'm sorry I'm acting this way. I know you're trying to help. But you don't have to be so gentle with me. I'm not going to break. So please, rip—"

"As you wish, Daisy girl," he drawls in my ear.

The tear and the scattering of buttons is deafening. The dress falls, and as it pools at my feet, my hands automatically raise to my bare chest. I had forgotten that the bra was built into the dress and not on my body.

This is also the moment I realize I am standing in front of Luke wearing nothing but a lacy white thong.

Maybe if I don't move, I'll become invisible. Or he'll take pity on me and find one of the very few doors in this cabin and lock himself in it until I can get my clothes out of my bag and change.

My racing thoughts come to a halt when I feel warmth on my lower back and hear a growl loud enough to make my bones shake.

Then I feel his hands on my left thigh.

Only then do I realize there was one more thing left on my body.

My garter.

That is until Luke rips it clean off me and escapes with it out the sliding door without a backward glance.

Chapter Six

LUKE

I'M POKING THE FIRE to death.

Hoping that if I move the logs long enough, I'll no longer see the spot where I threw the scrap of fabric that read "Mrs. Fischer" that clung to her thigh.

I have no reason to be this irrationally upset. I got dressed this morning knowing I would be attending her wedding. That I'd have to see her in a white dress. And that she'd walk down the aisle to a man who didn't deserve her.

It killed me knowing that she was going to marry him.

Still stings now that she hasn't taken off his ring.

But when I had her standing practically naked in front of me, all smooth skin and the soft curves I've dreamed about, I felt like I had died and gone to heaven. Only to be dropped into the pits of hell when I saw his last name wrapped around her skin.

The thought of her almost taking his name had me raging hotter than this fire pit before me.

So yes, for a split second there, I lost my goddamn mind and tore it off her body. And since I'd already lost all sense of reasoning, I tossed it into the fire.

After I was sure the coast was clear and she was locked in my bathroom, I snuck back into the house and placed a pair of thick wool socks and a couple of Band-Aids on top of the kitchen island, hoping she would see them.

I'd made a mental note to give them to her as soon as I saw that her feet were hurting, but I'd gotten sidetracked when she begged me to undress her in the middle of my home.

The same home I'd planned on spending the weekend in, drowning my sorrows in beers and frozen pizzas while Daisy was supposed to be prancing around in a bikini on her honeymoon.

My mind still has trouble catching up on how we got here.

Specifically the part where Daisy was standing naked in front of me. And thank God she wasn't facing me, because after years of barely using most of my facial muscles and learning how to keep my emotions locked up tight, I somehow forgot how to close my jaw and keep my eyes above ass level.

For the last fifteen minutes, I've given myself the harshest pep talk known to man, the kind that would make some of my players cry if I unleashed on them, which I try not to do too often.

I'm supposed to be her friend.

She's fucking losing her mind over the stunt she pulled today. And I can't get my cock to stop stirring at the memory of her soft curves beneath my fingertips or the way she got goose bumps when I ran my thumb over an angry-looking mark on her skin.

Fuck.

Here I go again.

If I don't wrap my head around the fact that Daisy is off limits, and fast, I'm going to have to toss myself into the fire. Otherwise, I risk doing something stupid and hurting her.

I have my demons, and it's only a matter of time before the skeletons in my closet come back out to haunt me. And there is no way in hell I'd let any of that mess spill over onto Daisy, especially after what she's gone through.

I contemplate our next steps as I sit here, engaging in a one-sided fight with a small fire, trying to figure out if I should act as if nothing happened or get it out in the open and then convince her it wasn't a big deal.

Maybe I saw a bug on her garter and wanted to make sure she didn't get bit?

Surely she's not used to the critters up here and wouldn't question my actions too thoroughly, right?

Time ticks on, and I'm starting to wonder if she's come to her senses and driven off in my truck, having come too close to feeling like she was starring in her own true crime podcast with a caveman as a roommate.

But then I see her.

Coming out through the sliding door, wearing a graphic T-shirt and black leggings.

She's also wearing the socks I left for her, and somehow the sight has the tension in my chest easing.

She dangles two beers in her hands as she makes her way toward me. "This seat taken?" She points at the empty Adirondack chair next to mine.

"It's gonna cost ya." I nod at one of the uncapped beers.

Knowing that she walked through my kitchen and made herself at home makes me feel like she's not planning to make a run for it. At least tonight.

She hands me a beer before she takes a seat and makes herself comfortable. "So... I know I've been a complete basket case, and you're probably questioning why you ever made conversation with the weird, quiet girl at work. So I'm going to make things easier and fly out of here early tomorrow morning. I thought it over in the shower and decided that as soon as I can get a signal on my phone, I'll text Nick and let him know that he can ship me off to one of his houses. He's probably got one or two I don't even know about," she finishes in a rush.

"You want to leave?" I manage to keep the panic out of my voice somehow.

Her eyebrows furrow. "Well, no—I mean—" She closes her eyes, sighing deeply as she sinks farther into her chair. "Luke, I'm a mess. You're a good friend, but I don't want to dump all of my mistakes on your doorstep. You deserve to enjoy your time off without having to worry about me begging you to rip my clothes off." Her eyes snap open and look my way.

My eyebrows must hit my hairline and her mouth gapes open as she realizes what she said and how it sounded.

"I didn't mean it like that. Of course you wouldn't want to—and that's not, err—" She releases a frustrated cry as she buries her head in her hands. "Ugh, I'm doing it again. I'm hazardous to be around right now. It's as if I reset my personal factory settings and now my brain doesn't know the proper way to compute. If you want, I can ask Nick to send someone for me tonight. I've already made a fool—"

"Daisy," I interrupt, then wait until she lifts her head and rests her defeated eyes on me. "What do you want?"

Confusion mars her face. "What do you mean?"

I exhale slowly, trying my best to not influence her. "It's simple: what do you want? Do you want to leave, or do you want to stay?"

She shakes her head. "I'm imposing. You should be—"

"Not what I asked, Daze. I'll stay here all night until I get an answer. And before you start worrying about something I haven't voiced, let me be very clear here. You are not imposing. You have not made a fool of yourself. And every negative thought you've had about yourself tonight is flat-out wrong. So with that cleared up, I'll ask again. What do you want?"

She stares at me, and I can see her trying to put together the puzzle pieces where there are none.

"It's simple, Daisy. Stay here with me or go. What do you want?"

She stares off into the lake. "Making decisions has never been simple for me," she whispers.

"If you stay, it should be because you feel safe and comfortable here. Not because you think you'll be hurting my feelings if you leave. If you go, it's because you know there is somewhere that can give you exactly what you need right now. Take your time. You have options. You always have options. So when you're ready, tell me what you want."

She looks up at the sky lit up with stars, the kind that would be impossible to see in the city. She takes a sip of her beer and lolls her head to the side, facing me. "I want to stay."

I want to punch the air in excitement like I do when my team is on a winning streak. But I keep my body lax as I ask, "Are you sure? I promise you there is no wrong answer. This is about you and what you need. I only want to be the person who helps you get whatever it is you want."

She takes a longer sip of her beer, this time nodding along as she considers something. "There is one thing I need from you."

"Name it," I say far too quickly.

She starts to peel the label off the beer bottle. "What are the chances of you having complete memory loss after seeing my ass? And does drinking this beer help move along that process?"

I groan as I tip my head back and run my free hand over my eyes. I didn't expect her to bring it up tonight, much less erupt into giggles.

"I promise to keep myself fully clothed from here on out. I know I scarred you for life back there." She smiles as she scoots her socked feet under her legs and looks into the fire.

I remain quiet until the silence stretches long enough for her eyes to find mine over the crackling fire pit.

"Scarring me? Daisy, trust me. I have many feelings about what I saw back inside my house, but scarred, sure as hell ain't one of them."

The easy-going smile slips off her face as her cheeks turn rosy. She turns her attention back to the fire. "So, um, what now? I saw a pizza in the freezer. We could throw it in the oven. Unless you're not hungry. Although you're always hungry. Not that it's a bad thing. You are still training like an athlete, and you..."

She continues to ramble as I take a long pull of my beer, but my attention is shot when I notice her nipples are hard under her shirt. Fuck, she's not wearing a bra.

It's going to be a long fucking night.

I clear my throat. "Pizza sounds good. How about you get that going while I put out this fire? We can watch a movie while we eat. Sound like a plan?"

The relieved look on her face answers before she does. "Perfect." She stands, and I bite the inside of my cheek when she turns and looks around, most likely searching for something to tidy up like she usually does. But all she's doing is giving me a view of her ass in those curve-hugging leggings and bringing back the memory I will in fact never forget. "Need any help putting out that fire before I go?" She smiles, knowing damn well she has no clue how to do so, but in true Daisy fashion, she would find a way if I actually needed help.

Little does she know that between her leggings and her thin T-shirt, she's only stoking the fires of my desire for her, which is doing the exact opposite of helping.

"All good. Let me know if you need help with the oven." I tip my beer in the direction of the house.

She rolls her eyes and smiles, then makes her way up the few steps onto the deck and finally inside my home.

I'll have to wait a few minutes before I get to work on putting out this fire.

Because if I stand now and Daisy looks out here, she'll know that I'm a terrible friend.

Because friends don't get hard when told not to think of their friends' naked bodies.

Or when thinking about how they'll be alone under the same roof for the first time ever.

No, no they don't.

So I sit back and allow myself to finally come to terms with the truth I've suppressed since the moment I laid eyes on Daisy.

I want to be much more than just her friend.

Chapter Seven

DAISY

It takes Luke an eternity to come back inside the house.

Who knew putting out small fires took so long.

The pizza is already cut and cooling on the counter. I've uncapped fresh beers and set them on the coffee table in front of the massive TV, and I've wiped down every surface I could get my hands on, even though they were already immaculate.

I wiggle my toes in relief. I don't know how Luke always reads my mind, but the Band-Aids and warm socks were lifesavers.

The same can't be said for the leggings I'm currently wearing. Since they are my "going out" pair, and not my "lounge in my bed" kind.

I eye the hoodie I left draped over one of the kitchen stools beside me. I used it as a pillow when I fell asleep in Luke's truck, and it felt so soft and cozy. It smelled like him too, and I found myself acting like a total creep as I took more than a few deep breaths and nuzzled into it while he drove.

What do you want?

It's such a simple question, but my mind always manages to make it as complex as humanly possible.

I'm always thinking of every possible outcome of the decision I make and how it could influence those around me.

A fun little party trick I picked up when I was a kid trying to get my dad's attention, and not the disapproving kind.

It doesn't take a rocket scientist—hell, not even a second grader—to know that I have daddy issues. And even though I'm an advocate for therapy and have been going for years, I still haven't managed to rewire the part of my brain that prevents me from feeling guilty when I feel like I've let someone down. Even if I logically understand the circumstances to not be my fault, my mind treats me like I'm public enemy number one and searches every avenue possible to reconcile the issue, even if it means disappointing myself.

That is, until I ran off into the woods with my best guy friend and shut off my phone, thus shutting out the world. Seems like I've run so far that the guilt has yet to catch up with me, even though I know many difficult conversations are still meant to be had.

I stare at Luke's hoodie one more time.

What do you want? continues to ring in my mind.

It seems so silly to be this tormented over something so trivial, so without another moment of hesitation, I grab the hoodie and pull it over my head. It hits me right above the knees after I've pulled it down my body.

I can see that Luke is still circling the firepit, so I bend quickly and pull down my leggings right then and there.

Damn, a girl could get used to this kind of relief.

I fold them and place them inside the bag that I've put in the linen closet.

I hear the sliding door open as I walk back to the kitchen.

"I promise I'll go on a grocery run tomorrow morning. I thought I'd have time on the drive up here, but it got dark and—"

Luke stops dead in his tracks.

His eyes darken as they assess me from top to bottom.

Shit. I fucked up.

I should have asked him if it was okay to put on his clothing.

Duh. What kind of person takes people's hoodies without asking?

Probably girlfriends and wives. Not friends and current runaway brides.

Am I giving him *Silence of the Lambs* vibes right now?

Because the way he's looking at me feels like he's holding himself back from taking off at a sprint.

"I'm sorry. I shouldn't have put this on. You gave it to me to protect my privacy, and I put it on because my leggings were too tight. Again, a me problem. I'll take it off right now."

He moves slowly, inching closer my way. Looking at the article of clothing as if he's never laid eyes on it before.

"You want to wear my hoodie, Daisy?"

"I-I can—"

He shakes his head twice. "Answer the question I asked. Not the one your mind is fumbling to answer."

I clamp my lips shut.

My brain is trying to give him an honest answer, but my heart is almost beating out of my chest with the tone he used on me. It wasn't mean, because I know a mean tone when I hear one. It was commanding. As if he was trying to wade his way through my thoughts and straight to my desires.

And if I give too much thought to how I squeezed my thighs when he spoke, then he'll be waiting a very long time for my answer.

"Daisy."

"Yes."

He arches a brow. "Yes, what?"

"Yes, I want to wear your hoodie. If that's okay with you," I add quickly.

His lips twitch as he takes another step my way, bringing us toe to toe. He picks up one of the strings around the hoodie's neck and gives it a soft tug. "Consider it yours."

Our eyes meet for a long moment, and I stay rooted to the floor when he turns and ambles to the living room.

Long enough to remind myself he's talking about the hoodie, and not himself.

"Pretty please? I promise I won't make you learn the secret handshake with me. Unless you want to. If so, we can start practicing tomorrow on the dock."

Luke sighs deeply. "*The Parent Trap*? Really? Don't you want to watch something with murder or suspense? That usually seems to make you nice and chipper."

I hit him with a small throw pillow as we sit side by side on the couch.

He showered quickly before dinner, and he's now wearing a long-sleeved navy henley and gray sweatpants.

While he was in the shower, I lined up every rom-com I've ever watched and prepared my pitch for each and every one of them.

So far, I've pleaded my case for six of them on three streaming services. And while I have yet to land on an option both Luke and I seem excited about, I do realize he hasn't actually said "no" to any of my suggestions.

Just the usual grunts and shrugs that he reserves for the rest of our friend group.

I tap my phone to check the time. "Look, it's almost midnight. If we don't pick something soon, I'm going to be watching the inside of my eyelids instead." I tap my phone one more time to make sure I haven't missed any calls or messages.

Nothing.

"Oh, crap. Hold on." Luke stands suddenly and makes his way to the front door. He flips up a switch that looks different from the rest of the light switches in the house, and my phone starts to buzz uncontrollably. "This place is a dead zone for cell signal, which was fine by me when I bought the place. But I figured it might be necessary to have access to the outside world when absolutely necessary, so I had a cell booster installed. I keep it off since I'm usually up here to be alone. Should have remembered to turn it on when we got home. But I guess I was, uh, distracted."

I point in his direction. "Memory loss! It's the only thing I've asked of you. And for a place to stay, I guess. And your hoodie. And to watch *The Parent Trap*, but the most important one on that list right now is memory loss, Luke."

"I'll get us some water while you decide whether you want to tackle those messages tonight."

Oh, right. That.

Between my cozy socks, soft hoodie and the comfy couch, I've almost forgotten that I imploded my life less than eight hours ago.

The power of self-care, I suppose.

I decide to bite the bullet and at least try to prioritize responses for the people that need them most.

Thank God Luke turned on the cell booster when he did, because it seems as though Nick was close to sending the National Guard our way.

I shoot him a quick text letting him know that I'm fine and should have regular phone service from here on out. But if I happen to lose signal, he should not send a small rescue team my way, since I am safe and sound.

He of course bombarded me with rapid fire responses, but Luisa's "I'll handle him, glad you're safe and taking time for yourself" text seemed to have settled my dear older brother.

Next, I wince at the number of messages I've received from my father. It's sad that he's texted me more today than he has in the last two years.

FATHER:

> Make sure not to wear too much makeup. There are many publications here, ready to cover the wedding story on their front pages.

FATHER:

> The wedding planner cannot find you. Where have you taken off to? Now is not the time for theatrics, Daisy.

FATHER:

> Are you still in the building?? The guests are becoming restless and it's not polite to keep us waiting. Today isn't all about you.

FATHER:

> Answer your phone this instant. Where are you?

FATHER:

> This is embarrassing. The priest had to tell the guests that his organist became ill and is currently looking for a replacement among his staff. We've bought you time, but now you need to get here and immediately apologize to Damien and his family for your tardiness.

FATHER:

> This is unbecoming for our family, Daisy. We will have words when you finally decide to grace us with your presence.

FATHER:

> DAISY

FATHER:

> WHERE THE FUCK ARE YOU????????

FATHER:

> Silly girl. What have you done?

FATHER:

> Seems like you have more of your brother's antics in you than I thought. Not that you deserve to know, but the guests have been informed that no wedding will be taking place today, and we will be reaching out with further information soon. Damien has handled himself with grace throughout this ordeal. You better come back on your hands and knees and hope he gives you the opportunity to make this right. I've never been more disappointed in you.

"All right, that's enough." The phone is snatched out of my hands. Not that I could really read anymore through my tears. "Daisy, talk to me. Are you okay?"

Luke sits next to me, pulling my hands into his rough, calloused ones. The feeling shouldn't be as comforting as it is, but I find myself leaning into his side for support.

"Want me to turn off the cell booster? Or we can make things simpler by blocking him. No one deserves to speak to you that way and continue to have access to you." His hands gently squeeze mine, but the ferocity in his eyes is anything but soft.

I open my mouth, but nothing comes out.

You'd think I'd be used to my father's cruel commentary, but his scathing words are usually delivered in a teasing tone or with a shoulder squeeze. That physical contact is probably the closest thing I've gotten to a hug from the man in the last decade.

But there is no context or nuance on the planet that could help soften the blow.

I've embarrassed him. Publicly.

And I may have deluded myself over the years thinking that maybe, just maybe, he could come to treat me with the same love and adoration fathers do in the heartwarming movies I like to watch. And that it would somehow fill in the void in my chest caused by growing up without a mother, since she passed when I was a baby.

But at the end of the day, one thing I know for certain is that my father reveres his image and money above all else. And today, I have cost him both.

"Daisy, talk to me." Luke wipes away tears before they have the chance to roll down my cheeks. "You've had a long day. Let me get you to bed. I'll be here on the couch if you need anything."

He tries to move me to stand, but his last words snap me out of my brain fog.

"What do you mean, couch?"

He looks momentarily confused. "I only have one bed."

"Yes, I'm aware. I was here for the grand tour." I wave around us.

He releases a deep breath while shaking his head, his face no longer looking panicked. "And that's where you'll sleep." He raises a stern brow.

"Absolutely not. I am not taking your bed when I've already derailed your entire getaway."

"I already told you I was already planning on being here. You're not derailing anything."

I stand and he quickly follows suit. I don't know if I'm fired up because of those text messages from my father, or if I'm just itching for a feeling other than sadness. Either way, I'm ready for a showdown if it comes to that.

"You're sleeping on that bed, *Coach*." I point back toward it. "There's no way around it. You can save the chivalrous spiel for another day. You've done enough rescuing as it is." I fight the urge to stomp like a petulant child.

He runs a hand across his thick beard. "Hmm, is that so?"

I smile triumphantly and nod. "Yes. Besides, I'm smaller than you. Most of the human population is, I suppose, so that doesn't say much, but it means I'll fit much more comfortably on the couch than you, anyway."

Looking down at the couch, I can already pick out the exact spot I'll curl up on.

Suddenly, Luke's knuckles lift my chin, guiding me until I'm facing him, his lips mere inches from mine. "Daisy, there is a better chance of me calling your ex-fiancé myself and giving him the location of my cabin, than me allowing you to sleep on a goddamn couch when there is a perfectly suitable bed a few feet away."

I'm shocked into silence, and it seems as though he's in no rush to fill it.

Neither of us has moved an inch, and I can feel Luke's deep breaths on my lips.

This is ridiculous. One of us should move away from the other right about now. But Luke only regards me as if he has all the time in the world.

What do you want?
I can almost hear him taunting me as his eyes stay on my lips a touch too long.

That should be enough to have me taking a step back.

To let him win this battle and move on with our night.

But lacking a backbone is what got me into this mess to begin with. And if there was a single person I could practice being assertive with, it would be Luke.

So with his words ringing in my ears, I finally break the silence.

"Luke."

"Mm-hmm." He hums slowly.

"I want you in that bed."

His breathing halts, and I swear a million emotions flit through his eyes before they darken.

He releases a low groan before answering. "Thank you for telling me what you want, Daze. But my stance hasn't changed."

I can read between the lines, and I don't hesitate to respond. "Well, I guess it looks like I'll be sleeping with you tonight." His eyes widen just like mine, and I take a step back, bumping into the coffee table. His arm is instantly at my elbow to steady me if need be. "I mean, we'll be sleeping in the same bed. Sleeping. Like the mature adults that we are. Not that there will be mature adult things happening. Because that's not what—"

His booming laugh breaks the tension and interrupts my pathetic word vomit, and I drop onto the couch, no longer having the energy to verbally spar. "Add that to the list of things you're obligated to forget. Start a tab at this rate."

His laughter eases as he settles back on the couch next to me. His eyes glimmer with delight as he picks up the remote and turns my way. "Never gonna happen."

"Ugh, because you enjoy watching me squirm?"

"No, because it's impossible for me not to memorize every single thing about you."

He freezes midway to handing the remote to me. I think he just experienced his own version of word spillage for the first time. Ever.

He reverts back to the silence.

The place I notice he's most comfortable in.

I take the remote out of his hand without looking at the TV.

"Daisy, I—"

"Luke."

"Yeah?" he asks worriedly.

"I want to watch *The Parent Trap*."

The lines on his forehead smooth over as he leans into the back of the couch. He smiles as he nods at the TV. "Guess it's settled then."

"Yeah. Guess so."

Chapter Eight
DAISY

I KEEP MY EYES closed as I snuggle deeper into the warmth beneath me and release a content sigh.

Luke's bed is much more comfortable than I would have imagined, although firmer than I expected.

Hmm, come to think of it, I don't even remember coming to bed. Did we even finish the movie? I'm sure I would have remembered teasing him about the infamous handshake scene.

I struggle to recollect any of those memories when I notice that the bed is moving. Rising and falling slowly.

"Morning. Are you aware that you're a very aggressive cuddler?" Luke's chest rumbles beneath my cheek as his voice comes from somewhere above my head.

I squeak as I bolt up, quickly discovering that I was indeed cuddling Luke. More like I koala-latched and pinned him beneath my body, really.

We're still on the couch, but the morning sun lights up the entire cabin, letting me know that we've slept here the entire night.

Well, I slept. Apparently, Luke was held hostage.

"I'm so sorry." I scramble to my feet and cover my mouth with my hand.

Luke offers me an easy smile as he stretches lazily. "What are you doing?"

"I have morning breath. And I was mouth breathing on top of you." I scrunch my face and try to remember if I did anything embarrassing in my sleep, which is fruitless, since I was knocked out like the dead.

He crosses his arms, looking way too good for someone who spent the night on a couch with a feral cuddler. His eyes crinkle softly as he runs a hand through his beard.

In pictures, the beard makes him look tough and unapproachable. But I've been up close and apparently much too personal with Luke lately. I know for a fact that his beard looks soft, and I wonder what it would feel like beneath my fingers.

Or maybe even somewhere else.

I shake my head, immediately banishing the inappropriate thought. When I look back at Luke, his eyes are zeroed in on me, as if he caught what I was thinking about.

But that's impossible, right?

"You okay there, D? You're looking a little flushed."

Was that a mocking tone?

I move my hand to my cheek, and sure enough, it feels like I'm burning up.

"Oh yeah. Totally fine. Just your average day. Waking up on my friend's chest after probably spending the night drooling on his shirt and all that."

He makes a show of running a hand down his shirt and back up. "No drool detected."

"Small mercies," I mumble.

"But you do snore quite a bit. Reminds me of a chainsaw I have in the shed that needs replacing."

I clap my hands and hook a thumb over my shoulder. "Okay. Great. Cool. I'm gonna go for a walk. Down that dock, and I'll keep going until I hit the bottom of that lake, where my dignity currently lies. So if you don't mind…" I turn to face the back sliding door.

I don't even make it a step before Luke is behind me, placing a hand on my stomach and pulling me toward his laughing chest. "I was joking, Daisy. You don't snore."

I huff. "Never figured you as a chipper morning person, Coach."

"Yeah, well, I guess I never had a reason to be," I turn in his arms. Somewhere in the back of my mind there are muffled words about putting space between us, but I find myself getting lost in the twinkle in his light blue eyes instead. This close I can see that one of them has a bit of green near the bottom of the iris.

"What? Runaway brides pinning you down on the couch is what Sunday morning dreams are made of?"

He shrugs. "Don't knock it till you've tried it. Now, c'mon, we're going on a field trip."

Chapter Nine
LUKE

She does snore.

But it's more of a cute kitten purr.

But I'll keep that little detail to myself.

Tucked away safely where I keep everything else I've memorized about my Daisy girl.

Chapter Ten

LUKE

After dressing Daisy in my oversized clothes and baseball cap, I was satisfied she was incognito enough for us to leave my home and head into town.

"This is ridiculous. No one will be looking for me around here. We're basically in Montana at this rate."

I give her an unimpressed look. "Remind me to pick up a map for you to study while I'm at the store."

"Luke, look at me." She stretches her arms wide, showing off the clothes that basically swallow her whole. "I look insane. I can't walk into the store like this."

"I know," I smirk. "I can pop into a store and grab a few more things for you to wear while you're hiding out in my truck. How's a week's worth sound?"

She attempts a little growl. "A week? Are you out of your mind? It's not like you can take a vacation at the beginning of the season, *Coach*, so that you can keep me in the Monarchs' version of the witness protection program."

Try me, I think to myself.

"Our previous game faced delays due to weather. Unprecedented major snowstorms in the Midwest have thrown us off schedule, so I don't have a game till next

Saturday. Which would make our stay at my cabin..." I wave at her.

"A week," she grumbles, but she fails to hide her smile as she does.

"Exactly." I tap her nose. "Besides, even if you already had a full wardrobe, I think it's safest for you to stay in the car while I grab whatever we need."

"But how will you know—"

"Oh, how little faith you have in me, sweet Daisy." I pull out my noise-canceling headphones while I nod at her phone. "We'll be on the phone the entire time. Not sure there's enough of a signal for a video chat, but if there is, I can turn it on and show you what they have at the market. It's not big by any means, but I'm sure we can get the basics."

"You seem awfully excited about playing secret agent, so I guess I'll play along." She sighs dramatically.

"Good sport. Now let's head over to the garage. I moved my truck in there in case we got hit with some unexpected rain," I lie as I look out into the clear blue skies.

I think it's best if Daisy avoids a certain part of my property.

Because if Daisy walks out my front door and actually pays attention to what's out there this time, she'll know that lying about my feelings is what I've been doing since the moment I agreed to be her friend.

I never thought that clothes shopping for a woman could be so torturous.

But when Daisy shyly whispered the fact that she was currently going commando and needed more underwear, I nearly ran the truck off the road.

I parked away from the main entrance and strode inside the women's section of a store that I figured would have everything she needed. I had a cart full of bras and panties for her by the time she called to bashfully give me her sizes.

I looked down and grinned at my selection, because I didn't need her to tell me she was a C-cup or that she typically wore size medium or large panties. I've spent enough time studying the curves of her chest and hips to know.

I grabbed soft T-shirts and the stretchiest leggings and shorts I could find. Cozy oversized cardigans and fuzzy socks. If she lets me have a say in it, then gone are the days where Daisy will have to feel uncomfortable in anything she wears.

A saleswoman tries to come over to help, but I grunt and shake my head. I've forgotten how chatty I can be when I'm around Daisy. But that shuts down immediately when I'm around others. It's something only she seems to bring out in me, and I'm perfectly fine with keeping it that way.

When I'm satisfied with the haul, I pay and make my way to the car.

Daisy is staring at her phone when I open the back seat of my truck. "Jesus Christ, did you rob the place? That is way more than a week's worth."

"There was a sale," I deadpan.

I finish loading the bags and shut the door. I walk over to Daisy's door and knock on the window. She lowers it and I rest my forearms over the door, using my body to block any view of her.

I nod at the phone in her hands. "Any word yet?"

She knows who I'm referring to, but I refuse to speak his name near her. "Nope. And at this point, I'm wondering if maybe it's socially acceptable for my fiancé to ghost me after I used nude lipstick to break up with him." She winces.

"Ex-fiancé," I correct before I can tuck the caveman inside me back where he belongs.

"Right. Ex-fiancé." She nods as she nudges the engagement ring on her finger.

The sight still kills, but that's my burden to bear, not Daisy's.

I'm about to push off and walk into the small grocery store a block away when her hand unexpectedly keeps me in place. "You wanna know the saddest part about this?" She lifts her left hand, and I force myself to keep my eyes on her and not the ring. "A part of me is waiting for some kind of permission to take it off. Like I should be expecting an email confirmation to tell me that it's okay to remove it and return it to its rightful owner." She smiles sadly as she tilts her head. "And the pathetic part about it? I don't think I know what role I'm supposed to play now that it's all over."

"Daisy—"

She raises her phone and shows me the last text message from her father.

FATHER:

> CALL ME IMMEDIATELY. WE ARE NOW IN FULL CRISIS MANAGEMENT MODE. IF YOU'RE NOT AT DAMIEN'S HOME BY 5PM, YOU'LL BE SORRY. DON'T KEEP US WAITING. YOU KNOW CARMEN WOULD BE SO DISAPPOINTED BY YOUR ACTIONS.

I want to throttle her father through her phone. Hell, I might even take Nick up on the ride on his jet he offered so I can get my hands on him quicker.

But Daisy refocuses my attention by keeping her phone angled toward the both of us as she taps the screen a few times before hitting the "block contact" option.

"I may be a little lost right now, but I have one firm boundary that I'd never let anyone cross, and it's using my family or loved ones against me. He's well aware that I still struggle with the fact that I never had a mother growing up. He's most likely used that fact to lure me into the fucked-up relationship we have. I'm not completely oblivious. But he made a grave mistake assuming he could speak about my mother's emotions on her behalf, when I know for a fact he was never truly there for her." She tosses the phone onto the center console and leans back, pulling down the bill of my baseball hat. "I may have no clue who I am or who I'm supposed to be, but I know for sure that I won't let my father speak to me that way."

I know I shouldn't touch her, especially at a time like this, but my body is incapable of withholding comfort from her. I lean into the truck and wrap my fingers behind the back of her neck, allowing my thumb to brush over her cheek.

"You're Daisy fucking Stonehaven. You're the first person people call when they need to feel safe or seen. The most supportive sister and friend who would drop everything at a moment's notice to be there for the ones lucky enough to know you." I pause, eyes imploring hers. "And the only person who was able to bring a soulless dead man back to life." She sucks in a shallow breath, but I don't stop. "But Daze, the two people who should have cared for and protected that big, beautiful heart of yours the most decided to take advantage of it instead. I know it's not my place, and there are details of your relationships with them that I'm not privy to, but honestly..." I nod my head toward her phone. "Fuck them. Your dad chooses to berate you instead of being concerned about your well-being, and your ex..." I chuckle darkly, accidentally squeezing the back of her neck and angling her face toward mine. "Let's just say, if you were mine, I would be scouring every inch of the earth for you until I had you back, safely in my arms."

"Luke." Her voice cracks, but I'm not done.

"But it's all right, because that people-pleasing version of you decided to get gone and buried the moment you let me toss your wedding veil out my truck window."

She cracks a watery smile. "It was a very expensive veil. I'm sure Damien's mother had a conniption over that alone."

Her ability to joke loosens the tension in my chest, and I release my hold on her.

If you would have told me five years ago that my heart could beat for someone like this again, I wouldn't have believed it. After tragedy struck me and my former team, I was sold on the idea of living in solitude, holed up in my cabin alone for the rest of my days.

Yet here I am trying to infuse a bit of life into the woman who singlehandedly handed me back mine.

"Who you want to be or act like is completely up to you. I'll be here, every step of the way. And I mean it. Because whoever wants a bit of your attention is now going to have to go through me. I'm going to be on you like a rash."

She chuckles. "Love the visual."

"Thought you would." I smirk.

She bites her thumbnail as she asks, "So does this new Daisy get freshly baked chocolate chip cookies and ice cream by any chance?"

I narrow my eyes at her. "You saw the bakery two streets over on the drive in, didn't you?"

She shrugs. "This new and improved version of me doesn't feel compelled to answer that question."

I bark out a laugh and quickly cover my mouth, not wanting to draw attention to us. "Something tells me that this new and improved version of you is going to give me a lot of attitude." I quirk a brow. "And that was supposed to be a surprise. We're picking up a dozen cookies and ice cream on the way home so you can eat them on the drive back."

She points her beaming smile my way, and I know I'm a goner.

"Then let's hurry up and get our groceries. I have about ten recipes I want to try, but I need to know if you can find all the ingredients." She sits up, then stops. "Oh, right. Incognito shopping." She grabs her phone and starts typing away.

A second later, my phone rings in my pocket.

"Answer it. We've got some cookies with our names on 'em."

Chapter Eleven
LUKE

I RACE DOWN THE aisles as quickly as possible to get back to Daisy.

I can hear her mumbling along to the music in my car, and the sound is almost enough to lessen my rage against her father.

Almost.

"Oh, get tomato paste. If it gets cold at night, I was thinking I could make carne guisada. Or sancocho if I'm feeling adventurous. Maybe some rice and beans with pollo frito. I mean, if you're in the mood to eat that stuff too."

I pick up a few cans of tomato paste. "I'm in the mood for anything you want, Daisy. I'm not a picky eater, you know that."

"Make sure to get enough meat. You're not picky, but you can inhale food quicker than I can make it."

I crack a smile because she's not wrong. "Clear out the meat section, noted. Anything else?" I ask.

"Hmm, no. I think the list I texted you has it all," she says, followed by singing the tail end of a song playing on the radio.

I look through the list on my phone and double-check that I have everything. I don't want to make another trip into town if we don't have to.

Unless she wants more freshly baked cookies, of course.

I start heading toward the butcher area when I realize I should probably get Daisy a box of cereal. She's mentioned she likes to eat it for dinner or as a late-night snack on nights she doesn't feel like cooking. And while I don't mind cooking every meal for us, I know her colorful cereal might be a bit of a comfort meal for her, so I turn the cart until I'm facing the array of options before me.

I'm about to grab a brand I know is her favorite when a sugary voice besides me speaks. "Um, excuse me." I turn to the woman in brightly colored athleisure. "Do you think I could borrow your height for a moment? I need that box right there and I can't..." she makes a pitiful attempt of stretching onto her tiptoes. "Can't manage."

I easily grab the boring-looking cereal, something Daisy would wrinkle her nose at, and hand it to the lady.

I go to snag three boxes of Daisy's cereal when I notice that the music playing in my headphones has been turned down significantly and Daisy is no longer singing in my ear. Instead, all I hear is her shuffling around in her seat.

"Why thank you!" The woman next to me says a bit too loudly.

I nod and try to steer my cart away, but she hops in front of it. "I'm sorry to bother, but are you new around here? This is a small town and all, and I'm pretty sure I wouldn't have forgotten someone like you."

"Oh, I'm sure she wouldn't," Daisy faintly grumbles.

I smirk to myself. Daisy is always sweet. Doesn't have a bitter bone in her body. Maybe I'm edging closer to the line of delusion, but I swear I hear a little jealousy in my ears.

And I think I like it.

The woman rests her free hand on my cart, keeping me in place.

I shake my head. As much as I would love to hear what Daisy sounds like riled up for me, I would never do that to her. "Sorry, but I gotta get going. Got some cereal to deliver."

I bypass her question and start to maneuver around her, but the woman is undeterred.

"Oh, my nephews love that stuff. Do you have any of those, or are you a single dad by any chance?" She looks me up and down, and I fight a full body tremor.

"Jeez, can people not take a hint anymore?" Daisy huffs.

I bite back a smile. Only Daisy gets to see those.

I think of ignoring the question, but feeling a little reckless, I decide to have a little fun instead. "Nah, it's for my wife."

Daisy sounds like she's choking on air while the woman before me looks like I've slapped her.

"W-wife? But you're not wearing a ring." She sounds indignant.

"Oh my God," Daisy all but yelps.

"Yeah." I look down at my bare ring finger. "We're not really ring people. We have an appointment to get tattoos instead. Cool, right?"

Her mouth opens, but nothing comes out.

"Anyway, have a nice day. Enjoy your raisin and nut medley... rabbit food."

I leave her slack-jawed as I maneuver through the aisles.

"Hey, Daze?"

"Uh, um, yeah?"

"Turn up the radio. They're playing your favorite song."

Chapter Twelve
DAISY

I'VE SPENT MOST OF the day cooking up a feast.

I told Luke it was a thank-you for letting me crash at his place, but in reality, I needed something to keep me occupied.

Because something is shifting between us.

He's still being the same kind and courteous man I know him to be, but when I walked out of the bathroom in the band T-shirt and cutoff shorts he bought me, I swear the look he gave me could light my new clothes on fire.

And if I'm being completely honest, I liked the thought far too much.

I almost laugh at the ridiculousness of it as I finish chopping the veggies and toss them into the sancocho I settled on for tonight. Ever since I started hanging out with Luisa and Isabella's families, I've become obsessed with our shared Dominican culture.

My mother was unable to teach me about my lineage, so I feel immensely grateful to my new friends and sister-in-law for letting me tag along and helping me embrace being a proud Latina. I have no living family members on my mother's side, therefore there was never anyone out there I could reach out to in an attempt to help me feel closer to my Mami or my culture.

And it kills me.

Because it makes me feel like I'm a fraud.

Like a fake Latina who's trying too hard to assimilate to a culture she wasn't raised in. Even after I've fielded questions about my "exotic" looks all my life. Like I'm a plant or an animal, especially since my last name is Stonehaven and my father lives in the UK.

It's probably why I've always felt like I'm just something to look at—with thinly veiled confusion that brings up more questions than answers. Which is why I've always tried my best to beat people to the punch before they have a chance to get curious. It's part of why I'm usually offering myself up for odd jobs and going the extra mile for strangers and friends and why I always have a solution handy.

If I can be useful, if I can make everyone around me happy, maybe they won't look too closely and see the cracks under the surface. If I'm helpful, they won't notice all the missing pieces I came without. Or how I hope I'm fooling them all by playing out a role. The ones I've come to emulate from books and movies, hoping no one catches on that there is nothing original or special about me.

Maybe I can sell them on the fact that I'm naturally this way. That I know how to be cheerful twenty-four seven so that they won't see my sadness or my fear of never being enough.

And maybe, just maybe, if I keep fussing and fluttering around the ones I care for, eventually something will stick. I'll figure out who it is that I'm meant to be, and no one will ever have to know that I was faking it the whole time.

Nick tries his best to remind me of the bits and pieces that he remembers of his childhood with our mom, and I take every morsel of information and weave it into my being.

And I desperately try to keep a positive outlook. Knowing that I lucked out with an amazing brother and an extended family in his in-laws now that he had the good sense to lock down Luisa.

But if I'm honest with myself, it's still not enough.

I put the lid on the sancocho as I lower the volume on the music on my phone. Maybe listening to my mom's favorite artist, Juan Luisa Guerra, the day after I ran away from my wedding wasn't the best idea after all.

I run my hands down my face. I need to stop being such a Debbie downer. It's not like it was all bad. I had the most incredible nannies growing up. There were a couple who rotated in and out of my life. A few were even from the Dominican Republic.

Their presence in my life was immeasurable. Some of my fondest memories include practicing speaking Spanish with them growing up. Or learning little old-school Dominican tricks for taking proper care of my curls. From using pure cinnamon in my conditioner to help with hair regrowth after learning the hard way the dangers of heating tools, to creating my own little concoctions with rosemary and other natural ingredients to use every few weeks to keep my hair healthy and shiny.

And while I did study Spanish in high school and college, nothing could compare to the speed and complexity of Dominican Spanish. I find myself laughing when I'm home alone, recollecting words that aren't in the Spanish dictionary but are a staple in my friends' vocabulary.

Speaking of my friends.

LUISA:

> Proof of life check-in before your brother calls in the Navy SEALs.

ISABELLA:

> Leave the girl alone. She's probably having hot lumberjack sex.

LUISA:

> Nick read that over my shoulder and now I think he's going to fly his plane himself. Hold, please. I need to make sure I'm on the life insurance policy.

I blush fiercely as I answer, knowing my brother will probably sneak his way into reading my response.

DAISY:

> I am alive. No need to send in the SEALs. And no lumberjacks have been defiled. Currently cooking up a storm.

I attach a picture of the boiling soup, and in seconds my phone starts lighting up.

LUISA:

> Don't give your brother another reason to want to crash your mountain getaway. Damn, that looks good.

LUISA:

> Also, hi. Nice to hear from you. How are you feeling?

ISABELLA:

> Tell Luke I'm ready to wife you up, because dayummm.

ISABELLA:

> Oh wow, now I look like the asshole for not asking how she's doing first. Thanks, Luisa.

ISABELLA:

> Just kidding!! How are you, Daisy? Any word from your ex?

I don't really want to get into it all but figure it's easier to send a voice memo to bring them up to speed. I mention my father's text, how I blocked him, and how Damien and his camp have been radio silent. I leave out anything that has to do with Luke, because I know they'd notice the change in my tone.

I'm a lie detector's wet dream because I can't lie for shit.

As expected, their support starts pouring through the group chat. I never had friends like this growing up, so it's still taking some getting used to. It's strange having people in my life who actually care about me instead of the last name I was born with.

I promise to keep them in the loop and to send more food and nature pictures while I'm here, then put my phone away.

I notice that it's been a while since I last saw Luke. He headed outside in what looked like a bit of a hurry when I tried to playfully show off the outfit he got for me.

Or maybe he has better things to do than babysit me.

There's nothing left for me to do but wait for the soup to simmer for a long while, so I decide to grab a beer and bring it out to him. I haven't really heard much noise while he's been out there, but I have been listening to music while cooking.

As I approach the fridge, I stare at the postcard and magnet of the Adirondack Mountains I cheekily put on his refrigerator. He wasn't exactly thrilled to learn that I'd left his truck for a few minutes and ducked into a mom-and-pop shop to pick up these little souvenirs.

I told myself I wanted to start collecting things that bring me joy, and these old-school postcards and cheesy magnets did just the trick. I'm clearly still on the journey of trying to decipher who I really am versus who I've been molded to be, and this small purchase made me feel like I was moving a step in the right direction.

But if I'm being honest, I probably hopped out of his truck and into the store because I needed to walk around and get some fresh air. Especially after hearing a woman shamelessly flirt with Luke. Followed by him saying that he was buying cereal for his wife. A wife who apparently loves the same kind of cereal I do.

I must be getting altitude sickness. I have no idea what the elevation is here, but I'm sure that's a thing. And it must be a reason my mind is suddenly all over the place when it comes to Luke. My friend.

Friend. Friend. Friend, I remind myself as I open the refrigerator.

I'm surprised to find that he bought ciders as well as everything on my list. I'm not exactly a huge drinker, and I've mentioned that ciders kind of feel like grown-up apple juice, so they're easier for me to tolerate.

I smile as I grab two and make my way out back. I tuck a beer into the crook of my elbow as I open the sliding door before holding it steady in my hand again.

And thank God for that.

Because had I been looking at what was waiting for me beyond these windows, I might have shattered both beers on the ground.

Actually, I'm sure of it.

Because a few yards before me stands a shirtless Luke in low riding Wranglers, wiping the sweat off his brow with his forearm.

His chest glistens in the warm afternoon sun as my eyes trace over every divot and pronounced muscle on his body.

But I almost swallow my tongue when I realize there was one little fun fact I was kept completely in the dark about when it came to Luke.

He has tattoos. Lots and lots of tattoos.

I've never questioned why he's always worn those long-sleeved sweat-resistant, shirts under his uniform, even in the summer months. But I guess this is why.

My eyes eat up the small scatterings of cursive handwriting and artistic designs that trace up his biceps. They adorn his ribs and pecs too, curling around his shoulders and leading down his back. Tiny sparrows, roman numerals, and abstract art decorate his skin perfectly.

But the ill-fated death to my new panties comes when he picks up a small piece of wood and places it on a tree stump. He then bends and picks up an axe.

The fact that I'm at a secluded cabin in the woods with a white man wielding an axe should have me searching for my survival skills.

But damn if this view wouldn't be a good way to go out if it's my time.

There could be a pack of wolves running my way and I wouldn't even notice at a time like this.

Luke expertly lifts the axe over his head and swings it down, perfectly cutting the piece of wood in two. I don't know if there's a certain form for chopping wood, but it seems like a ten out of ten from where I'm standing.

I shouldn't be ogling him. The man is simply doing some manual labor, and there are about a million and one reasons why letting my mind go down this path is a bad idea, but I can't help myself from staying rooted to the spot and living a little, even if it's just for a few minutes.

Imagining what it would feel like to be pinned down by that body, worked over by those hands. To trace each of those abs with my tongue until I drift down and taste—

"Daisy girl, you thirsty over there?"

My eyes snap up from Luke's abs to his face.

His very smug-looking face.

Oh God, how long has he known that I've been watching him? I must have lost track of time since I'm sure Ginuwine's "Pony" song played on a loop multiple times as he worked log after log.

Stop thinking about his log, woman.

Yet my eyes take a quick detour down and back up again.

Enough time for Luke to quirk his brow, as if to say "gotcha."

Enough time for me to turn on my heel and bolt back into the house like an idiot.

Enough time to decide that I am indeed thirsty, and that I'm going to be needing both of these ciders for myself.

Chapter Thirteen
LUKE

I'm not going to tell her that I picked up chopped wood in town.

Or that I'll have to pop two painkillers for the sore muscles tomorrow.

Won't even mention that it's going to rain tonight and we'll have to stay indoors.

Because all that matters is that I caught her watching.

Chapter Fourteen
DAISY

I think Luke's fucking with me.

I'm aware that I did pull out all the stops with today's dinner. Hell, even I'm impressed with how quickly I've been able to mimic Luisa's aunt's sancocho.

But does the man have to moan after every sip?

Or look me in the eyes as he softly blows on the steaming broth?

And the way he's sucking on the boned meat is downright pornographic. He could probably teach a class in the art of doing that kind of work with one's mouth.

"Why are you frowning at me, Daze?"

"I'm not," I respond a bit too quickly.

He smirks. "If you say so." He takes a spoonful of broth and yuca and then digs into his side of white rice and moans. Again.

"Is that really necessary?"

He wipes his mouth with a napkin, eyes looking far too amused for my liking. "Care to elaborate?"

I roll my eyes as I push my half-full bowl away. "I've shared hundreds of meals with you, and I have never heard you yipping and yapping so much in my life. A simple 'compliments to the chef' would suffice."

He raises his hands in a placating manner. "My apologies. I wasn't aware I was being so... vocal. But damn, Daisy. That is the best sancocho I've ever tasted in my life. I've been fed by a lot of Dominican and Puerto Rican moms while working in the MLB, so believe me when I say I know a thing or two about the subject."

My manners get the best of me, so I simply nod and say thank you.

"Something on your mind, Daisy girl?" he drawls, running his finger down the condensation of his beer bottle.

I stand up and point at the smirk on his face. "Aha! That. Right there. What is that?"

He leans back in his stool. "My face."

"Oh, no you don't. You've been doing it all day. You're messing with me, aren't you?"

He brings the bottle to his lips, speaking before he takes a long pull. "You're going to have to be more specific for me."

I wave around in his general direction. "You're just more, more... seductive and grizzly, I guess."

His brows furrow. "I'm a bear now?"

I release a frustrated breath as I dig my hands into my hair. "You know what? Maybe you're right. Maybe I'm the one who's a bit off-kilter. After all, I am the crazy woman who ran away from her own wedding. I do seem to have a case stacked against my sanity."

"Hey, don't—"

"Maybe it's because we're having an extended sleepover and my brain wasn't ready to see you shirtless and tatted while watching you do lumberjack cosplay."

"Lumberjack cosplay?"

"Or hear you talk about having a fake wife when you never talk about who you're dating."

"No one, and you know that," he says lowly. I keep that detail tucked away for later because I'm unable to put the brakes on my rant.

Although I really wish I could, given what I reveal next.

"You know what? It probably is all my fault," I say, nodding. "How were you supposed to know that the very specific combo of buying me freshly baked cookies followed by chopping wood would send me into a tizzy? It's not like you're aware I haven't had sex in years or that the only way I'm ever able experience an orgasm is with a rechargeable little toy that I didn't realize I should have packed in my toiletry bag for survival in the wilderness after leaving my ex-fiancé at the altar," I say all on one breath, leaving myself gasping for air.

The tiny person in my brain who is responsible for drafting all of my coherent thoughts must be off on holiday, because a moment too late, I realize what I've said and slap a hand across my mouth as I shut my eyes tightly.

I wait for it.

The shock or confusion that's sure to come.

I count my breaths and wait for the pity.

Instead, I jolt at the sound of Luke's stool scraping across the hardwood floor. His measured steps are silent in his socked feet. His warm hands on my shoulders gently turn me to face him.

I sigh as I drop my hand and open my eyes, resigned to face the inevitable, but I'm taken aback by the look on Luke's face.

Pure and unfiltered anger.

My wide-eyed gaze must clue him in to how he must look, since he reels it in significantly. Then, in a soft voice, he says, "You're going to have to explain this to me. Because I can't for the life of me understand how you were engaged for a year and *living* together and never—"

"It's not because I didn't want to," I start, seeing a flash of something on his face before he schools his features again. "I'm not a virgin or saving myself for marriage, but he said that it would make more sense to wait until we were hitched since he was running his campaign on "family values" and didn't want to feel like a hypocrite. So he gave me my own room in our apartment and said we would have a shorter engagement. I guess I went along with it and we never... well, yeah," I say, ashamed of my naivety.

"That sounds like a crock of shit to me. Because if I—" He stops short as he grits his teeth.

"If you what?" I push. If I'm going to lay it all out there for him to see, he's going to have to stop filtering himself around me as well.

He shakes his head. "This isn't about me. It's about you not being treated the way you should have for far too long. Not feeling cherished, appreciated." He hesitates slightly. "Pleasured."

I suck in a shallow breath at the sound of that word from his mouth. My eyes dip, chasing the view as well when his hands squeeze my shoulders and my attention is brought back up to the set of baby blues that seem to have taken on a darker hue.

"Pleasured. Well, I um..." I clear my throat and take a reluctant step back. "That's going to be a task for me since I can't, uh..." I scratch behind my ear as I shake my head slightly.

"I don't even know how we got here. We were talking about my cooking, right? Must be the ciders. How much alcohol is in these things anyway? Must be going straight to my head."

He crosses his thick arms over his wide chest, looking none too impressed. "Not even 3 percent. Everyone knows you have a low tolerance for alcohol, and I didn't want you to have to deal with hangovers on top of everything else on your plate. So if you don't want to talk about this, then tell me it's none of my business. Because we've never bullshitted one another before, so we aren't going to start now that the truth is being laid out."

I bite my lip at his tone, and his eyes seem to lose the same battle mine did a few moments ago when they dip to my mouth.

"Luke," I hedge, not knowing how to respond.

"Daisy, did—did you love him?" he asks, voice cautious.

I drop my head. This isn't the first time I've been asked this question, and the fact that it needs to be asked at all is telling. But I've always had my answer ready and practiced for those around me who clearly had their doubts.

I think back to that night a few months ago during Isabella and Luisa's bachelorette party, when my loved ones tried to ask me the very same question.

"Everything okay, Daisy?" Nick asks, worried.

My head snaps up. I scan our small crew while putting my fake smile back on display. "Yep. Just thought it was normal for couples to be a bit off before getting married. Only finding their footing later on like you guys did. But it seems like you guys were playing a completely different game from the one I pictured." I force a laugh.

Luisa's fingers tap on the table a few times before she stops and straightens in Nick's lap. "Daisy, you don't have to answer this if you don't want to. But..." *She looks around the table, meeting everyone's eye before settling on mine.* "Why are you marrying him?"

My eyes widen, but my focus is momentarily drawn to the glass of water that's threatening to shatter in Luke's white-knuckle grip.

"Wh-what do you mean? Why does anyone get married? I mean, well, besides you guys." *I fake chuckle as I pull the neck of my sweater down an inch.* "Because I love him, of course."

Luke stands abruptly.

"Where are you going?" *Mateo asks.*

"Quick walk."

"But you left your coat on your chair," *Isa yells after him.*

"Don't need it," *he says as he steps into the frigid December air.*

"What was that about?" *I ask.*

"Oh boy," *Isabella mumbles under her breath.*

Nick simply shakes his head. "Daisy, I'm your brother and I love you, but level with me, please. Is Dad pressuring you in any way to get married to Damien?"

"No," *I say before he's done asking the question. The look on his face tells me not to bullshit him, and I raise my arms slightly.* "He's, kind of... Well, you know Dad. He's been stressed the last couple of years with his business. And having contracts stateside, with the government, would help immensely. The fact that Damien and I were already dating seemed to please him. And he seemed so damn thrilled when Damien proposed, even if it was a bit sooner than I expected, and—"

"Daisy, do you hear yourself? Our sorry excuse for a father is absolutely manipulating you."

Luisa tries to intervene. "Daisy—"

"No, stop. I know what you think of me. What you all must think of me. That I'm some kind of idiot. Some weakling who can't make choices for herself. But you're wrong." My eyes latch on to Nick's with a force I've never set on him before. "And I'm sorry, brother, but you can't possibly understand where I'm coming from. You had a decade with our mother. Our sweet, caring, and beautiful Mami. I never got that. I got a rotation of nannies and a father I would see twice a year at most. I only have one parent left, and while I know he will never win any best dad awards, he's all I've got."

My heart threatens to crack down the middle, feeling so exposed.

"Oh, Daisy," Luisa says softly, but I shake my head.

"Please don't. The last thing I need is your pity. I'm a poor little rich girl who has daddy issues. There is nothing original or extraordinary about me. My job was a handout from my brother. I live in my fiancé's apartment, which doubles as a storage unit for his accolades and is the place where he rests his head a handful of nights each month. My college degree, the one I'm not even using, was paid for by my absentee father.

"All I have that is truly mine are my choices. And as dumb as they may seem to all of you, they are still mine. And if I'm making a huge mistake, well, I guess that's my mistake to own."

"Daisy—"

"We don't—"

"You shouldn't—"

The chill at my back signals that Luke has returned and likely heard every word I said. I feel him at my side before he even speaks.

"You don't love him, Daisy." Luke's words silence us all.

I cross my arms in defiance, but the harsh tone in my voice has all but disappeared. "How would you know? You won't even RSVP for my wedding."

He leans closer, hands resting on the top of his vacant chair. "You really want me there, D?"

I jut my chin out and nod after a few beats.

The chair creaks under his hands. "Then I'll be there." He grabs his coat and tears out of the restaurant.

The secret pathway of the thoughts I harbored in my heart, kept far from my brain, clears as I finally answer Luke honestly. "I—I think I loved the idea of what our lives could have been together. The bits and pieces he promised me along with the gaps I knew I'd have to fill. The same way I learned to do with my relationship with my father." I release a deep breath. "I wanted a family. A husband and kids. To create the home I never had growing up. Knowing that even though he wasn't the perfect man, I'd be able to experience motherhood and get to be the mom I wasn't able to have. Offer children the warmth I wasn't freely given, the safety in secure arms. The support I needed while I was alone at boarding school." I shake my head. "But honestly, Luke. No. I don't think I really loved him. And before you go off and judge me, it's probably because I was struggling to love myself too, okay?"

I think back to that night a few months ago, when Luke flat-out told me in front of our friends that I didn't love

Damien. I was furious at him for the very first time in our friendship.

Because he was right. And I hated that of all people, he was the only person bold enough to say it to my face.

The truth, while freeing, also has me feeling like I'm sinking farther into myself. The parts that aren't shiny and perfect. The ones that would make it easy for the people in my life to walk away if they really knew how close I was to losing my mind while living the life that felt like a true and utter lie.

I expect him to give me his version of tough love. To tell me I'm wrong for convincing myself of so many untruths.

Instead, his face softens. "I get it. I've been in your shoes before. It's why I hid from the spotlight for so many years before deciding to join the Monarchs team last year. It's—it's why I ran."

I try to hide my shock. Luke's never talked about his tragic past with me. Or anyone else on the team from what I've overheard.

It feels grimy to know something about a person based on the articles written about them instead of hearing it straight from them. Yet there was no way to look up Luke online without being faced with the devastating headlines that seem forever synonymous with his name. But I still won't pry or ask for details. That'll all have to come from him.

I place my hand on top of his on the island, and he turns his over, intertwining our fingers. My soft, small hand, in his rough calloused one feels oddly familiar, as if we've done this countless times before.

"Thank you for telling me, Luke. I know you don't like to talk about the past."

He stares at our hands, studying them for so long that I think he's about to change the subject altogether when he finally speaks. "You know what, Daze? I think it's time I start shedding some of my past and try to start living a little." His eyes lift to meet mine. "Because something tells me if I don't take advantage of the opportunity presented before me, I might live to regret it."

"What do you mean?"

His head bows slightly and his closed eyelids twitch softly. I almost convince myself that I can hear as he counts in his head. When his head raises and eyes meet mine, they seem clear, lighter than moments before. "Before we get into me and my demons, how about we figure out how to put yours to bed?"

"Nothing's happening in my bed," I quip before I'm able to reel it in. And then I remember something he said—or rather stopped himself from saying. "When I told you I never slept with Damien and that we had separate bedrooms, you started to say something but never finished."

His eyes narrow slightly. "You sure you want me to answer that, Daisy girl?"

There it is again. That slow drawl that lacks innocence.

I lift my chin. "I asked, didn't I?"

He leans in closer, his attention floating between my eyes and my lips. "I was going to say that had it been me"—his voice drops even lower, taking on a gravelly tone—"there wouldn't be an inch of your body that hadn't been marked by me. You'd never have to wonder what it felt like to come completely undone. And trust me, Daze, you'd have to beg me for mercy to stop the onslaught of orgasms I'd give you." A slow smirk appears under his beard. "*That's* what I was going to say."

"Oh." I drop my eyes as a deep blush creeps up my neck.

Am I breathing? I think I am. But I can't be quite sure.

Because that was... whoa. Not what I was expecting him to say. And now that he has, I want to dare him to do it. I want to see if he's actually telling the truth or saying it for the sake of my tattered self-esteem.

I want him to put his hands on me. I want to feel the power that he so easily wielded with that axe earlier. See if it can break the spell my body has been under and actually allow me to feel pure and unrestrained pleasure by hands that are not my own.

To know firsthand if what my friends and romance books speak of actually exists. Because if it does, I have a feeling only someone like Luke would know how to crack my code. And the longer I look at him, the less he's starting to look like a friend.

A part of me wants to solely focus on this sexual attraction, but I won't even bother lying about the feelings that are fluttering around my chest. And how lovely it might feel to not have to force or fake them.

And I know that our time alone here is limited. Hell, it's barely begun. But I can see myself feeling greedy for his attention. Especially now when his free hand cups my cheek, forcing me to look him in the eye as he speaks. "You're going to get everything you want out of this life. That I can promise you."

I attempt to clear my throat, as if his words haven't set my world on fire. "Oh yeah? How can you be so sure?"

He speaks cautiously, his words measured. "Because I'll be the one to give it to you if you let me."

Is he saying what I think he's saying?

In my defense, it's much too hard to focus on words when his hands are on me and I'm enveloped in his dizzying pine and sandalwood scent.

Before I can make sense of his words, he points at the stool I was sitting in before I decided to spill all my secrets. "But we've got time, Daisy. So for now, we'll watch another movie, one that you'll hopefully stay awake long enough for me to mock you for choosing. And I'll bring you a bowl of cereal to snack on even though you say you're full, and I'll…" He trails off, biting his tongue it seems.

"And you'll what, Luke? No bullshitting, remember?" I snark, playfully throwing back his words.

"And for the time being, I'll pretend like I don't know that you've never come on a cock or with a head buried between your legs." I gasp, my thighs clenching at the vision he's put in my mind. "Remember, you asked for it." He releases me, nudging me back toward my seat. "Now sit back down and finish your food before you go putting any more ideas in my head."

He walks away, but not before I hear him mutter, "At least not until you're ready for me to act on them."

Chapter Fifteen

LUKE

WHAT IN THE ACTUAL fuck?

I'm trying to focus on the movie Daisy picked for us tonight, but I can't stop replaying our conversation earlier.

She didn't love him.

They never had sex.

Not that it would have mattered to me, since Daisy is a grown woman and should be worshipped every second of every day. But knowing that she's been deprived of pleasure for all her life makes me want to throw my fist through a wall.

The fact that I haven't touched anyone since I first laid eyes on her makes it feel like some cruel joke from the universe that has already done a number on me.

Had I known the details of their relationship or her lack of satisfaction, maybe I could have helped her talk through her feelings. She might have come to a conclusion about that doomed relationship sooner.

Or maybe I'd have been too blinded by the possibility of being the first man to make her come and gone insane—

"Do you think any less of me now that you know the truth?" She interrupts my thoughts. My response is delayed since I'm slightly distracted by her long curly hair. She took a lengthy shower after dinner and came out with her hair in a wet bun.

Throughout the night, she's unraveled it bit by bit, and now she's shaking the curls out, creating a stunning halo around her delicate face.

And the fact that she's wearing my hoodie again, even though I bought her more than enough clothes to wear, isn't helping my concentration.

"What? Of course not."

"Most people would assume I'm a brainless bot, following some weird Stepford wife handbook."

"Well, I've never been accused of acting like most people. And I take that as a compliment."

She rolls her eyes. "You know what I mean. I feel so dumb, especially since I was well aware that my brother and my friends could see that I wasn't happy. No matter how hard I tried to put on a happy face. Everyone knew, and I beat that dead horse until I couldn't. Until I ran. Like a coward."

I slam my glass of water on the coffee table a little harder than intended. "Yeah, you're going to have to do me a favor and stop talking about yourself like that. Otherwise I'm gonna have to do something about it."

She lifts a questioning brow. "Oh yeah? Like what? Force me to recite words of affirmation to myself in the mirror?"

I bite my tongue. Because none of the thoughts that ran through my mind were close to being appropriate.

Her eyes narrow as she scoffs. "There it is again." She stands, but I manage to pull her back down by the back of my hoodie.

But instead of the couch, she ends up landing on my spread open legs. Any higher on my lap and she'd have felt my dick twitch at her proximity.

She gasps as she repeatedly looks at my face and where she's fallen to. "I'm on your lap."

"Great observation skills."

"I-I should move. Um, right?"

I shrug. "You've got legs. Use them if you want. Or don't," I challenge. "Now what were you going off about before you almost stomped out the room?"

She crosses her arms, eyes drifting down once more before she meets mine, staying put. "I wasn't stomping."

I almost smile. She's being defiant. Stubborn. All the things she's never allowed herself to be.

"Why are you smiling like a weirdo?"

Whoops.

"I like seeing this side of you, that's all. Now tell me what's got your panties in a bunch."

"You can't say stuff like that when you've actually bought all my panties. I'm sure there's a rule somewhere about that," she mumbles.

"Ah, yes. Another rule. You just love following all of those, don't you?" I tease. "Now go on."

She bites her lip. "Well, now it seems silly."

"I'm waiting."

She throws her hands up, causing her ass to move down farther to my crotch, and I internally curse. "Fine. Earlier you held back from saying something. Just like my brother and all of my friends do. They think I don't see when they have silent conversations with their eyes. I act like I don't notice because I don't want to make things awkward. But... but it makes me angry. No—frustrated. Because everyone acts like they have to treat me with kid gloves. Like I'm this fragile little Daisy that is going to wither away if I'm told the cold, hard truth to my face." She huffs as she studies me, looking for a reaction.

"I don't think you're fragile, Daisy. In fact, we all know you're strong as hell. I mean, you had to deal with Nick as an older brother all of your life. For that alone you deserve the Nobel Peace prize," I joke.

She shakes her head sadly. "No, you don't get it." She sighs. "For so long, I've been 'Nick's little sister' or 'the youngest Stonehaven,' but never just Daisy. No one looks at me as a woman in control who can make her own decisions. And trust me, I know that I've done things to help me earn that reputation, but sometimes I wish people wouldn't censor themselves around me. Or try to placate me. Hell, I'd settle for the truth, knowing it'd hurt my feelings because it meant I was respected enough to be spoken to straight up. But instead, I get the proverbial pats on the head and patronizing smiles."

"Daze—"

"I love my brother, really, I don't know that I would have made it this far in life if he weren't a constant fixture by my side. But I fear I'm always going to be playing the role of little sister to him." She deflates slightly.

I try to control my breathing. What I want to say and do are at odds. I've spent the entirety of our friendship keeping my thoughts about her hidden. I slipped earlier during dinner, but even that could be played off as a hypothetical.

A very descriptive and sexual hypothetical.

But now I need to brace myself. Because what I say next will have no chance at being misinterpreted.

I slowly turn her face toward mine with my thumb and forefinger. "Daisy, I'm sorry you've felt that way. And I apologize for any part I've played in exacerbating those feelings." She nods, opening her mouth to speak. But I don't need another autopilot response from her. No, I need her to listen for exactly what she asked for. "But I need to be crystal clear here. I don't see you as some fragile kid sister who can't endure the hard things in life. Do I want to shield and protect you from anything that might cause you harm? Absolutely. A frightening amount, actually. But when I look at you, I'm not thinking about your last name. Honestly, half the time you're talking, I can barely remember my own."

"What do you—"

I chuckle darkly. "Daisy. If you shift your ass any higher, you're gonna feel exactly how I feel about you, and that should answer your concerns about me thinking you're too fragile. Because there is nothing soft or gentle about the thoughts running through my mind when you're sitting on my lap."

Her cheeks brighten, but she doesn't move an inch. Her eyes drop and I feel her tense the exact moment she spots the outline of my hard cock pressed along my thigh.

I test my luck and lean forward to speak into her ear. "If unfiltered responses are what you want from me, then that's exactly what you'll get."

I feel her tremble, and I know for damn sure she's not cold in my hoodie.

"You good there, Daze?"

She nods repeatedly.

"If you keep looking at it, it's only going to get bigger."

Her ass is off my lap as if it's been lit on fire. "I—I wasn't, um—"

I tsk. "The no bullshitting goes both ways, Daisy."

I stand too, keeping my eyes on her roaming ones as I readjust myself.

"I, uh—" She waves at my crotch. "Well, I've, um—"

"Out with it."

"Okay, fine. I've never seen one that big before, happy?"

"Very. But you haven't actually seen it, just to be clear."

Now she's bright red, and I'm dying to know if the rest of her body flushes a pretty pink under different circumstances.

But I'm not going to push it, especially since from now on all she'll get from me is God's honest truth, no matter how filthy that may be.

"Now sit your fine ass down on the couch and keep watching your movie." I walk away, needing a moment for my dick to calm down.

"Wh-where are you going?" I hear the slight desperation in her voice, and it perks my cock right back up.

"To get you a bowl of cereal."

And attempt to find wherever I left a sliver of my sanity.

Chapter Sixteen
DAISY

"I promise I don't bite."

I throw a fluffy pillow at Luke's laughing face.

I'm usually the chatty one of the two of us. But ever since Luke broke down whatever barriers he kept around me and spilled his unfiltered thoughts, I've been lost in my head.

His massive erection also didn't help my two remaining brain cells either.

Now we're getting ready to sleep in the same bed and Luke has decided that now is a perfect time to develop an uncontrollable sense of humor.

I keep scowling his way, but I secretly love it. Or I would if my mind wouldn't keep circling back to his dick every five seconds.

"C'mon, we're just sleeping. I promise I'll be on my best behavior."

"I am fine. Totally fine. This is normal. Friends share a bed all the time. This is basically a sleepover."

"When do we start the pillow fight?"

I chuck another one in his direction and immediately regret it because now I have none.

I ignore his chuckles as I slide into the comfy bed and bring the covers up to my chin, laying my head on the flat bed.

I feel the bed shake as he gets in beside me, his arm brushing up against mine as he settles in.

"You're massive," I grumble.

"Why, thank you. Although I must admit that is quite forward of you."

"No! I meant you're taking up the whole bed. Never mind." I groan as I cover my face with my hands.

I feel him hovering over me and after a few moments decide to woman up and meet his gaze head-on.

His hand comes down and cradles the back of my head and slowly starts to lift me toward his face.

I forget to breathe as I willingly let him pull me closer.

It takes longer than I care to admit for my mind to register that his other hand is sliding a pillow under my head. I release a shaky breath as I stare at his concentrated focus on me.

"Perfect," he whispers, his breath floating over my lips.

"Thank you."

He nods slowly, his eyes traveling over every part of my face. "Good night, Daisy."

"Good night, Luke."

He retreats back to his side of the bed. "No more teasing. I promise. You can rest easy. I won't cross this invisible line in the bed." He points up and down the minuscule gap between us with mock seriousness.

I huff out a laugh. "Yeah, you better stay on your side or else." I say while secretly hoping he doesn't.

I'm so warm.

Correction, I'm hot. All over.

I must still be dreaming, because I've never felt this good while awake.

Like I'm on the cusp of euphoria even though my skin feels like it's too tight for my body. My body shifts, instinctually searching for the release that's just outside my grasp.

There.

I moan as the pleasure builds, teasing against my core.

I move again, canting my hips wantonly in search of more of the same feeling.

And I get it. Even stronger this time. It's accompanied by another deep moan.

But this one doesn't come from me.

My brain jolts awake and my eyes snap open.

Oh. My. God.

Luke's eyes stare back at me with an intensity that should have me shooting off him in record speed. His jaw is clenched as his nostrils flare.

He's shirtless, and his muscular arms are flexed as his hands are fisted behind his head.

What the hell is going on?

I feel something twitch between my legs and gasp at the feeling on my oversensitive center.

And then all the pieces slowly start to click.

Because I've somehow woken up on top of Luke.

Correction, straddling Luke. And it would seem as though I've been dry humping him while I slept.

Dry. Humping.

Dear God.

I need to move. I need to apologize. Yet my body and mind seem to be on a two-minute delay. "Luke... I—"

He shuts his eyes tightly as he tips his head up and whispers my name in a gravelly voice. "Daisy."

"I'm so, so—"

His loud groan interrupts me, followed by another jolt.

By Luke's very large and very hard dick.

A quiet mewl escapes my lips at the realization, and Luke's attention instantly drops back down to me.

He flexes his hands but keeps them exactly where they are as he demands the unthinkable. "Finish."

My eyes widen. Surely I misheard. "What?"

He sucks in a deep breath, as if reining in whatever control he has left. "I said, finish. You've been riding me for the last ten minutes, and if I hadn't made a sound, you would have come already. So go ahead, use me. Finish what you started."

My jaw drops at the same time my body accidentally bears down on him.

Our eyes latch on to one another the second our moans intertwine.

"Luke," I whine.

This has never happened to me before. I've never been so aroused that I couldn't think straight. Couldn't focus on anything besides rocking against the hardness between my legs and wishing there were no clothes between us.

"Daisy, before you get in your head, answer me this, and answer it quickly." I nod once, and he continues. "Do you want to come?"

I bite my lip and nod again.

"Words, Daisy. I'm going to need you to use them," he grunts.

"Yes, Luke. I want to come," I admit shyly.

He exhales sharply. "Good. Now use me. Take what you need, Daisy. Get yourself there." I look down and see that Luke's sweatpants have a damp spot. I'm almost overcome with embarrassment when Luke speaks again. "Yes, Daze, your pussy is fucking drenched, but you can't take all the credit. I've been slowly leaking in my underwear feeling your heat on top of me. And if we're not careful, we might be the only people on the planet to make a baby while keeping our clothes on."

I shake my head as I discreetly rock myself on top of the wet spot. "Your cum between my legs won't be a problem. I'm on birth control," I say mindlessly, growing more brazen as I slowly continue my ministrations.

I swear his chest vibrates as he brings his hands to the headboard, a whispered "fuck me" escaping his lips before he speaks directly to me again. "Widen your legs. Make sure your clit is rubbing on the crown of my cock, and don't stop until you're coming on top of me."

I scramble to do what he says. I bear down and rock over him shamelessly as my hands come to rest on his tatted chest.

I'm burning up, feeling like I'm about to burst.

"Fucking hell, look at you. Riding me so fucking well." His voice growls as he somehow manages to take over without laying a single finger on me. His hips thrust up once, twice, brushing the spot where I need him most, and that's all it takes.

I shut my eyes and detonate.

I come harder than I ever have before, screaming his name at the top of my lungs as my nails claw into his chest, my legs shaking beneath me.

My body continues to ride out the high, and him, with abandon.

My eyes fly open when Luke stills below me with a masculine-sounding grunt, the vein on his neck looking strained as he jolts one last time under me.

Oh God, Luke came too. In his pants.

His chest rises and drops heavily beneath my hands, my fingers having created small crescent moons on his skin with my short nails.

He watches me cautiously as we catch our breath. "How do you feel?"

A quiet laugh escapes my lips, followed by another one. The motion has me accidentally brushing up against Luke again, and we both hiss.

"Oh, you know, the usual. Not bad for rubbing up on my friend in my sleep like a true creep and coming all over his pants. How's your Monday morning going?"

He shakes his head, lips twitching. "If anyone's the creep here, it's me. I was awake. I could have stopped you."

"I don't think I gave you much of a choice."

"We always have a choice, Daisy," he says softly.

"Yeah, but you didn't even touch me." I fear a tiny bit of disappointment bleeds into my tone. I quickly try to overcorrect. "Not like you would, of course. Because you're my friend, doing me a favor." I wince at my pathetic choice of words as I finally find my strength and move off Luke to stand by my side of the bed.

I eye the mess between his legs and feel my face burning up.

It's now his turn to stand, but his eyes are locked on mine as he rises to his full height and walks around the bed. I need to tilt my head back to maintain eye contact, and I'm glad for it, because it means I won't be caught ogling him again.

"You're right, I didn't touch you." His knuckle taps under my chin once, forcing me to angle my face higher as he lowers his.

My eyes dance between his lips and eyes. "Exactly. Because we're fr-friends."

He shakes his head once, his nose faintly brushing mine, voice dangerously possessive. "As much as I'd love nothing more than to fuck that word out of your vocabulary, I won't. Not while you're still wearing his ring."

I quickly peek down and stare at the monstrosity that I've yet to take off. The ring given to me by the man I'm supposed to be waking up to instead of dry humping my fr—Luke.

Would Luke really have crossed that line with me? Does he want to be more than—

"Get out of your head and into the shower, Daisy," he says roughly.

I look back up, raising a brow. This orgasm must have given me superpowers, because I feel emboldened instead of embarrassed. "Oh yeah? Or what?"

A devilish smirk unfurls on his face as he leans closer, his beard tickling my ear. "Or I might change my stance and take that ring off your finger myself."

Chapter Seventeen
LUKE

She bolts faster than a freight train.

I chuckle darkly as she squeaks behind the closed bathroom door.

She must have fried my brain, because nothing about what happened was amusing.

I'm supposed to be keeping Daisy safe from the men who want nothing more than to manipulate her into being a mindless puppet, yet here I am selfishly bending her to my will.

Asking her if she wanted to come, telling her to use me.

Jesus Christ.

I quickly make my way outside. When I installed the outdoor shower, I never expected to need it to wash off after coming in my pants like a randy teenager. I turn the water to cold and strip. I don't even flinch when I step under the spray, the coolness bringing a welcome relief to my tense muscles.

I told myself to keep the shower quick, but visions of Daisy on top of me keep playing on a loop and I lose track of time.

The way she ground down on me.

Wearing my hoodie, while making those sounds.

I know it's a losing fight when I wrap my hand around my hard cock and pull tightly.

Doesn't matter how cold the water is when I can still remember the smell of her arousal and how desperately I wanted to lower my head and have a taste for myself.

I growl at the thought of licking her clean, claiming her in every way I can. Knowing that she's on birth control nearly did me in when visions of my cum leaking out her warm cunt flashed before my eyes.

I hear the crunch of leaves behind me and nearly chuckle.

Of course she would venture out here at a time like this.

I rationalize that she's already seen me come once, but is it really necessary for me to turn around as I continue to stroke my hard length as her shocked eyes meet my heated ones?

No, but I do it anyway.

Her jaw drops, and I see the apology on the tip of her lips. Doesn't mean she takes her eyes off my dick for a second as she starts. "I'm so—"

"If you try apologizing at a time like this, I'll have you on your knees before you can blink."

She shocks the ever-loving hell out of me when her eyes heat and she licks her lips, as if she's dying for a taste of me too.

And I'm done for. I come with her name on my lips.

My release lands a few feet away from her sneakered feet. Her eyes watch intently as I come undone for her.

Her gaze slowly rakes up my body, not showing an ounce of her usual bashfulness when she speaks. "Should I get you a towel or…"

"No need. Seems pointless to cover up now, doesn't it?"

She bites her lip, a habit I might need to break if I want to survive the next few days around her. "While I can't say I didn't enjoy the show, I came out here because your phone was ringing nonstop. Apparently, the poop emoji is calling you?"

She lifts both our phones in her hands and the emoji of the single most annoying person in my life tries to call me again.

But I don't pay it any mind, because even after coming twice, my cock is still pointing right at Daisy, and she's doing a shit job at not staring right back.

If one of us doesn't find some semblance of control, I fear I might be pulling those soft leggings off Daisy and bending her over the nearest tree stump.

The phone goes off again. I'm about to say something to break my naked standoff when Daisy's face goes ghostly white.

Because the phone currently ringing isn't mine, but hers.

And the name clearly legible from where I stand belongs to the man she was supposed to marry.

Chapter Eighteen

DAISY

I don't answer.

Not the first time he calls or even the second.

I sit on the kitchen island, staring at my phone, not knowing what to do.

This morning, after I unraveled on top of Luke, I felt like a part of myself that had been hidden for so long had finally been freed.

I was able to embrace my sexual side without feeling shy or awkward about it. In control while also being guided by Luke.

The moment I came, my brain chemistry altered in real time. And after my shower, instead of coming up with a million reasons why I should apologize and never do that again, I was tracking down Luke to make sure he was okay... and to feel out the situation and see if we could have a lot more mornings like those, but with a little less clothing.

And when my literal wet dream came to life right before my eyes, I realized I was still a bit in over my head, but I didn't run like I usually would have.

That is, until the one person I'd been hoping yet dreading to hear from finally decided to call me.

And I get it. I don't have much of a leg to stand on here. I left him at the altar. I should have come to my conclusions about our relationship much sooner and expressed those feelings in a far more appropriate manner. But we're here now, and in true Daisy Stonehaven fashion, right when I get a taste of something good, something I think I might deserve, here comes the person who had way too much control over my daily life, all for the sake of his image.

Control I should have never given up in the first place.

I bounce back and forth between the guilt of my own wrongdoings and wanting to make everything right again for everyone else. Attempting to figure out if there is a way to allow myself a moment to seek my own happiness without being a selfish and terrible person.

"What do you want to do, Daisy?" Luke asks as he places a glass of water next to me, fully clothed now.

My circular thinking halts at his nearness. He's not within reach, and a part of me wishes he were.

But if I know Luke like I think I do, then I know he's giving me the space to figure my shit out. Because as much as he likes to pretend that he's a growly grump, the man is a total teddy bear under it all and is putting my needs and feelings before his own.

My phone rings again, and this time, I reach for it.

"I'll give you some privacy. I'll be outside." He lightly squeezes my knee as he walks past, and I almost call out for him to stay.

Then I realize there's nothing stopping me from doing just that.

"Luke?"

He turns, eyes raking over my face intently.

I ignore the constant ringing from my phone. Damien can call me a fourth time for all I care.

"Would you—"

He's already making his way back to me, pulling out a stool and sitting between my swinging legs. After the morning we had, one would think there would be a sexual undertone to our closeness, but Luke's unwavering silent support is all I can focus on.

"I'll stay."

I nod. "Thank you."

"You're not weak. Nothing he says can break you. Remember that." He places my right hand in his, and I revel at the comforting contact only he seems to provide.

I release the breath that was caught deep in my chest, pick up my phone with my free hand, and answer.

"Damien, hi."

Silence greets me for a moment before a dry chuckle vibrates through the phone. "Daisy Stonehaven, as she lives and breathes."

I feel Luke's hand tense in mine, so I know that he can hear Damien even though the phone is pressed against my ear.

I clear my head and focus on my main priority. Apologizing and moving on. "Damien, look. I'm sorry for how—"

"Save the apology for the cameras, Daisy. You were supposed to be here yesterday. I had a crew waiting on standby for our first sit-down interview after our wedding made national news." The sound of him loudly crunching on something, probably pistachios, makes me think I'm mishearing him, because he's not making sense. "Thank you for the bump in the polls, by the way. The picture of me looking like a heartbroken jilted groom has done wonders for the female demographic between the ages of thirty-five and fifty-five."

My face scrunches up in confusion. "What are you talking about? Cameras? Did—did you not see the note I left on the mirror?" Oh God, does he still think—

He snorts. "Ah yes, we all saw your little arts and crafts presentation. But I'll have to ask that you keep the theatrics to acting when the interviewer asks about why you got overwhelmed about the grand production of our wedding. And don't forget to mention that you also asked me to consider a more intimate affair the morning of the wedding. We need to make it clear that you never set foot into the church, and since no one saw you in your big white dress, it shouldn't be a hard sell. We need my male voters to not see me as weak, so you'll clarify that you didn't technically leave me at the altar. Instead, you were waiting for me at home to have a private service first, followed by the big party." I'm stunned by his words, only able to hear the beehive of activity around him. He must be surrounded by his entire campaign team.

"I don't—I don't understand, Damien. I broke up with you. I'm sorry for the shitty way of doing it, I truly hope you know that, but I—we're not—"

"Oh, but we are." His voice whips out in a sinister tone. "Because I'm taking over as your handler in regard to you and your media responsibilities. Your father promised he had it all under control, but clearly, he's done a shit job of it, and the gamble is too big at this stage in the game to have another fuck-up. We can finish this conversation in person. I'll have a car sent for you if I must. But I truly don't have the time to hold your hand through all the details. That's what my assistant is for." He pauses before humming in delight. "That and fucking me, of course." He chuckles when I gasp. "I assumed your father told you about our little arrangement, but I'm guessing he fell short in performing that task as well?"

The phone nearly slips out of my hand. I feel as though a tight fist has wrapped around my heart.

My father? A handler? His assistant?

But then every moment of our relationship starts to flash before my eyes. How he always flipped his phone over while having dinner with me or flat-out denied me access to it when I wanted to download a podcast I thought he'd enjoy.

The sudden change of plans, the unexplained extended nights away...

I guess the clues were all there, if I had only dared to look close enough.

I now understand that me running from my wedding wasn't a rash decision but rather me finally listening to my intuition. It's one thing to know something is wrong, but when your blinders are up so high, it becomes easier to ignore them... until you can't.

I'm frozen in place. All I can feel is Luke's shaky hand in mine.

When I look down, his shoulders are almost to his ears, and it seems like his entire body is brimming with rage. He's looking at the ground, but I can only imagine the look on his face.

He draws circles on my hand with his thumb, but even that motion is erratic, as if it's taking too much concentration to focus on that small act and not my disaster of a phone call.

I know it's going to take more than a moment to unravel everything Damien has so callously revealed to me. But I need to walk away from this conversation knowing that I've said all that I've needed to while also giving him a piece of my mind.

"I don't know why you're telling me this. I know you're upset, and you have every right to be, but honestly, are you fucking kidding me right now?"

Luke's head snaps up at my change in tone.

I'm no longer feeling guilty, sad, or remorseful.

I'm fucking incensed.

"I have no clue what you and my father have conspired behind my back, but that is now none of my concern and I am none of yours. Therefore, I won't be needing that car you so *chivalrously* offered and I won't be crying crocodile tears for votes. So you can ignore the little doodle I drew on that mirror and take *this* conversation as the official ending of our fucked-up engagement. Oh, and while I'm at it, fuck you too." I raise my voice.

I'm about to hang up when I hear his stupid laugh over the phone.

"My, my, so she does have a backbone," he all but purrs. "Had I known you had this ruthless side to you, I might have considered fucking that attitude out of you after all. I wouldn't even have minded the little extra meat on your bones, might be a nice change from all the coked-out models I tend to prefer." My grip on the phone tightens. "But while this verbal foreplay is getting me hard, I really do need you back within the hour, because even though I wouldn't mind fucking you now, I'm still not going to risk losing the Latino vote that you've all but handed to me on a silver platter, *mi amor*."

Luke stands, sending the stool he was sitting on flying back in the process.

The grip on my heart loosens slightly at the sight of him running his hands through his unruly hair, eyes set on my phone, probably ready to snap it in two.

But what neither Luke nor Damien are aware of is the overwhelming sense of power that is coursing through my veins the longer I hear Damien speak.

Because I've played every possible scenario of this very conversation in my head repeatedly since the moment I ran from that church without a backward glance. And every scenario ended with me feeling like a pile of crap while curled up on the floor crying.

I never could have anticipated the venom coming from the man I had foolishly convinced myself I could be happily married to.

Couldn't have fathomed my father having a hand in orchestrating my obedience for political gain.

And as I stare at the man standing before me, looking like he's ready to burn every inch of the world that dared to harm me, I do the unthinkable at a time like this.

I laugh.

The action has Luke stilling before me, head tilted in confusion. Damien's cut off from wherever I left him in his unnecessary rant.

"Something funny, wifey?" Damien sneers.

"I'm not your wife, and I never will be. So call off your dogs and get your story straight. And by story, I'm referring to a little thing most humans with a soul call the truth. You were left at the altar. We are no longer getting married. And if you're feeling extra charitable, tell the people of New York that you're also a lying piece of shit. But feel free to run the wording by your chief of staff."

Damien is scoffing in my ear, at a complete loss for words. But I'm too focused on the sexy-as-fuck grin on Luke's face.

He places his hands on the island, bracketing me in his arms without touching me.

"Hang up," he mouths.

"Not yet. I'm having too much fun now," I mouth back, swinging my legs back and forth.

"You're out of your depth, Daisy," Damien says, his voice much less confident than when we started our call. "There will be repercussions for your actions. This is larger than you and me. There are powerful people backing me to ensure that I'm in that governor's mansion after this election. Now is not the time to throw a damn tantrum. And if you think you can take me down, don't expect to come out of this unscathed. Your big brother isn't the only one with connections. Do you really think I can't have you painted out as the villain in this story? It's so easy to pit women against one another. How long do you think until the internet trolls are out for your blood, Daisy? Hmm?" he spits.

My confidence starts to waver. I know how vicious social media can be. It nearly sent my friend Isabella into hiding for a few years to escape the worst of it.

But the alternative? Marrying Damien and standing by his side for the rest of my days, or at least as long as he deems me helpful to his image?

Absolutely not.

I hum and decide to go for the jugular instead. "Ah, yes. Go ahead, Damien. And tell me again how the optics of a white man in power going after his Latino vote—my apologies—Latina fiancée and trying to dismantle her impeccable reputation is going to go for you and the liberal voters you've tried your hardest to convince you're one of?"

"You fucking bitch!" He all but screams into my ear.

Luke tries to take the phone, mouth already open, but I easily dodge it, leaning my head on his shoulder, my satisfied gaze clashing with his ruthless one.

I click my tongue. "Yeah. Well, it's a good thing I like the ring of 'bitch' much better than Mrs. Fischer anyway. Have a good life, Damien. Or don't. Needless to say, I won't be voting for you. Goodbye."

I hang up and drop the phone to my lap and release the biggest breath known to man, landing in Luke's warm embrace in the process.

He speaks into my curly hair. "Daisy, I am so fucking proud of you. You—you... God, I think I'm speechless."

I chuckle into his chest. "You've never been accused of being a man of many words."

He pinches my side, and I erupt into a fit of giggles as he continues his merciless assault.

I manage to slide off the kitchen island and escape, putting a hand up between us before he attempts to come at me again while I catch my breath, walking backward toward the living room.

"Hold on. I need to make one more phone call before my life potentially goes up in flames."

Luke cocks his head. "Your father? Am I getting a front-row seat to that verbal lashing as well?" He rubs a hand over his chest. "Not going to lie, Daisy. You telling your ex off... it was doing things for me."

I look down quickly, wondering if what he felt was physical.

He quirks a brow. "Caught ya."

I shrug. "As you said, nothing I haven't already seen."

His jaw actually drops at my comment, and I feel unstoppable.

But before we take this any further, I need to clue my brother in to the media shitstorm coming our way.

Nick picks up on the first ring. "Need the chopper?"

I pause. "You have a helicopter? Actually, don't answer that. I'm calling because I just got off the phone with Damien."

"Shit. Luisa!"

I roll my eyes. Of course my brother is looping in his wife. He knows she would rake him over hot coals if he failed to retell the conversation accurately and wants her to hear it straight from the source.

"It's Daisy. She spoke to Damien," he says, slightly out of breath. Sucker probably ran up the ridiculous number of stairs in his brownstone.

"Shit. Daisy, are you okay? Do you need us to come up there?" Luisa asks.

Luke's booming laugh takes us all by surprise. "Oh, she's fine, all right. She told him to fuck off and threatened him if he decided to smear her name in the media. Which he probably will find a way to do, given that he's a grimy excuse of a man."

Silence.

"Did Coach just laugh?" Nick whisper-shouts into the phone.

Luke rolls his eyes. Looks like I'm rubbing off on him.

Well, I actually did this morning.

"Anyway," I say, more to myself than anyone else. "I wanted to give you a heads-up. And he also admitted to fucking his secretary and models who are fond of cocaine. And he mentioned that dad was playing some role behind the scenes in keeping me compliant for him. So all in all, it was a pretty informative phone call."

"He fucking cheated on you?" Nick shouts through the phone. "He dared disrespect you and put you at risk for—fuck. Daisy, do you want us to send a doc—"

"No need. They never fucked," Luke says, a bit too smug for this conversation with my brother.

"I—what? I don't know how I feel about knowing that information. Luisa, how do we feel about this?"

She clears her throat. "Well, first, we feel relieved. I will have follow-up questions, answers to which I will not be sharing with you, my dear husband. But honestly..." She pauses. "There was no way Daisy was getting dicked down with the way she's been acting all year, so I guess it tracks?"

I feel my cheeks go bright red as my brother goes on about not needing to hear those words in regard to his little sister ever again.

While Luke runs his thumb over his bottom lip, lost in thought.

When his heated eyes meet mine, I can only imagine he's thinking about his wake-up call this morning.

"Yeah, so this has been great. But I'm gonna go now and act like that last part of the conversation didn't happen with my brother on the line. Okay? Cool. Thanks. Love you guys. And sorry in advance for whatever shit Damien slings our way. Bye!"

"Wait!" Luisa says, sounding more businesslike. "Thanks again for setting up the new pitching coach with everything he needs, Luke. Especially since you're the one who unexpectedly took time off for the first time since you signed your Monarchs contract." There's a sly tone in her voice.

I look at Luke. "I thought you guys were off because of weather delays?"

"We are," Luisa answers for him. "But that doesn't mean the team doesn't have scheduled practices and tapes to go over with their manager or that they don't have to come up with strategies for the lineup of teams on their calendar. C'mon, Daisy, you've been around long enough to know that the boys don't just show up on the field on game day." She chuckles.

"Right," I draw out as I look at an unapologetic Luke.

He shrugs, even though she can't see him. "Gotta use that time off at some point, right, boss?"

"Mm-hmm, sure," Luisa singsongs.

"My ears are still covered. Are we still on the dicking down conversation?" Nick asks.

"And that's my cue to go. Bye, guys."

"I'll update the girls via the group chat" is the last thing Luisa says as I hang up and toss my phone on the couch.

Luke takes a step closer to me. "Did I mention how proud I am of you, Daze?"

I lift my hand, halting him in his tracks. His brows furrow, but I need to ride this high I'm feeling and do what needs to be done before I've wasted any more valuable time in my life.

"Ask me." I take a breath for courage. "Ask me what I want, Luke."

His face shifts into his signature, unreadable mask.

Cautiously, as if holding his breath, he asks, "What do you want, Daisy?"

I flip my left hand over so it's facing him. "I want to take this atrocious, gaudy-looking ring off my finger and never set sight on it again." I pull the ring off in one single tug—it was never sized correctly to begin with—and let it drop to the floor with a clink.

Silence greets me as his entire demeanor shifts.

I know exactly what I've done.

I've thrown down the gauntlet.

He said he wouldn't touch me while I still wore another man's ring, and now I'm going to test if those words ring true.

"Ask me again."

"Daisy—" he rasps, his voice barely recognizable.

"Ask me."

His jaw clenches beneath his beard. "What do you want, Daisy?"

I stare at his lips as I reply. "I want you to kiss me."

Chapter Nineteen
LUKE

I'm on her in an instant.

One hand on her hip, bringing her flush to me, the other in her hair, angling her face up to mine. "Say that again for me."

She has the audacity to smirk, the look in her eye already claiming the victory she must know she has over me. "I said I want you to kiss me, *Coach*."

"Thank fuck." I barely let the last word leave my lips before I'm swallowing her surprised gasp.

And finally, finally, I get my first taste of my Daisy girl.

She's sweet, like I knew she would be, mixed with this morning's café con leche.

I lick along the seam of her lips and she opens for me, letting me explore every bit of her my tongue can reach.

Her fingers grip my T-shirt tightly, keeping me close to her as her soft lips travel over my bruising ones. As if I would move a millimeter away from this heaven. The only way I'm stopping is when she tells me to.

Daisy has full control of me, and it's about damn time she figured that out.

She moans into my mouth and my cock answers like she's released a siren call for him.

Then Daisy's phone starts to ring again.

"That might be my father calling from a different number," she pants before her lips claim mine once more.

"I don't doubt it," I say as my lips move across hers.

My phone dings once, then four more times.

"That's for sure Luisa. The only person to text me with multiple messages for a simple sentence. She knows how much it annoys me. Or maybe my sister, I've been ignoring her calls."

"Must be." She gently pulls my bottom lip between her teeth and I decide to tug on hers even harder.

I don't realize I've been moving us along until her back hits the front door, causing her to arch deeper into our kiss.

Our phones continue to chime and ring nonstop, and Daisy releases a cute-as-fuck growl below me.

"What do you need? Name it and it's yours." I kiss the corner of her mouth, then continue a path down her neck, then back up behind her ear.

"Did you ask me a question?" She sighs dreamily and I smile against the sweet scent of her skin.

"Daisy." I say her name like a prayer. One that's finally been answered for me.

"I want everyone to leave us alone. I want this moment to be... only us." She sags against the door.

I pull myself up enough to see her face. Her swollen lips carry the evidence of our mutual assault, her blown out pupils are laced with desire, and her chest rapidly rises and falls beneath my touch.

I want to memorize every single part of this moment, and like I promised, I'll give Daisy everything she asks for.

"Wait. I haven't asked you a single time what it is that you want." She bites that lip that I've decided now belongs to me. "I should have asked you sooner. What do *you* want, Luke?"

"Isn't it obvious?" I raise my hand, not taking my eyes off her, as I switch off the cell booster, sending us into blissful silence, only our ragged breaths to be heard in my quiet cabin. "You."

Chapter Twenty

DAISY

I'm kissing Luke.

My Luke. The man who has silently stood by my side through it all.

And he's kissing me back like a man starved.

When he turned off the cell booster, and in turn quieted all the noise coming from our phones and the outside world, something inside him snapped.

"This is your two-second warning I promised you."

"What?"

Luke swoops down and lifts me into his arms by the back of my thighs, giving me barely a moment's notice to loop my arms around his neck and hold on for the ride.

"Bed or couch?" he asks gruffly.

My mouth answers before my mind can work itself into knots. "Bed."

Luke doesn't release his hold on me as he walks us over, then slowly lowers me to the bed, spreading my legs wider with his body as he crawls over mine, hovering over me without giving me all of his weight.

"You tell me when to stop and we stop. Got it?" he whispers gently over my lips.

"Yeah. Same. But I'm hoping that's not anytime soon." I pull him down to me with more strength than I knew I possessed, causing him to drop his weight onto me, and I reclaim his lips with mine.

I feel his hardness pressed between my legs and moan when he brings it closer to where I need him.

Is this really happening? Am I really going there with Luke?

He bites down on my lower lip, as though his thoughts are reprimanding mine for ever having any doubts.

Yes, yes, we are. They chant back to me.

"Talk to me. What do you need? Because if left up to me..." He slides his hands under my T-shirt and holds me by the waist, his fingers inching dangerously close to my bra.

"Off." I nod.

"Yours or mine?" I spot the smirk he's trying to hide, but I'm too far gone for subtleties.

I push against his chest, making him rise up on his knees. "Both."

He pulls his shirt off easily with a practiced tug from the neckline behind his head and tosses it to the side.

He opens his mouth to speak, but I point my foot at his jeans. "Those go too."

He grins as his eyebrows raise slightly. "Bossy. I like it." He slowly pops the button, then teases me with the unhurried pull of his zipper. I sit up and manage to remove my shirt and leggings just in time to catch the scowl on his face. "I was going to do that." His eyes stay locked on my barely covered chest.

I purse my lips to keep a small laugh from escaping. "I could use some assistance with this bra if you're still feeling helpful."

His face turns predatory as he leans over me, placing rough kisses all over my chest, keeping his eyes on mine as he unhooks my bra and slowly slides it down my arms.

Having his attention is intoxicating. It's unlocking a part of me that's always felt too shy to ask for what I wanted. But with Luke, it seems as though I can't stop doing just that. "I want to feel you everywhere."

His eyes darken as they lower to my chest. "Like here?" His thumb brushes over my hardened nipple, and I bite down on a moan. "Like this?" He slowly traces the outline of my nipple three times before pinching it, eliciting a surprised gasp from my lips.

Then he lowers his head and continues his discovery of my body with his tongue.

I arch into his mouth as he moves over to my other breast, giving it the same attention.

He continues his journey lower, kissing my stomach as his hands play with the edges of my panties.

His hands stop moving. "You're trembling." His concerned eyes meet mine as he leans back on his haunches. "Tell me again, what do you want, Daisy?"

What I don't say is that my body is vibrating with need. With the knowledge that nothing will ever be the same after today. That although I'm scared of ruining our friendship, there is no way in hell I am spending another minute of my life refraining from reaching for the things I want with both hands.

I don't know if it's the ache between my legs or the possibility of us stopping because Luke thinks I'm not ready for sex that has me speaking up, but I find the courage to spread my legs a little wider, showing the dampness coating my white cotton panties. "What do you think, Luke?"

My skin heats as his searing gaze focuses on the indecent scene between my legs.

"Fuck. Me," he groans as he runs a single finger over the wet spot on my underwear.

My eyes almost roll to the back of my head at the sensation. "That was going to be my answer to your last question." I raise my left arm and let my fingers trace over the tattoos that have been ingrained in my memory ever since I saw him shirtless and wielding an axe.

My fingers trail lower, following the path of light brown hair until reaching the waistband of his boxers. I'm about to tug them down when his hand wraps around my wrist, halting my movement.

"I don't have any condoms, so these should stay on until I can head into town and buy an entire store out." His voice sounds pained but steady.

"We don't need them." The words rush out of my mouth before I can explain properly. "I mean, if you don't—I, uh."

He goes still as he towers over me. "Daisy, be very careful about what you're going to say right now."

"We can wait, of course," I rush. "But I wanted to let you know that I've been tested and I'm all clear, and I haven't had sex since... well, it's been a very long time. And you already know I'm on birth control."

"Painfully aware." He reaches down and readjusts himself as I carry on.

"I want to respect your boundaries, and it's totally fine if you want to use condoms, but I wanted to let you know that I'm okay if you want to—"

He continues to grip himself through his boxers and grits his teeth as he speaks. "I'd never put you at risk, Daisy. I'm all clear as well and haven't even looked at another woman since the second I laid eyes on you."

"What? That's so... so swe—"

I gasp at the sound of my underwear ripping. "Rude."

"Yeah, well. I'm not feeling very *friendly* right now." His eyes challenge mine as he rips the other side of my thong and pulls the lousy fabric out from under me. "Much better."

"Just because you bought them doesn't mean you can tear them." My voice quivers at the end as I watch him stare down at my most intimate part.

"So fucking pretty. Just like I knew your pussy would be."

He raises up to his knees, his eyes looking between me and the erection that's bound to break through the fabric of his underwear. "Go on, then. Take me out."

I don't have to be told twice.

I pull his boxers down to his knees and watch in amazement as his hard length bobs mere inches from my face.

I know I shouldn't stare. I already got an eyeful of him this morning.

But his dick commands all my attention as it juts out toward me, a thick vein running along the side of it as a drop of precum swells at his tip.

I wrap my hand around as much of him as I can, rubbing my thumb over that raised vein. He seems to grow harder when I give him one tentative stroke down, then back up. My jaw drops slightly as he twitches in my hand, and I lick my lips at the thought of tasting him.

He seems out of breath even though he hasn't moved a muscle. "Careful, Daisy. You're putting too many thoughts in my head."

My hand squeezes at the word "careful." That's all I've been doing my entire life, and it has done me no favors.

So, no. I won't be careful. And I'll be damned if he tries to hold me back. "I don't want you to be gentle."

"Daze," he warns.

"I want you to mark me. Leave evidence of every place you've touched along my body so I know that this is really happening," I all but beg.

I give him one last tug before I release him and lean back on my elbows, leaving myself exposed and open for him.

"I want you to fuck me like you plan on breaking me, Luke. Because that's exactly what I want to do to you."

Chapter Twenty-One

LUKE

My shock is quickly overtaken by lust.

I chuckle darkly. "Is that so?"

When I spread her legs wider with my hands on her knees, she completely loses the ability to speak. But I have no issue telling her with perfect clarity what I intend to do with her.

"This what you're after?" I run the tip of my cock over her clit, and she whimpers. I continue teasing her as I lean down to speak directly into her ear. "I'm going to fuck you bare. Fill you with my cum until it's leaking out of you and then rub it all over your clit to get you off again. That sound like a plan to you?"

She nods frantically.

"Words, Daisy. Tell me now while I can still hear you. Before your thighs are pressed against my ears and you're too busy screaming my name."

"Oh, God." She tries to lift her hips and put an end to my teasing, but I'm not done yet.

Because she already ruined me for anyone else, so I think it's time I returned the favor.

"First, you're going to learn what it feels like to come on my fingers and tongue." I crawl down her body, and she starts to protest. I tut. "Trust me, I need to work you over before I have you bouncing on my cock, Daisy girl."

She all but swallows her tongue.

Good.

Because if she thought she was going to break me without me shattering her in the return, she was gravely mistaken.

I take a detour and suck a nipple into my mouth, nipping at her hard tip before continuing to lay kisses along her waist and hips until I'm settled in the spot I would happily call my new home.

I spread her open with my fingers. Her hardened clit has teased me enough, so I swipe my tongue over it to satisfy the hunger I've had for far too long.

Sweet and sinful. Like I dreamed she would be.

Her back bows off the bed, but I keep an arm banded across her hips to keep her pinned down right where I want her.

She yelps as I bury my face in her pussy, and I look up at her to make sure she's okay. "My beard. Is it bothering you?" Fuck, I should have thought about that. I want her to enjoy the very first orgasm that she hasn't had to give herself, and I'm not about to let a little facial hair get in the way. "Want me to shave it? I have clippers with me."

She stares down at me with a lethal glare. "Touch a hair on that beard, and you and I are going to have problems."

I run my tongue over my top lip, reveling in the taste of her ferocity. "Noted."

My mouth is back on her, sliding down to her opening, and I groan at how soft and wet she is for me. I slip a finger in and curse at how tight she is. I'm going to have to recite game plays if I don't want to blow my load before I've even gotten the chance to sink into her.

I manage to introduce a second finger while keeping my tongue properly occupied on her needy clit. I pump my fingers in and out while curling upward.

She tries to silence her screams, but I won't be having any of that. Those screams now belong to me.

"You can be as loud as you want. Stop holding back, Daisy." I slap her clit with my free hand before licking the sting away. Her walls tighten around my fingers, and I take that as my cue to suck on her clit and work her over even harder.

"Oh, God. Luke! I-I'm comin—"

Her words end on a scream as my tongue laves over the essence that's made a mess of my beard and her pussy.

I rise up to my knees to get a good look at what I've done. She's spread open and boneless on my bed. Her curls create a halo around her head as her chest rises and falls heavily. She looks blissed out of her mind, and I feel the same way. We could call it a night right now and I would still feel more pleasure than I've ever had during any other sexual experience in my life.

I lean over and trail my way back up her body, leaving gentle kisses on her sweat-slicked skin. When I'm within reach, she grabs my face with both hands and kisses me deeply, tasting herself on my lips.

My forearms bracket her face against the soft bed as I lose myself in her kiss.

I feel one of her hands trail down my face, caressing past my chest, drifting lower until it wraps around my cock. I lift my head slightly, breaking our connection. "Easy, Daisy. We don't need to rush this if that was too much for you. Trust me, my cock wants nothing more than to fuck you until the sun comes up, but we can focus on you today. Please believe me, the taste of your pussy on my tongue is enough to have me coming any second now." I chuckle as I kiss her nose, cheek, and forehead before placing a chaste kiss on her lips.

But instead of a sweet and sexually satisfied woman beneath me, I'm met with a pissed-off Latina. "You're turning into Mr. Nice Guy when I told you I wanted you to break me." She starts to move her hand up and down my length with assured strokes.

"I was probably too rough. I need to lotion your thighs in case my beard—"

She runs my cock over her wetness, and for a moment I forget how to breathe. "You promised to fuck me, Coach." Her other hand lightly scratches down my chest and abs. I hiss as they continue to travel over my ribcage and up my back.

"You're not too sensitive?" I ask, but even I can see how close I am to breaking as I thrust into her grip.

"Stop treating me like I can't take it." Her hand leaves my back, and for a moment I think she's going to stroke my cock with both hands. But it continues to dip even lower until she's cupping my balls.

I groan as I feel myself slowly leaking over her fingers. "You're tight, Daisy. Maybe I should eat you out one more time."

She hums. "Might take you up on that later, but right now, I want to feel all of you." She kisses me once more before she delivers the final blow. "Make it fit, *please*."

All traces of worry vanish from my face as my cock hardens impossibly further. I smack her hand away and replace it with my own, notching myself at her opening. "Like this?" I push in, just the tip, as she sighs below me. "That good enough for you, Daze?"

She shakes her head.

"Hmm, how about now?" I push in a few more inches, her pussy stretching to make room for my size. She winces and I stop, but I don't dare ask if she can handle it. She told me to make it fit and that's exactly what I plan on doing. She takes two deep breaths and nods. "Words. Use them," I grit through my teeth. I wasn't lying when I said I could come at any moment. Even more so now that I'm being enveloped in Daisy's tight heat.

"More, please. Keep going," she pleads, and I concede.

I slide in and out of her gently until the look of discomfort on her face transforms into one of pleasure. Then I push in farther, giving her more of me.

"Like this?" I continue to pump in and out of her, slowly inching my cock deeper. "Your pussy trying to take all of me tonight?" I taunt.

She whimpers and closes her eyes, nodding.

"Use." *Thrust.* "Your." *Thrust.* "Words." *Thrust.*

"Yes! Luke, God you're so fucking big. Keep fucking me just like that." Her nails dig into my skin.

"Good girl, Daisy." Her eyes flare with heat at the praise, and I smirk at her reaction. "You're taking my cock so well." Her nails start scratching up and down my back, and the thought of getting those marks permanently tattooed on my skin crosses my mind.

I look down and curse loudly. My hand shoots out and grabs her from behind her neck and hauls her up until she's bracing her hands on the bed. "Look at you." My voice doesn't even sound like my own anymore. "Were you playing pretend all along? Because the way your pussy is creaming all over my cock tells me that you were fucking made for me."

She looks down at where we're joined and her face burns bright. "Oh my God! I can't believe—I—"

"Don't you dare be fucking embarrassed," I scold, releasing my grip on her neck once I see she's got a steady hold on herself. "Your cum is letting me fuck you deeper. Like this." I hook one of her legs over my forearm and open her wider to me, closing in on the last few inches that kept my pelvis from reaching hers.

"Yes, Luke," she whispers.

"Louder," I grunt as I power into her.

My free hand finds her breasts, squeezing and plucking, finding that it synchronizes with the way her pussy is choking my cock. My mouth wants to join in on the fun, so I abandon the leg that's kept perfectly open for me to tease her nipples between my teeth. I pull on them, then move up and find a soft spot beneath her ear and bite down. My tongue lashes out when her cries threaten to send me over the edge. My hands find purchase on her hips, digging into her soft skin to the point where I know they'll bruise.

Her tits shake with every thrust, and I feel the sure signs of her impending orgasm.

"This cunt is so greedy for my cum, isn't it?" I taunt as I feel the vein in my neck pulsating. "Go ahead, Daisy. Come for me. Fucking *break* for me."

She tightens around my cock until I see stars, and she comes loud enough to shake the windows in my home.

I never stood a chance of holding out any longer.

I come on a roar, her pussy milking the cum out of me, as if claiming its rightful place.

She slumps back on the bed, sliding off my cock as she digs her hand into her hair, trying to catch her breath. She's glowing, a light smile playing on her parted lips as she looks well and thoroughly fucked.

I place my hands on my hips and look heavenward, because what the fuck did I just experience?

I'm feeling pretty damn good about working her over like that. So it's safe to say I'm shocked as hell when she leans up, puts her hands on my spread thighs, and slowly licks our cum off my cock.

My brain has ceased all usefulness as I keep still, not daring to move a muscle.

Her tongue runs from my base to my tip in languid strokes, moving blindly as her eyes are locked on my wide ones. She gives one final swirl around the tip of my cock before sucking the sensitive tip and coming off it with a *pop*.

She licks the corner of her mouth before she smirks at me and seals her fate with eternity in my bed with two simple words.

"Good boy."

Chapter Twenty-Two

DAISY

"Does that thing ever go down?" I ask as I soap up my body in the shower.

Luke looks down at his hard cock, then back at me. "I have you naked and all soaped up in my shower after fucking you in my bed. What did you think was going to happen here?"

I roll my eyes and continue to run my hands over my sensitive body. "I thought we were getting cleaned up," I say innocently as I turn my back to him and smirk.

I feel his heat on my back before his hands snake around my waist and travel higher and claim my breasts.

I hum, resting my head on his shoulder as he gives me the world's most thorough rub down.

"Shit, when did I bite you?" Concern laces his tone as he turns me around, fingers brushing lightly against my skin as he starts to catalog all the marks blooming on my skin. His brows furrow. "I was too rough."

I lean up on my tiptoes and nudge my wet nose with his. "It was perfect." He doesn't seem convinced as his eyes continue to survey every square inch of my body. I dig my fingers into his hair and bring him down to my lips. He softens slightly, but I can still feel the tension in his body. "But more importantly," I say, waiting until his eyes meet mine, "it was exactly what I asked for. Thank you for listening to me and trusting that I knew my limits."

He shakes his head. "You give me too much credit. You weren't in my head. God, the things I said to you…"

"You will be saying again and again if I have things my way."

And I mean it.

I've never had someone talk to me that way during sex. To the point where I was sure I was going to orgasm from his words alone. But damn am I glad he delivered with his entire body as well.

His lips twitch. "You liked that, huh?"

I shrug nonchalantly as I step into the water, making sure to avoid getting my hair wet. He watches me rinse, and I swear he's trying to follow the trail of every drop of water on my body at once. "See something you like, Coach?" I taunt.

He hauls me out of the water and presses me up against the warm shower wall as he chuckles. "Oh, my sweet Daisy girl. You don't know what you've done. Go ahead, keep teasing me. Because now that we've crossed that line, there will be no chance in hell of you ever waking up without my hands, face, or cock between your legs. I don't care if I need to steal your brother's jet so you can fly across the country to every away game. I don't think I'm capable of ever waking up without you lying naked in my bed."

He trails kisses down my neck and places an extra gentle one over the spot where I know he's left a mark.

"You say that, but something tells me you're a big softie and you're just jonesing for a cuddle."

He perks up. "With you? Always. Actually, I'd like to make an amendment to my previous statement. I want to wake up wrapped around you every morning. Hear your little kitten snores as you burrow into me and stick your cold feet on my legs. Then we can move onto fucking." He smiles widely as he plants a kiss on my lips.

I want to wake up wrapped around you every morning.
Every morning?
Now wouldn't that be something.
And since I can't help myself from potentially putting a damper on a perfect moment, I don't stop from running my mouth. "You sure that's what you want?" And I want to kick myself for sounding so fucking needy.

Where the hell is the woman who told her fiancé off and ripped off his hideous engagement ring with a flourish?

The one who told this man to fuck me like he wants to break me.

Am I really asking for validation at a time like this?

Luke rises to his full height, his eyes carefully roaming over my face like I've become accustomed to. As if he can scan my inner thoughts and respond to them directly.

He sighs, shaking his head. I think I've well and truly fucked it.

But then his hand cradles the back of my neck while his thumb rubs my cheek, all the way down to my bottom lip and back up, repeating the same path over and over again.

"You're asking yourself if I want you, while I'm secretly begging to know if I can keep you."

"Luke." I breathe his name, taken aback by the sincerity in his words.

Keep me?

I've been so caught up in the chaos of the toxic men in my life that I haven't even allowed myself to think of life beyond today.

Yet the thought of staying cradled safely in Luke's arms has me tightening my grasp on his forearm.

"I'm sorry. I shouldn't have said that." He places a chaste kiss on my chin. "You have more than enough on your plate." He pauses, and I feel him emotionally retreating, unable to meet my eyes. "I'm such an idiot. The last thing you need is someone like me, with my reputation—"

"Hey, Luke." I press a finger against his lips. "You're going to have to do me a favor and stop talking about yourself like that. Otherwise I'm gonna have to do something about it." I parrot his words from last night back to him.

"Daisy." He sighs, resting his forehead against mine.

"Would you?" I whisper.

"What?"

"Keep me?"

A pained growl sounds before me right as Luke's lips crash down on my own.

I know I have a lot going on, most of my problems currently being kept at bay since shutting off our cell signal. We probably need to figure out a whole lot of things before we can freely walk out of this cabin as a couple. I need to handle with the aftermath of my failed engagement and deal with my father. All while ensuring that my relationship with Luke doesn't negatively impact the Monarchs.

But he's dead wrong about whatever misconceptions he's let fester about himself. And I'd be the dumbest woman alive if I let this man walk out of my life based on what other people might say.

I've lived most of my life in a contest with myself. Worrying about the opinions of strangers. Trying to appease people who have no idea that I'm bending over backward for them. And shrinking into a version of myself that was unrecognizable, all in hopes of being appealing enough to garner a little love and affection.

But for the first time in my life, I feel like giving myself permission to put my wants and desires first. Perception be damned.

My hands roam down his chest until I wrap them around his stiff cock.

"Daisy, you must be sore." He places his hand above mine but doesn't push me away. He's letting me make the final call regarding what my body can handle, and it furthers my resolve.

We slowly stroke his cock together, and I'm certain the moisture running down my thighs is no longer shower water.

I release him only to turn around and lift my foot onto the shower bench. "I want you to take me from behind. Slowly. I want to feel you like this."

He presses his front against my back, and together we line him up to enter me. "Slowly," he reiterates with a soft warning.

I need to rise to my tiptoes to get the angle right, and once I do, he pushes in fully with one slow motion.

The knowledge that his body fits perfectly inside my own sends tingles down my spine.

I place my hands on the wall in front of me as his left hand cradles my breast and the other starts to press firm circles on my clit.

I instinctively clench around him, and we both moan.

"Dammit Daze. You feel so fucking good. Taking all this cock all over again."

"Fuck, Luke. Your hands." His thumb runs back and forth over my pointed nipple as the other plays between my legs. "I feel you everywhere."

"Good. Now you know how I feel," he murmurs against my neck before he kisses me there.

It's all-consuming. The sex. The feelings. This version of Luke who was here all along. And the knowledge that he wants to keep me, keep us.

"Oh, Luke."

"I know, baby. I feel it too. Come for me."

My cries bounce around the small bathroom before his loud groans join me over the edge.

He places soft kisses along my spine before slowly easing out of me.

I yelp quietly, but it's too late, he already heard me.

"I'm fine—"

He throws me a look that has me shutting up as he detaches the shower head and carefully cleans between my legs. Using his hand to cradle me so the water doesn't directly hit my oversensitive clit as he works diligently to set me right.

He rinses his half hard dick off before shutting off the water.

"Daisy, I want you in my hoodie and on the couch eating cereal while I lotion you up and take care of you. If you thought I was—what was it you called me?—a growly bear before, see what happens when you don't let me take care of my woman."

Chapter Twenty-Three

LUKE

"I can feed myself, you know," she grumbles as I feed her a spoonful of cereal.

I wanted to cook something hearty, but I don't think my body is quite capable of being more than a few inches away from her.

Daisy's in my hoodie again, and the sight has something shifting in my chest. And the fact that she's only wearing a tiny thong underneath has something shifting in my pants.

I internally chastise myself as she uncrosses her legs and I see slight redness between her inner thighs.

I wordlessly drop the bowl onto the coffee table and head to the bathroom, where I see a travel-size body lotion in her toiletry bag. When I realize there's more than a handful of different brands, I decide to grab the entire bag and bring it with me to the living room.

She arches a brow. "Are you in the mood for a skincare tutorial? Because I gotta say, I've been dying to see you with pink undereye patches."

I hold the large Louis Vuitton pouch to her. "Which lotion can I use for your legs?"

Her face softens as she digs around a bit and she pulls a small bottle out. "This one is extra hydrating and smells nice."

I drop the bag next to her and take the lotion from her hand. I take a quick picture of the brand with my phone and make a mental reminder to order a few dozen of the largest size they sell so I can always have it on hand for her.

I don't want to risk putting all my weight on the coffee table, so I take a seat on the cushion next to hers and wrap one of her legs around my hip, then drape the other over my thigh, opening her up to me.

Fuck, I'm going to have to do this as quickly as humanly possible.

I was so distracted with the thought of tending to the marks between her thighs that I forgot that I would be massaging her close to my new favorite spot on the planet.

She's wearing a nude cotton thong, and at first glance, it really does look like she's wearing nothing at all.

"Why are you mean mugging my pussy?"

I jerk back, completely caught off guard by the giggle in Daisy's voice. "I'm not."

I warm the lotion in my hands before applying it to her inner thighs.

"Mmm, that feels good. I like your hands on me," she murmurs while lifting her hips slightly.

"Daisy," I warn.

"What? I can't be honest with my masseuse?" She opens her legs a bit farther, and I have to grip her thighs to keep them in place.

"Daze, I'm quite literally tending to the marks I left on your body after burying my face in your pussy. You can't possibly be teasing me at a time like this." I squeeze her moisturized thighs.

She simply shrugs. "What can I say? You unleashed a sexual monster. I guess this is now your burden to bear."

"You can't be serious—" The sight of a damp circle in the center of her panties has me clamping my mouth shut.

She must know what's caught my attention because she keeps going. "If you think for a single second that the feel of your beard brushing up and down my pussy wasn't one of the most exhilarating moments of my life, then I suggest you try again so I can make sure to convince you properly this time."

"You—" I shake my head. "You're sore. I heard you earlier. You were in pain. I never want to be the reason you're hurting."

She smirks. "I am sore... so maybe you can kiss it better?" She bites the corner of her lip, and before I know it, I'm hauling her by the back of her thighs.

Her squeal turns into a deep moan as I dip my head and pull the flimsy thong aside with my forefinger, then take a long lick along her wet seam. "Like that?"

"Yeah, just like that," she says breathily.

I peel her open with my fingers, exposing that needy little bud I can't get enough of. I place a kiss right on her clit, knowing the whiskers of my mustache are tickling her there as well. "There. Did I kiss it better?" I tease. "Or does my girl need more?"

"Please, Luke." Her voice cracks with need.

I keep my eyes locked on hers as I place my lips over her clit and suck. She throws her head back as she shouts incoherently. I nip at her thigh until her head tips back down at me. "Eyes on me if you want to come."

She nods frantically as I get back to work, swirling my tongue over and around her bundle of nerves, keeping the same cadence I quickly learned she liked before.

Her fingers run through my hair as if to keep me in place. It's cute that she thinks I'd rather be anywhere else. "You're coating my tongue. Give me more, Daisy. I want it all."

The sting of her pulling my hair only riles me up further as I relentlessly work her over with my tongue. She comes seconds later on a scream that sounds like the most beautiful symphony.

She slumps back on the couch as I lazily run my hands up and down her thighs, feeling the little body twitches the orgasm has left in its wake. I force myself to cover her up with the pathetic scrap of material and ignore the raging hard-on in my joggers.

I don't bother moving us as I reach back for the bottle of lotion and start reapplying over the redness that's burning a touch brighter than before. "Look what you made me do. Now I've got to start over," I chastise.

"Dammit, Luke. You really have created a monster," she mumbles to herself, and it takes me a moment to realize I haven't stopped grinning.

"In you go, you sexual fiend." I pull up the comforter and guide Daisy into bed.

"Who, me?" She bats her eyes innocently as she settles on her pillow.

I round the bed, tossing all the pillows I know we won't need onto the floor. Because tonight I fully intend on sleeping wrapped around her. Hope she's okay with the amount of cuddles coming her way.

I turn off the lights, and we're basked in the midnight moon's glow. These windows can be set to go completely blackout, but I've always enjoyed feeling like I'm sleeping outside, under the stars. Not being caged in by the four walls that always seem like they're one bad headline away from closing in on me.

I lean back, and before I'm able to call her to me, Daisy rolls over and drapes herself across my chest, burrowing into my side like a perfect puzzle piece.

I exhale deeply, relishing the feeling of my hands roaming freely over her back as her fingers trace over my tattoos.

Some of them have deep meaning and others I got when I was young and stupid. I haven't inked myself in five years, and I've missed the feeling of the needle on my skin. Of coming up with an idea and having an artist bring my vision to life, even if it's a simple doodle.

Over the last year, I've had to stop myself on multiple occasions from getting new ink. I even walked out of an appointment after telling myself I would look like a complete lunatic for getting a certain flower tatted on my chest.

But having the real thing, the woman currently rambling sleepily between yawns, is better than any ink I could have gotten.

Besides, this woman is buried under my skin far beyond where ink can reach.

Her musings stop and her breathing evens out. Her cheek is pressed to my chest with her arm wrapped around my middle.

I realize in this moment what a gift I've been given. To have a woman like Daisy trust me with her body, and hopefully her heart as well.

Unfortunately, it's also in this moment that the dark thoughts decide to rear their ugly heads again. I try to take a few deep breaths without waking her and think of a few things I can see, feel, and smell.

Daisy, Daisy, Daisy.

But it's no use.

I should have known that true peace could never exist for a person like me.

It's the reason I ran away all those years ago.

Why I don't keep close relationships and prefer my solitude.

It's how I know for a fact that I don't deserve someone as amazing as Daisy, but fuck if I'm too desperate and selfish to make myself walk away when I know I should.

So instead, I close my eyes and let the demons come for their pound of flesh as my mind replays that horrible night on a loop. I suppose it was only a matter of time before they threatened to drown me whole, even as I try to focus on every one of Daisy's exhales.

The hours pass in agony as I relive the past while trying to cling to my future.

But I guess that's the life I'm due when I'm the reason two people are dead.

Chapter Twenty-Four
DAISY

Fuck, I'm sore.

I stretch lazily as I take a mental inventory of the damage. I know it's pointless, since there is no chance I'd forget a single second of what went down between Luke and me yesterday. And as much as I'd like to sit and reminisce about the kinky thoughts he's set off inside my mind, I have more pressing matters to attend to.

Like figuring out why the fuck I'm alone in this bed.

I really wasn't lying when I said he unleashed a sexual monster in me. For all of those years I had to repress those feelings because I never felt comfortable enough with a partner to reveal myself that way or was stuck in a sham engagement that should have never happened to begin with.

Either way, it's left me alone, grumpy, and horny on this fine, beautiful Tues—Wed—... what day is it? Who cares. I sit up and immediately spot Luke standing out by the dock with what seems to be a coffee in hand.

The sight of his broad back against the beautiful backdrop of the lake and colossal trees almost takes my breath away. His body seems like it was meant to be here, as if he were built by the mountains that surround us.

I break away from my ogling session to do my business in the bathroom and put on cozy leggings, then pull on an oversized cardigan over my cropped T-shirt, knowing that the spring mornings up here in the mountains still tend to be nippy. I don't bother making myself a coffee, instead pulling a throw blanket over myself as I head outside.

I'm taken aback by the sudden gust of cold wind. I don't understand how Luke is simply in a T-shirt and joggers. He must be absolutely freezing.

He turns right as I reach the bottom step of the deck and quickly makes his way to me.

I have a witty remark about waking up in bed alone, but it dies on my tongue when I see the look on his face.

"Hey, what's wron—"

"It's cold. Let's get you inside." He places his empty mug on a railing as he tries to lead me back into the house, but I'm not budging.

I drop the blanket despite his sound of protest and gently cradle his face, my thumbs slowly brushing over the dark circles under his eyes. "What's wrong, Luke?"

He sighs deeply, but his tired eyes won't meet my determined ones. "More importantly, are you okay? How are you feeling? Do you want me to turn on the booster so you can call someone? I don't want you to feel isolated. Should I call Luisa? Or maybe Isabella, since she isn't the friend that's married to your brother?"

I'm confused by his words, and because he's rambling when he typically tends to communicate well with as few words as possible.

"I, what? I don't understand." I shiver against a brutal gust that has Luke cursing under his breath one moment, then hoisting me over his shoulder the next.

"Luke, what the hell? Put me down and tell me what's wrong," I huff. I kick my legs and haphazardly try to smack his ass.

I'm enveloped in the warmth of the cabin and the still warm sheets when I'm deposited onto the bed carefully. His hands run up and down my arms, then cup my hands in his as he blows warm air onto our fingers.

I manage to free one of my hands and place it behind his neck, gently pulling him down until our foreheads touch. "You're scaring me. Please tell me what I did—"

He jolts, but my firm grasp keeps him in place. "Don't you dare finish that sentence, Daisy. You are perfect. Far too perfect for someone as tainted as me, and yet I still took every bit of you I was allowed without a moment's hesitation because I'm a selfish man who's spent an obscene amount of time wanting you. When, instead, I should have been protecting you from my darkness."

His darkness?

I may not know everything about his past, but I know for damn sure that Luke is a good man. The fact that he wouldn't even touch me after helping me run from my wedding simply because I was still wearing my engagement ring tells me he is ruled by honor, no matter how displaced it may be.

And while I know I need to tread carefully with what I say next, I have to nip this in the bud before we start creating obstacles for ourselves. Because once we are out of this cabin, the real world is going to slap us in the face with what's coming our way, and I need to know that we're in this together.

"Luke, talk to me. I have a pretty good idea of what you're referring to, but I'm not going to push. What I will ask instead, is for you to allow me the same respect you've always given me and include me in whatever conversations are going on in your head. Because when you don't, you come up with assumptions I'm not privy to, and it leaves me feeling... lost."

He clears his throat, lifting slightly to press a lingering kiss on my forehead before straightening out of my hold. "You're right. I'm sorry for freaking out on you. I should have..." He shakes his head, placing his hands on his hips. "Fuck, I need to be better. You didn't deserve to feel like that. You deserve—"

"And I'm actually going to stop you right there, babe."

He stills at the term of endearment, which was actually my intention, to shock him out of whatever doom spiral he is in.

Unfortunately, I am well acquainted with those.

"I've had a couple of back-to-back freakouts since you busted me out of that church parking lot. I don't see you holding a grudge over any of those. Granted, one of those instances had you ripping me out of my wedding dress, but I digress."

"Daisy—"

"I'll let you speak. I promise. But we're going to try this thing where you don't tell me what I deserve or can handle or should want. And I'm going to listen to your feelings and take your past into account and give you grace. Then we can take it from there. How's that sound?"

He looks like a deer in headlights. Not the exact reaction I was going for, but this whole speaking up for myself thing is new, so I'm bound to be graded on a curve, I guess.

He gulps audibly. "All right. Well, then, first things first." He fidgets with his hands, something I've never seen this man do. He's solid and determined in everything he does, which tells me he must be nervous. "Do you, uh, regret anything from yesterday? Anything at all?"

I huff as I cross my arms over my chest. "Yeah, sure. When you didn't let me go down on you after you ate me out on the couch."

"Daze."

"No. I don't regret a single thing. Only that it took us too long to get out of our own way and see what was standing right in front of us. I regret that I spent so many lonely nights in a loveless relationship with a horrible man when I could have been cuddled up on the couch watching a movie with you or cooking up a storm while dancing in your kitchen or up here in your cabin celebrating Valentine's Day by not wearing a stitch of clothing for an entire weekend. Those are my only regrets, Luke." I take a fortifying breath, because the little voice in my head that told me we were too good to be true must be conspiring with Luke's. "But—but if *you* are having regrets—"

"Don't." The word lands like a whip. "Don't you dare let my fucked-up behavior make you second-guess anything about the time we've spent up here." His voice is brimming with barely controlled passion.

And there he is. My Luke. My protector. My saving grace.

But the thing about knights in shining armor is that they might need some saving every now and then too.

"All right, then why don't you tell me what this is really about? What triggered this? Because last night, when I fell asleep in your arms, I thought everything was perfect."

"It was." He rushes to add, "It is. It's just..." He takes a seat next to me and pulls my hands into his trembling ones. "When you fell asleep in my arms, everything felt right. I've never had a moment of extreme contentment like that, like when I felt you breathing softly on my chest. But that was also the same time that memories from my past resurfaced and kept me up all night. Running through everything that happened. The reason I left the sport... Why I fell off the face of the earth."

He squeezes my hand and I squeeze right back. "I'm here. You can talk to me. But only if you're ready." My thumb brushes over the back of his hand as his eyes take on a faraway look.

"That night. When she... and he..." He sucks in some air. "It's all my fault. Their deaths are on me."

My eyes threaten to fall out of my head at the statement. I may not know the ins and outs of what transpired that night a few years ago, but I do know the facts.

Two people got in a vehicle while under the influence of alcohol.

Their car crashed against a lamppost and they were pronounced dead on the scene.

And those two people were Luke's girlfriend and his best friend.

Chapter Twenty-Five

LUKE

I hate reliving this part.

But Daisy is right. She doesn't need me making the calls on her behalf. I'll tell her the full truth, and if by some miracle she decides she still wants to stick around, then I guess it'll be on my ass to work on myself so that I can be the kind of man worthy to stand by her side.

"She was my ex-girlfriend," I say out loud for the very first time. "That night, while I was out celebrating our World Series win with the team, I broke up with Mindy. It was a dick move. I had been putting it off for months, but I was so laser-focused on getting that win that I didn't want to add any potential distractions like her posting about our breakup all over social media and overshadowing all the hard work the team had put into the season."

I brace myself to find judgment on her face. When I find none, I summon the courage to continue. "We were young. Met at a charity event and hit it off immediately. She understood my lifestyle and supported me during the beginning of the relationship. But as the season went on, she got a little more brazen about asking for money, complaining about the fact that the other WAGs had more designer bags than she did, and hardly made it out to any of my games. I told my best friend Jack about my concerns, and he told me to keep my head in the game and deal with the drama after one of us made it to the World Series. The kicker is that we both made it, but on opposing teams."

"So the night you won..."

"He lost. The game and his life."

"It was a tragic loss. They were both so young and should still be here, but I'm failing to see where the fault of their untimely passing lies with you, Luke," she says gently.

I start pacing, not able to sit with the energy coursing in my veins. "I was an asshole. I was too focused on the sport and let my responsibilities as a boyfriend fall to the wayside. I didn't even bother breaking up with her in a respectful manner. And what did it lead to? Two drunk people getting in a car together and—"

I can't even say it out loud. But the look on Daisy's face tells me she already knows the rest.

"From what was reported," she hedges, "they had been secretly seeing each other for months...behind your back."

I close my eyes at the onslaught of memories. Of all the times they lied to my face while probably laughing behind my back. The betrayal that has nowhere to go because in the end, they died. Everything else is irrelevant.

"The newspapers didn't have to report everything from the police report. The fact that she wasn't wearing a seat belt and that he was found with his pants unzipped around his thighs is not something a parent should have to learn when they're in the midst of planning a funeral."

She winces, which only confirms that she knew that morbid fact.

"While I was partying with my team, my ex and my best friend were getting drunk on my tab and getting behind the wheel and putting others at risk as well. And when it was all said and done, I'm supposed to be looking like some sort of grieving widower, even though I was toasting to being single while they lay dead in a ditch. And afterward, any time I cursed their names in my head, the burning hot rage turned on me, because how could I be upset at two people who couldn't answer for what they'd done? And as much as I hated what they did, I would have never wanted that outcome. I wish I could have moved on and dealt with a scandal in the gossip headlines. Instead, I was alone. I trusted no one. I ran here and bought a thousand acres of land that I had no clue what to do with, only to build a cabin fit for one because who the hell would I ever trust enough to share my space with again? Who would ever want to associate with me?" My voice cracks on the last word, and Daisy is up and catching a tear before it even has a chance to run down my cheek.

I gulp audibly. "A part of me always knew things were never right with my ex, yet I kept her along for the ride anyway. Almost everyone deals with some form of infidelity against them at some point in their life. But Jack? He was more than my best friend. He was a mentor. Someone I looked up to, confided in." I suck in a fortifying breath, revealing what I've been too ashamed to say out loud. "Before we sign our contracts, we're warned by everyone with a pulse to look out for gold diggers or people in our circles who will try to scam us out of our newfound wealth. But never in my life could I have imagined a betrayal like this coming from someone I thought was more of a brother to me. And if a brother could do that to me, so easily cast aside his loyalty and respect for me, then I guess my only real value in the world are the numbers in my bank account and the one on the back of my jersey." I release the breath stuck in my throat. "So I ran. And if I'm being honest, I haven't stopped running since."

Daisy's grip on my face tightens. "I'm so sorry, Luke. But you're wrong. Your finances are the least impressive thing about you. You carry honor like a second skin, and anyone who is lucky enough to be around you knows they're in the presence of greatness when you enter a room." Her worried eyes sweep my face. "You didn't deserve any of that," she coos as her hands magically touch me exactly where I need her. "And I won't pretend to understand what you must have gone through, but I can promise to help you process it all from here on out. If you let me in."

I laugh humorlessly. "If I let you in? Daze, you've somehow broken down all of my fortified walls with your smile and that special dose of kindness only you possess. When we first met, you sat through so many lunches where I was a wordless grump and offered to bring me a special blend of tea because you thought my grunting responses were due to a tickle in my throat when in reality, I was an awkward, disgruntled man who didn't know how to act around a woman as beautiful as you."

Her lips twitch. "In my defense, it was flu season and you guys could be taking better care of yourselves when you're out there on the road." She runs her fingers through my hair, bringing my forehead back down to hers. "But you were one of the first people to speak to me without an agenda. You couldn't care less about who my brother was, what school I went to, or what designer I was wearing. Instead, you asked about the social media segment I created for the Monarchs and offered to get mic'd up even though you're notoriously known for hating press conferences and having to deal with the media."

"I wanted to support you any way I could. It was the only way I would allow myself to stay close to you without crossing any boundaries."

"Yeah, and now look at you. In the past few months I've seen you dance at my brother's wedding, help light an ungodly number of candles for Mateo's proposal to Isabella, and even attend a joint bachelor and bachelorette party."

"I stormed out of that last one," I grumble.

"Yeah, I suppose you did." Her small smile makes an appearance, so I dip low and kiss her on the corner of her mouth, relishing the feel of my mouth on hers again.

"I'm sorry," I breathe over her lips, my shoulders slumping.

"The only thing you should be sorry for is not delivering on those morning cuddles." She pauses, eyes searching mine. "How are you feeling right now?"

I sigh. "Better. Relieved... and scared. Because I know these feelings don't simply go away. I've wrestled with them for years in therapy, and I thought the worst was behind me. But now there's you, and I'd never forgive myself if I caused you heartache because my heart no longer worked right."

Her sweet smile warms me from the inside out before she speaks. "Your heart works just fine, Luke. I promise to be gentle with it as long as you promise to be patient with mine."

"Patient?" I almost laugh. "I've spent the last year wanting something I knew I couldn't have... and now that you're giving me the time of day, knowing all the good and bad thoughts that run rampant through my mind and somehow still want to stick around... hell, I think I could find cause to keep you locked up in this cabin for the rest of our days."

"Offering to kidnap and keep me in the woods? Who knew you were such a romantic?"

I feel my lips tug up slightly and realize only Daisy has the power to do that to me. "What do you say we start our morning over and I make breakfast so we can eat in bed? Where I promise I will cuddle you after I put the both of us into a food coma."

She nods. "I'm going to have to charge you extra for those cuddles now. In the form of more chocolate chip cookies. I saw the cookie dough you tried to hide behind the milk carton. And then we can watch a thriller. I think we could use a little true crime as a distraction."

"Nothing gets past you," I accuse playfully. "And I've got the podcast you like paused and ready to go on my phone so we can listen while we cook. Or rather, while I cook and try not to burn the place down while you sit on the island and drink coffee in my hoodie."

"Oh, this calls for an outfit change? Who knew you had a flair for the dramatics, Coach. Going overboard for a morning movie and cuddle." She laughs as she leads me to the kitchen.

If only she knew how overboard I can truly go.

Maybe it wouldn't be such a bad idea for her to walk out the front door. Then there'd be no question about how deep my obsession for this woman goes.

Chapter Twenty-Six
LUKE

I thought there was no better way to wake up than yesterday morning.

But as I look down at Daisy napping soundly on my chest, her legs tangled along with mine as a movie plays on the TV and our empty breakfast plates sit on the coffee table, I know that this is what perfect mornings are made of.

I'm aware that life outside these walls won't be easy.

But I know beyond a shadow of a doubt that I'll do everything in my power to keep her right where she belongs.

Here with me.

Chapter Twenty-Seven
DAISY

The next few days are a blur of food, cuddles, and sex.

Lots and lots of sex.

I can't seem to keep my hands off Luke now that I'm able to touch him whenever I want.

He still tries to be gentle with me, but all it takes is a little taunting from me, and whatever thread of control he believes he still holds snaps. That's the side of Luke I seem to be addicted to. The part that isn't trying to hide himself from the world. The part of him only I get to see.

But then there's the side of him that he's kept under lock and key for so many years, and it's finally starting to come up to the surface.

He's slowly allowing himself to talk about the night that changed the trajectory of his life. The feelings of betrayal caused by not only the two people who should have been the most loyal to him, but by his former team as well.

I had no idea there were teammates who were aware of his ex's affair but kept their mouths shut because they wanted to make sure Luke kept his head in the game. He considered many of those guys close friends, even brothers. Which was another reason he had no qualms about walking away from the MLB at the height of his career.

How he's been able to be such a solid grounding force for the Monarchs is beyond me. While he won't be winning any Miss Congeniality contests with the guys, there is no question that his team knows he's always there for them.

I've seen firsthand how he's handled the team after facing a brutal loss. How he takes certain players aside and offers them private words of encouragement away from the cameras. How he allowed players like Martinez to keep his phone in the dugout in case there was an issue with his daughter.

And while the media does him no favors and says he's rough around the edges, I will disrespectfully have to disagree.

Because as I look up at the man sitting next to me on the couch with pink undereye patches while rewatching *The Parent Trap*, I can't help but grin. The world would have a field day with my current view.

He looks down at me, not changing his usual grumpy expression, and winks. "Stop objectifying me, woman. We need to try to get through this movie fully before you pounce on me."

I giggle as he pulls me tighter into his side.

And in that moment, I allow myself to admit what my heart already knows.

I'm falling in love with my best friend.

We've turned the cell booster on once a day to send proof of life to my brother and friends. They're usually pics of the lake in the morning sun or the meals we cooked the night before.

But yesterday Luke took a selfie of us with the cabin in the background. I'm in my new favorite cardigan, hair going wild in the wind, smiling like a fool as he holds me close from behind, grinning up at the camera.

My only warning was the mischievous look he sent my way before I heard a swoosh from my phone.

He sent it to the group chat.

He didn't write a message along with it, but I think our faces might have been confirmation enough, because my phone started blowing up immediately with messages from the girls.

While Luke's buzzed five times with messages from my brother.

NICK:

> YOU MOTHERFUCKER

NICK:

> I'm sorry. I meant welcome to the family. I know it's been a long time coming. I'm genuinely happy for you guys.

NICK:

> Though I'm sure it doesn't bear repeating that I'm your boss and could easily fire you if you so much as cause a momentary wrinkle on my sister's face.

NICK:

> Still very happy, of course. Please disregard the prior message. This is not my wife texting on my behalf to rectify my lack of decorum.

NICK:

> But I know people, and don't you forget it, Coach Weston.

That last message got a chuckle out of Luke.

And to be honest, I was a bit relieved to get that out in the open with the people who matter most in my life.

Even though I know what Luke and I have is true, a small part of me couldn't help but worry about what they'd say.

I'm technically supposed to be on my honeymoon, and here I am falling in love with my colleague.

And while I know that thought lacks more than an encyclopedia's worth of context, I still can't help but feel like I'm going to be judged once everything is out in the open.

My relationship with Damien was tailor made for public consumption, and now I want to hide and protect myself and Luke from whatever onslaught may come our way. He's had a rough go at it, and while I know the things people will say about me are inevitable, I am much more worried about how he will handle being on the dark side of the press once again.

But for now, I have bigger issues to tend to.

Like where the hell am I going to live once I get back to the city?

Every time we've turned the cell booster back on, I've half expected a barrage of messages from Damien or my father's assistant since he's still blocked.

But there has been nothing.

Radio silence.

And it's terrifying.

I'd rather know exactly where the boogeyman is hiding than wonder when he's going to pop up.

I allowed myself to google my name once before I wisely closed out of the tab.

So far, there is a lot of chatter about the wedding that wasn't, but everyone seems to be waiting on a statement that Damien has promised to give "in due time."

So far, the running assumptions are that I was a runaway bride. *Ding, ding, ding.*

Or that he cheated. Which is also true, but not the reason there wasn't a wedding, since he informed me of that morbid tidbit after the fact.

And finally, there is talk of me being silenced by some political mastermind behind the scenes, and we're all staying quiet until I get a payout.

While that last one is way off, all this attention seems to be paying off for Damien's campaign since everyone seems to be tuning into what is going on in his personal life.

I shake my head as I open the rental app on my phone and try to focus on the task at hand.

After thirty minutes, I give up and shut off the cell booster abruptly. My mind won't let me focus on square footage and rental agreements when it's too busy thinking about how the hell I'm supposed to leave this perfect bubble I've been living in and deal with the outside world.

Luke looks up from the cutting board where he's finished slicing a perfectly toasted grilled cheese.

"What's wrong? Did he text you?" He pulls down the tea towel that was resting on his shoulder and throws it onto the island, eyes lasering in on my phone.

I place a hand on his chest as I shake my head. "No, I'm just trying to figure out where I'm going to live after we leave this magical place. All the apartments I like are too far from the stadium, and the ones that are close by are way too sterile looking and pretentious. I want something warm and inviting like Nick and Luisa's brownstone. But I don't want a place that massive just for me."

He places a hand on the kitchen island, standing abnormally still. He clears his throat. "So, uh, you're not going to move in with your brother and Luisa while you figure out where to go next?"

I scrunch my face. "I love them to pieces, but I would rather run up an astronomical bill at the Ritz than be around the couple that I swear will never slip out of the honeymoon phase. I've caught them on more than one occasion getting frisky in the middle of dinner parties at their place. Piece of advice, always stick to the main floor bathrooms. Anything on the second floor is apparently fair game for them."

He nods along, looking contemplative. "I see."

"Luke."

"Hmm."

"Spit it out."

He sighs. "You already know what I'm going to say. But I don't want to pressure you into staying with me. I know what we have is very new, and I am trying my hardest not to mess this up by pushing you too far, too quickly. Because if it were up to me, I'd have you moving in with me in a heartbeat."

I place a hand on his bearded cheek as I press up on my tiptoes and place a gentle kiss on his lips. A part of me thought he would suggest this, but I didn't want to assume he'd want me to become the official squatter of all of his properties.

"But," he continues, "I also know you well enough to know that you need your own place. Somewhere that you can call your own."

My heart soars at how deeply this man understands me.

I was already trying to line up the right words to express why it was important for me to have my own spot, but of course, he already knew.

Because this is Luke. My Luke.

"I want nothing more than to wake up in your arms every morning. And trust me, I will be enforcing an absurd number of sleepovers." I continue to smile as he feigns indignation. "But I also know that I owe it to myself to finally stand on my own two feet. To live in a place where I'm allowed to paint the wall colors that make me happy. Buy fun and colorful throw pillows that match the season. Have a mismatched gallery wall full of the faces of loved ones and pictures of me and my mom together before she passed. I want to be able to live in a home that tells the story of who I was, who I am, and who I strive to be. Because for most of my life my home has been more of a prison cell, and now that I'm finally out, I need a safe space where I can feel free."

He leans down and places a sweet kiss on my lips. "I know, Daisy. You don't need to explain yourself to me. And you're right. You deserve all that and more. And I think I can help."

He pulls his phone from his pocket, then walks over to the cell booster. He gives me a teasing look and switches it back on so he can use his phone. After a couple of taps, he's handing his phone over. The listing for a two-bedroom apartment with the most stunning views of the East River makes my jaw drop.

I start swiping immediately. The kitchen is decorated in warm tones of brown instead of bland whites and grays. The entire place has high ceilings, making it feel like you're anywhere but an apartment in the busiest city in the world.

And in the description, it says that there are only two apartments per floor, so I won't have to worry about privacy.

"Luke, this is amazing. How did you find this so fast?"

"My realtor has private listings I'm privy to" is all he offers, and I'm too busy salivating over the deep tub in the master bathroom to badger him with more questions like I typically would.

"This is probably already snatched up. Is it even for rent or sale? Do I need to send a deposit to show interest—"

"How about I shoot him an email with your number, and you two can go over the details? This is all you, Daisy. If you really want this place to be yours, tell him and don't let him take no for an answer. The rest we can handle from here. It's unfurnished, but that's probably best so you can pick out every single piece of furniture yourself. If you close the deal today, we can have a mattress delivered by tonight. So at the very least you have a comfortable place to sleep while you decide what you want to do with the place."

I throw my arms around his neck as I squeal. "Thank you, thank you, thank you." I kiss his cheek repeatedly. "The apartment is perfect. It's... it's a place where I can have friends over for game night!" I say excitedly.

He chuckles. "Hmm, only your friends?"

I nod along pensively. "You're right. My brother as well. We have been a great cooking duo as of late."

He catches on to my teasing. "I see. Anyone else missing from that guest list?"

I look up and to the side. "Oh, you're right! Silly me. I'm sure some of the Monarchs players would love—"

I yelp as he lifts me easily and sets me on the kitchen island, quickly settling between my open legs. I keep my arms right where they are, not showing an ounce of remorse as his face warns me of what's to come if I finish that sentence.

I blow a curl out of my face and sigh. "Well, I guess it might be nice to have a place where my boyfriend can come visit me when he comes home after a long stretch of away games."

His face loses all traces of humor.

Shit.

I was really feeling overconfident there, trying to slyly slide in that boyfriend comment undetected. Looks like I gravely miscalculated.

"I'm sorry. I shouldn't have—"

He pulls me in tighter, one hand now on the back of my head as if he's bracing to kiss me. "You calling me your boyfriend now, Daisy?"

I clear my throat, nodding as I dig deep for my courage. "I am. Is that crazy?"

His eyes smile as they rove over mine. "Not any crazier than me secretly pining for an engaged woman over the last year."

I smirk. "Yeah, I guess that was pretty certifiable."

He nips my bottom lip for that. "Guess I'll settle for being your boyfriend for now."

I raise an eyebrow at that. "Settle, huh?" I cross my arms over my chest, and he does the same with a twinkle in his eye.

"*For now.*" He grins, and before my mind can wrap itself around what he's getting at, he picks up his phone. "I'm emailing my realtor. Get your game face on, Daze. You've got an apartment to lock down."

Chapter Twenty-Eight
LUKE

It's our last full day at the cabin.

Tomorrow morning we start our drive back to the city since the Monarchs have a night game.

Daisy thinks we're already cutting it close by not showing up today for practice, but I wasn't having any of it when she suggested we head down sooner.

I'm going to be selfish and soak up every second I can get alone with Daisy without feeling an ounce of guilt about it.

I was worried about opening up about my past. It's dark and not easy for me to talk about with even my therapist on the best of days. I was scared as hell that reopening those wounds in front of Daisy would have her running for the hills.

But she didn't.

She stayed.

And when I woke up this morning, I felt lighter than I have in years.

I know the pain I carry will never fully go away. It's somehow shaped me into the person I am. But I'm hoping that with Daisy by my side, I can work a little harder to make sure it doesn't consume me more than it already has.

Because when you have someone like Daisy Stonehaven believe in you so wholly, it's hard not to believe in yourself as well.

She got the email confirmation yesterday evening that she got the apartment, and like I promised, a full bedroom set was delivered before we went to sleep.

I won't tell her exactly how I knew that apartment would be hers in a heartbeat. She'll come to learn of that soon enough, but my Daisy needed a win, and I'm glad I could have a hand in helping her get it, even if it means keeping her in the dark for a little bit.

We've been lying in bed since we finished breakfast, enjoying the view of the lake and trees in the midday breeze. Daisy traces the tattoos on my chest. The sensation usually does wonders in lulling me to sleep, but she feels tense in my arms, and I swear I can hear the cogs turning in her head as her fingers glide over my skin.

"Can you stop thinking so hard? I'm trying to enjoy my last midday nap with my girlfriend," I mumble into her hair.

"Sorry about that. Was thinking about... everything that's to come."

I pull her in closer, fully spooning her now. "Anything I can do to help?"

She shrugs. "Feed me pizza and tell me I'm pretty?"

"Now that I can do." I roll her over, pinning her under my body, my hair falling over my eyes as I look down at her. "You, Daisy Stonehaven, are the most beautiful woman I've ever laid eyes on. And your physical beauty." My fingers trace her cheeks. "These eyes. Those lips." I lower and place a quick peck over them, then push back up to continue tracing my hand down her side, over her hip and waist. "This body, every last inch of you. And yes, I mean every last inch." I wag my eyebrows playfully and she erupts into a fit of giggles at my silliness. "Only pales in comparison to the beauty you hold in that heart of yours that I hope I'm making a home in. 'Cause you sure as hell have made the place yours in mine."

"Luke." She raises my hand to my cheek.

I turn my head and kiss the center of her palm. "So how'd I do?" I smile expectantly.

She tilts her head side to side. "Meh, would have been better with pizza."

I tsk. "Knew I was taking a gamble walking into that empty-handed. My apologies. It won't happen again."

"Apology accepted." I'm off her and heading for the kitchen, grabbing a discarded henley and throwing it on, then preheating the oven.

Daisy meets me by the refrigerator, handing me the sealed pizza dough we've been meaning to use, along with shredded cheese, sauce, and a couple of Italian meats. "Let's try to use as much of this stuff as possible before we leave tomorrow."

I chuckle. "Don't need to tell me twice." I pop a slice of pepperoni into my mouth.

She tinkers with her phone until it connects to the built-in speakers around the house.

Her favorite Aventura song comes on, and I raise the volume substantially, filling the house with some pretty inappropriate Spanish lyrics. "Remember, I said you could be as loud as you want here," I rumble into her ear so she can hear me.

I don't miss the shiver that runs down her spine and smirk when I notice her cheeks have started to turn that pretty shade of pink I'm so addicted to. Daisy and I have fucked more times than I can count, and trust me, I've been fucking counting, but she never seems to lose that special brand of innocence that only she could pull off.

Like when she asks me to fuck her harder or acts like a brat, only to seem genuinely surprised when I give her exactly what she's been after.

She points a less than threatening finger at my face. "The oven is on and we're not burning this place down, so keep your thoughts PG until we've at least taken our pizzas out of the oven."

I take a pepperoni off the individual pizza she started making for herself. "Oh yeah? Or what?"

"Hey! Get your own." She rearranges the pepperoni on her pizza, reaching for the last one in the pack, but I snag that one too and toss it into my mouth unapologetically.

With more speed than I knew was humanly possible, she grabs the dish rag off the counter, revs it up, and whips it out, hitting me right over my left nipple.

I almost jump out of my skin at the jolt of pain, gaping at my vicious little pizza maker. She keeps on, feigning as though nothing's happened, even while she keeps a vigilant eye on me.

"Oh, you're going to pay for that, Daze." I slowly stalk toward her, already imagining her bent over my knee as she slowly starts to back away with her hands up.

"In my defense, you started it."

"Keep talking if you want. It ain't gonna help you out in the slightest when I get my hands on you." She puts the kitchen island between us, creating a false sense of safety.

"Luke, let's be rational about this."

I make it to the oven, keeping my eyes on her as I turn it off.

The chime works like a bullet at the commencement of a race, because she makes a run for it.

It's not the first time I've chased her around the cabin. It's how I ended up fucking her from behind against the maple tree in my backyard.

I dive right so I can catch up to her quicker when she makes a run for the back sliding door.

But that's when I realize I've made a mistake.

Because she seems to have learned well from our wicked games.

She grins back at me as she runs up to the front door, turns the handle, and runs out.

I panic and run after her.

This isn't how I planned for her to find out, and I hope she doesn't keep running for the hills once she sees what's out there.

I brace myself against the front porch.

She's standing in the middle of my driveway, catching her breath, still oblivious. I decide to keep a safe distance until I know how she'll respond.

What I didn't anticipate was my own reaction to seeing the woman I love standing before me with a breathtaking smile.

While standing in a sea of daisies.

Chapter Twenty-Nine
DAISY

I'M GIGGLING LIKE A madwoman as I burst out the front door.

I'm down the porch steps in a flash and instantly assaulted by the bright midday sun. I squint and raise my hand while my eyes adjust.

I can't believe I've never thought to run out this way before. Although if I'm being honest, I'm never really trying that hard to run away from Luke, because once I'm caught, it's always well worth my while.

But I love the chase, and I love seeing the determined look on Luke's face to get me back in his arms.

Oddly enough, I don't hear his footsteps pounding behind me, but that doesn't mean he's not on the prowl. Made that mistake once and almost ended up digging sap out of my nails.

"Daisy girl." Luke's voice halts my escape plans.

His tone is soft but unsure.

My head snaps up to see him leaning against the front porch beam, hands wringing the dish towel I held only moments ago.

The wind picks up, lifting my curls around my face.

A tiny speck of pink flies within my line of vision before it's gone.

It happens again, only this time it's yellow.

Then purple.

I tuck my hair behind my ears so I can see properly and take in the sight of Luke's meticulously landscaped circular driveway.

My body moves in slow motion as my mind registers what it's actually seeing.

Daisies. As far as the eye can see.

Beautiful little white daisies everywhere, perfectly intertwined with colorful, unruly wildflowers.

I forget to breathe as the wind tips them from side to side as though they're dancing just for me.

I walk over to the nearest bunch and run my hands over the delicate flowers.

Luke's shadow stands over me, and I look up in time to see him gently pluck a daisy out from in front of me and hold it between us.

I turn to him. "Luke, are these—"

"Daisies? Yeah. I planted them myself. One for every time you've crossed my mind."

My eyes widen. "B-but there's, like, hundreds—"

"Thousands," he corrects. My jaw drops slightly as he simply shrugs. "If I didn't have a day job keeping me away most of the year, there'd be more."

He's watching me intently now, trying his hardest to read the thoughts flying through my mind a mile a minute.

He reaches up and tucks the daisy in his hand behind my ear, tangling it within my curls. "Can't you see? It's always been you for me, Daisy." His hands cradle my face. "Every time I fell a little harder for you, this is where I would run to. And each time I left, my driveway held evidence of your existence in the world. In the only way I could have you."

He nods toward the blooms as he keeps his gaze on me. "Those daisies represent you. Innocence and joy. Elegance and beauty. But those wildflowers? Those are the parts of you that I was lucky enough to get a peek of when we were just friends. And I knew for a fact that you were a true wildflower. Not someone who was meant to be tamed and kept in a gilded cage, but rather free to run in any direction your heart desired. And on the days when I was barely holding on to any thread of decency, I would daydream that maybe this place might someday be the one spot in the world where you would want to run home to."

A tear runs down my cheek, but neither of us so much as breathes as the next words tumble out of his mouth. "I love you, Daisy. Long before I had any right to, more now that I have you in my arms, and for many lifetimes after we're long gone from this earth where these flowers are planted."

His lips capture my surprised gasp.

Did he say—

Yes. Yes, he did. Luke loves me.

And an overwhelming feeling of peace settles over me, knowing that come what may, I have this man's love to help guide me through the mess that awaits us.

I return his kiss with equal measure as his hands cradle my face with a level of gentleness that seems impossible for a man of his size.

"My Daisy girl," he says between kisses, and I feel the steady flow of happy tears run down my face as he slowly starts to wipe them away.

He eventually pulls back, placing his forehead against mine as we both take much needed deep breaths.

"You don't have to say it back. I've had one hell of a head start." He chuckles as he straightens and shakes his head.

But I'm not having any of that. I wrap my arms around his neck as I look up at the beautiful blue sky. I only allow myself one tiny second to curse the day I accepted Damien's proposal. I want to kick myself for not noticing Luke's feelings and ditching my old, empty life sooner.

But I can't find it in me to be upset, because now I know exactly what love is supposed to feel like. And lucky for me, it's with the man whose heart I want to love and protect more than anything on this planet.

I raise up on my tiptoes and pull him down so we're eye level as I speak, his hands coming to rest on my hips. "You may have had a head start, but my heart has always known it's been safe with yours. It's how, during this insane time in my life, I've been able to trust my instincts and feelings when it comes to you. And we may have only been just friends until a few days ago, but you've always been able to read me well. So go ahead, look me in the eye and tell me, Luke. How do I feel about you?"

His eyes fan over my face quickly, his gaze turning serious as his hands tighten around me when he finds what I have no desire to hide. "Say it."

A slow grin spreads across my face. "I love you, Luke."

My sentence ends in a squeal as he lifts me up and spins me around. I laugh as he stops and rains kisses down my face and neck. "I love you so much, Daisy. I swear on my life, I'll be good to you."

"You already are. And it may take me a minute to get my footing, but for the first time in my life, I feel like I'm at the helm of my future, and I can't wait to live it with you by my side."

It's then that I'm lifted bridal style, like the first night he walked me into his cabin.

He strides through the wall of daisies until we reach an empty patch of soft grass under a large oak tree. He sets me on my feet and wordlessly removes his henley with one effortless pull over his head. I don't need instructions to start doing the same, and in a matter of seconds, we're both naked in the warm sunlight.

He pulls me into his arms as he goes to lie down, but I stop him. "Wait, we should get a blanket or something. Your back might get hurt on the ground."

He simply smiles as he sits on the cool grass and guides me to straddle him. "I've been in a daze since the moment I first laid eyes on you." My eyes widen as he chuckles. "Yes, that's why I love to call you, Daze. And now? All I feel is your love all around me. I could be lying on a bed of fiery coals and I wouldn't feel a single thing besides your lips on mine. So stop stalling and let me make love to you," he pleads, and it's my undoing.

I bear down on him, and his hardness bumps against my wet center. I wrap my arms around him as his kiss threatens to consume me whole. I feel the breeze in my hair and the smile on his lips as I lift slightly, lining him up with my entrance, then slowly sink onto him. We don't stop kissing as I slowly start to ride him, my clit grinding against him as I rise and fall at a languid pace.

His hands run down my side before rising up again and cupping my breasts. Pinching my nipples into little peaks as I moan into his mouth. My speed increases as he continues to play with me, and soon enough he's managed to take over, even though I'm the one on top. Placing his hands on my hips, he keeps me in place as he pistons up into me at a brutal pace, hitting the sweet spot inside me that he knows will make me shatter.

And I do. We come together. Me screaming his name, him shouting "I love you" as he kisses my neck and breasts.

We lie on that patch of grass afterward, watching the clouds above us move and shift into shapes we can't decipher.

But we don't try too hard to guess what they look like.

Because we can't keep the silly smiles off our faces, and honestly, we don't even try.

Chapter Thirty
DAISY

It's our last morning at the cabin, and I'm currently refusing to move from my spot on the bed.

The one keeping Luke pinned under me.

"We can come back any time you want," he mumbles into my hair.

"I'm not done dissociating yet. So I have no idea what you're talking about."

His chest hums under my cheek. "You know what would make things better?"

"Do tell."

"Freshly baked cookies." In a flash, he's thrown the covers off us, planted me on my pillow and tucked my naked body back beneath the sheets. "Now stay your cute little ass in bed while I run into town and get you the last batch of the morning, so we can munch on them on the drive back." He takes off in search of his clothes.

I'm too busy staring at his bare ass to notice that he's being ridiculous. "Hey. Take those clothes back off and get in bed," I say grumpily.

He pulls up his jeans and chuckles while buttoning up. "Never gonna tire of those words coming out of your mouth,

Daze. But I am a man of my word, and I've promised my woman a sweet treat, so I must deliver."

He darts around the bed quickly. By the time I'm able to untangle myself from the sheets, he's already fully dressed and grabbing his keys.

"At the very least wait for me." I look around the disaster zone of discarded clothing, unsure of when I stripped out of any of those items since Luke and I have developed a habit of ripping them off each other's bodies.

He places a hand on my cheek and another on my hip, bringing me close to him. "I'll be quick. Thirty minutes tops."

I pout. "It'll take at least forty unless you plan on ignoring every speed limit in town."

He ignores my estimate as he carries on. "And after, maybe…" He clears his throat nervously, which suddenly has me on alert. "Maybe after, we can take a drive and I can show you a bit more of the property? I've got some ideas I want to run by you."

"Okay… You looked nervous for a second there. I thought it was something bad." I narrow my eyes at him. "I swear to God, if you declared your love for me yesterday just to show me your murder shed today, I'm going to be beyond pissed at you, Luke Weston."

His shoulders relax as his eyes shine with humor. "Daisy, you're cute."

"Thank you—"

"But a little bit psycho."

"What?" My jaw drops.

"It's endearing. Really. Suits your whole innocent vibe. And it reminds me not to piss you off since your true crime obsession has taught you over a dozen ways to make a body disappear."

"And don't you forget it," I grumble.

He slowly backs up to the front door, arms up with a sly grin on his face. "Be back soon. I'm setting the alarm, so stay inside. I don't want to worry about you going off looking for my murder shed, tripping over a raised tree root, and ending up with a sprained ankle."

"That only happened one time. Okay, two times, but I swear that root wasn't there the last time I checked."

He steps out but pops his head back in one more time. "Thirty minutes, and then I can properly praise you with warm cookies and an orgasm before we hit the road. How does that sound?"

I cross my arms over my chest as I lift my chin. "Like I'm okay with you breaking the speed limits."

I've pulled my hair into a high bun and finished packing our things, and I'm throwing on my cozy cardigan when I hear the alarm disengage.

I wash my hands and look at the time on my phone, then shake my head. "Really, babe? Thirty minutes? Is a box of cookies really worth getting pulled over for?" I ask as I walk out to meet him.

But I freeze when I get a look at the person standing in front of me.

The stunning *woman* standing in front of me.

Long wavy blond hair that almost reaches her ass. Sharp makeup that accentuates her pretty hazel eyes, and a smart camel trench coat that's tightly cinched at the waist and shows off her curves.

Who the hell is she? And how the hell did she know the code to get in here? Or that *here* even exists?

I love and trust Luke, so I'm trying my hardest not to jump to conclusions. But I'm also the kind of woman who'll only ever be 99.9 percent sure someone isn't a serial killer. Therefore, in my mind, there is always a chance something will go wrong.

I should be concerned that she might be a crazy ex. A silent assassin. Someone sent by Damien's campaign to cut off "loose ends."

But instead, I'm more concerned by the slight upturn of her lip as she scans me from head to toe and the way it hitches higher with every pass she makes.

Finally, she speaks. "Well, well, well. So this is why he hasn't been answering my calls."

"I—Who—"

Tires screech beyond the open front door, followed by a door slamming. Heavy footsteps run up the front porch before Luke's bursting into the cabin looking none too pleased at our latest arrival.

His chest rises and falls heavily as he seems to try to get his breathing under control. It's odd; I've witnessed Luke ripping people's heads off for small infractions on the field, so I would assume he'd be running mad if someone was breaking into his house. I'm even more surprised when his voice comes out calm, as if he's trying to make peace with this woman rather than sending her packing. What the fuck is going on?

"I told you not to come inside until I got here. Could you not follow those simple instructions?"

She full-on grins now, and I'm starting to feel like the odd man out. "Is she—" I stop, not knowing how to organize the mess in my mind. "Should I go?" I point behind me, as if my home is somewhere in the woods. A place I would happily run off to if I discover that Luke has a secret hot hookup who apparently decided to stop by.

"Daisy, it's not like that." He starts to make his way toward me, stepping into the space between me and her, when she makes a gagging noise.

"Ew. No. Gross!" She moves closer to me and sticks her hand out. "Hi, I'm Valentina. Luke's sister. And if this place had a decent signal, you would have seen me blowing up his phone. I'm pretty sure I'm listed as the poop emoji in his contacts." She snickers as I take her hand and slowly shake.

Sister. This is Luke's sister.

"H-hi. I'm Daisy."

He's mentioned her before, but now that I'm meeting her in person, I feel like there's so much more I should have asked.

As if she can read my mind, she interjects. "Oh, we're not related by blood—Thank God—because I love showing emotions far too much to respond in monosyllables like this one seems to prefer, and I fear that might be genetic."

"You know Mom doesn't like it when we say adoptive. Makes her weepy. Plus your parents always called me mijo," he grumbles down at her.

She smiles tenderly at that and lifts her fist up sideways. Luke taps it twice with his in a move that tells me they've done this thousands of times.

"Now that you've bulldozed your way into my home, would you please tell me why you're here instead of back in the city finishing up your move?"

She waves his comment away. "Moving boxes make for great coffee tables while I wait for my stuff to arrive. And besides, I was over in Burlington shooting a wedding and I needed to check in on you after I heard the news that she—Daisy—didn't get married." She loudly whispers the last part.

"Thanks for the breaking news," he deadpans.

She rolls her eyes, and I think I fall in love with her a little bit right then. "I'm a smart cookie. I put two and two together after Daisy was nowhere to be found in the tabloids and you were up here avoiding my calls like the plague. And I was fine with calling to needle you and see if you'd finally told her that you've been in lo—"

"Val." He stops her from continuing.

She pulls her phone out of her purse and unlocks the screen. "Anyway, I would have waited for the chisme when you got back like a good sister. But when I saw this, I knew I had to get up here and show you before you headed back into the city and went full King Kong or something."

"What is it?" he asks, extending his hand for her phone.

She pushes it toward me instead with a grimace on her face.

"It's Damien Fischer. He sent out his official statement. It's a save the date. To your rescheduled wedding. Two weeks from now."

Chapter Thirty-One

LUKE

Valentina takes the phone out of my hand before I have a chance to break it in two.

I snatched it from her because I needed to see the news for myself.

She's not marrying him, my mind chants.

Fuck, not this shit again.

I look over at Daisy, expecting her to be on the verge of tears. Instead, she looks like she could go on a rampage right alongside me.

"How. Fucking. Dare. He?" she seethes as she stomps over and flips on the cell booster, bringing her phone to life.

Unsurprisingly, Nick is the first call that comes through. "What the fuck?" she answers, taking her brother and me by surprise.

She places the phone on the kitchen island and puts it on speakerphone.

"D-Daisy? Are you okay? I'm assuming you've seen what Damien's posted? That fucking twat," Nick fumes.

"Yes. What the hell is he thinking? Even if I hadn't dumped him on our wedding day, a message that should have been crystal fucking clear, he told me all the horrible things he was doing behind my back, using me for votes, cheating, conspiring with my father. Like am I missing something here?"

My sister almost growls next to me as she hears this unfold. Guess some things do run in the family, genetics be damned. "Fucking scum," she mutters under her breath. Blood or not, we are alike when it comes to protecting the ones we love. And while I can't say this is how I expected the last day at the cabin to go down, I am happy to see her.

"No, Daisy. The only thing that is missing is a strongly worded cease and desist letter from my attorney. And if you want to stay out of this, I can have a statement out in five minutes as well. I'll use much more colorful language this time around too. I've got my team on standby ready to bury him with the accusations of infidelity alone. Family values, my arse," Nick spits.

I move closer to Daisy, needing to feel her pulse under my hand.

She's deep in thought, not responding to Nick or to me, but when my hand slips behind her neck, she leans into me and closes her eyes.

I kiss her forehead. "Everything's going to be okay, Daze. You're in control. What do you want to do?"

She opens her eyes and straightens, holding on to that anger that seems to be fueling her as she speaks. "The days of me staying out of it are over. It's time I step up and speak for myself, Nick. If Damien wants to embarrass himself further by planning a wedding without a bride, that's on him."

Nick is silent for a moment. "Wow, Daisy. I'm—" He sighs. "I'm so damn proud of you, sis. Trust me, I want to shield you from this shitstorm more than you'll ever know. Hell, I'd take delight in destroying your ex while I was at it. But I love that you feel empowered enough to do it yourself. But please don't go straight from Ms. Nice Girl to first-degree murderer. Even my reach might be limited when it comes to keeping you out of the slammer if you kill this guy in broad daylight." He chuckles, trying to bring levity to the situation, but my sweet little Daisy is too busy being a hellion to simmer down.

With the same commanding tone that her brother would usually use as the owner of the New York Monarchs, she starts. "We're coming back to the city for tonight's game. Because we all have a job to do, and dealing with Damien's publicity stunt is not a part of my job, at least not anymore. If he wants to make a fool of himself, he's free to do so. And when I have a clearer head on the matter, I will be releasing a statement of my own."

"Remind me to never piss you off," Nick mumbles to himself as he types away on a computer. "When do you think you'll have a statement ready by?"

She gives an incredulous look, as if he could see her. "After I talk to my girls. Duh."

I smirk at the thought of Daisy and her friends gathering and scheming ruthless ways to handle Damien. Almost makes me feel bad for the guy.

But not quite.

She hangs up, promising to swing by her brother's office once she gets to the stadium.

We both look at my sister as she tries to sneakily slip out the front door. "Sorry, I think I've caused enough havoc for today. I'll leave you guys to it. Daisy, it was nice to meet you. Sorry I was the bearer of bad news."

Daisy walks straight toward Valentina and doesn't stop until she's pulling her in for a hug. "Nonsense. This is my mess and it's about time I clean it up for once and for all. But I'm so glad I got to meet another incredible person in Luke's corner. Why haven't I seen you at a game? I know a couple of girls I'd think you'd get along with."

My sister pales at the mention of visiting the baseball stadium. The same way she does every time I've invited her out to a game or charity event.

I know she has a history. Our parents were best friends before we were born. Her dad was a famous Dominican baseball player turned team manager. He was still employed by the MLB when he and his wife passed away in a boating accident in the Dominican Republic while on vacation. Valentina was only fourteen. We've always been neighbors and had grown up together like family. When her parents died, her custody was left to my parents in their will. My parents later decided to formally adopt her, even though it wasn't legally necessary since by the time the paperwork was done, she was close to turning eighteen.

She split her time between our home and her extended family's in the Dominican Republic. She even spent the last two years of high school there, after she begged my mother to let her spend more time with her biological family. My parents agreed, but I knew something was off when she made the mid-semester decision.

I knew that she was seeing someone but never found out who. I'm five years older, so I never really knew many kids her age. I assumed a bad breakup had sent her running, but I could be off since that would be a bit extreme, even by teenage standards.

She never had a problem coming to any of my games when I got drafted into the league, but for some reason she flat-out refuses to come to Monarchs Stadium.

I'm no expert in trauma or grief by any standard, but given my own past, I know well enough to leave her be. She knows she can talk to me if she wants to, just how I know I can talk to her.

So much so that I spilled my guts about my feelings for Daisy just days before her wedding, after indulging in a few too many pity beers. It caused Val to ramp up her calls to check in on me.

Which is why I wasn't totally surprised to find out she was heading my way this morning. I just figured I'd beat her to the cabin so I could warn Daisy properly before my sister made her grand arrival.

I take in Val's tight smile and decide to throw her a bone. "I'm sure Valentina would love to meet you and the ladies at that bar your brother bought for Luisa. What's it called again?"

Daisy smirks, probably at the reminder of how insane and possessive her brother is of his wife. Shit, I think I might be like that too. "No Boys Allowed. Luisa thought it was fitting since the night he bought it for her, he had all the men kicked out."

Color returns to my sister's cheeks as she laughs with Daisy. "Okay, that is definitely a man obsessed and a story I will need to hear over drinks." Val sends me a thankful look.

"Sit down. Have some coffee and a cookie while I load up my truck and close up shop around the house. You're not driving back by yourself. I'll follow behind you to make sure you get back to the city safely."

Both Val and Daisy roll their eyes while smiling at one another. "Is he this overbearing with you too? I assumed he just had a thing for kidnapping runaway brides," Daisy whisper-shouts.

"Oh yeah. One time, he ran off one of my college boyfriends because the model of his car was recently recalled by the manufacturer and the poor kid had no clue. Luke chewed him out for trying to pick me up on our date in that "death trap," and the next day, I got a very politely worded breakup email. Honestly, I didn't blame the guy."

Fucking hell. They're going to gang up on me all the time now, aren't they?

"Yes, we are," they say at the same time.

"Fuck, did I say that—you know what? Never mind. Eat a cookie or don't. We're hitting the road in ten. Let's hope by then you two haven't conspired to run me up a wall."

Daisy tilts her head. "I'm thinking we can make it eight minutes if we really put our minds to it."

Valentina taps her chin, deep in thought. "Nah, I'm sure we can shave off some of that time if I start telling you about Luke's imaginary friend, Noah. Or maybe we can go full blast and dive into that time Mom told him he had to start doing his own laundry if he was going to put crusty socks in the hamper all the time."

Unsurprisingly. It only took them six minutes.

Chapter Thirty-Two

DAISY

I walk into Monarchs Stadium with all eyes on me.

We planned on this happening. It's why Luke is walking a few paces behind me like a bodyguard instead of a boyfriend.

We went back and forth about it on the car ride over. I wanted to hold hands, no longer concerned about Damien or whatever trash the media might feel inclined to write about me. But after running over a few scenarios with Luke, Nick, and Luisa on speakerphone, we thought it would be best for the Monarchs organization to try to minimize the public scrutiny. This will already be a media circus after all, since it'll be my first public outing since the wedding that never was.

These players work themselves to the bone for this team, and I already feel bad enough that my story is overshadowing the beginning of their winning streak. So I agreed to show up, using my usual entrance instead of the private one Nick had put in, and show the world that I'm back to work and it's business as usual.

Though my look is very different from the last time I was seen. I'm usually strutting into the office with a tweed suit of some kind and designer pumps, with my hair straightened in a slicked back ponytail.

But today? I'm taking full advantage of my brother and sister-in-law being the owners, knowing they won't have an issue with my lax attire. I'm wearing a flowy black long sleeve tunic that hits right below my ass, which is perfect because the leggings I'm wearing underneath do absolutely nothing to hide my tempting ass—Luke's words, not mine. I'm wearing my white Converses too, and my tussled curly hair is styled half up and half down.

The security guard did a double take when I asked to be let through because I didn't have my work badge with me. His answering smile hinted that he approved of my new look, and Luke's not-so-subtle growl behind my back let him know to keep those feelings to himself.

We round the corner to the executive offices, and with each step, I can feel Luke inching closer to me.

I know he was on board with keeping our relationship out of the spotlight for the time being, but up on this floor, only trusted personnel are allowed, and I wouldn't be surprised if he snuck us into his office to burn off some of the frustration that's been nipping at us since we left the cabin.

I'm about to suggest just that when an unexpected welcoming crew comes into view. I start laughing to myself, because I should have anticipated this.

Luisa and Isabella come barreling into me, giving Luke a split second to get out of the way before he finds himself engulfed in a very teary group hug.

"It's been eighty-four years," Isa starts, and I swat her and Luisa off me with a giggle.

Luisa takes one long perusal of me from head to toe. Then nods my way as she speaks to Isa. "Now that. *That* is a woman who's been dicked down."

Luke sounds like he's choking, while Nick shouts a pained "Angel!"

I'm about to throw in a very mature "Ha, take that. Now you know how it feels to hear about your siblings' sexual escapades." But the words die on my tongue as I realize that Mateo Martinez, Ace Middlebrooks, and Julian Vega are standing next to my brother as well.

If Mateo's grin gets any bigger, it's going to turn creepy. Whereas Ace and Julian are sporting identical looks of shock.

I should probably cruise my ass over to the HR department, because it doesn't seem like any professionalism will be found around these parts.

"Coach?" Ace points at Luke. "And our sweet little Daisy?" he asks in a dramatic whisper.

Julian simply shakes his head, feigning disapproval. He's the newest member of the team, having been acquired by Luisa in an impressive three hundred-million-dollar deal as our new first baseman. But he's seamlessly settled into the Monarch family and into the role of Ace's best friend. "You think you know people, and then they run off and forget that they have a team to coach."

Ace places a hand on Julian's shoulder. "Did you know that Vega over here couldn't remember whether he had to hit the ball with a racket or a bat? Poor thing was lost without you. Lost."

"So lost." Julian nods.

I cover my mouth with my hand to keep my laughter from breaking free. Luke steps closer to me, nudging my chin with his lifted knuckles. "You think these clowns are funny or something?" I see the tension melting from his shoulders and could kiss those two fools for distracting Luke from my current media debacle.

But I'm sure that wouldn't go over too well with Luke's current caveman antics, so I think I'll telepathically send my gratitude.

When I don't answer, Luke slips his large hand over my cheek and leans down, faintly brushing his lips over mine.

The women start to squeal while Nick attempts to break up our moment.

"Coach Weston. My office. Now. We clearly have a conversation that needs to be had... and some HR paperwork to sign," Nick grumbles the last part.

Luke nods, brushing the tip of his nose against mine. "Hmm, that sounds urgent." He turns, giving our little audience a blinding smile before he continues. "But I need to take care of something important first." His lips are on mine in a bruising show of longing and possession all at once.

"Ugh, fine. I'll be waiting in my office." Nick stomps off.

"All right, boys, keep your mouths shut and get your asses on the field before Coach has us crying in the weight room." Mateo says, ushering the men off.

"We'll wait for you in Luisa's office. Take your time. No rush at all," Isabella all but sings as the last footsteps fade.

And then it's just us again.

Me in Luke's arms, his lips doing wonders in helping me forget everything I need to deal with today. And as the kiss deepens, I have to force myself to escape this man's clutches. Otherwise I'll be putting on a whole other show in front of our coworkers.

Luke protests. "Why did we come back here again? I think if we leave now, we can make it back to our cabin before midnight."

I try not to lose myself in his use of "our cabin." Although it certainly feels like ours after the week we had.

Sitting out back sipping beers by the firepit. Watching endless movies on the couch. Cooking meals while dancing in the kitchen. Making love surrounded by daisies under the big oak tree.

But we have a game tonight, and I need a debrief with my girls and set my past in its place before I can focus on my future with Luke. So I take a step back.

Luke watches me with the intensity of a hunter.

I point at his chest. "You have a job to do."

He nods. "Hands, mouth, or cock? Your office or mine?" My body flushes with heat, but my eyes narrow in his direction as I take another step back.

"Oh, no you don't. You get your ass on that field, *Coach*. We need to make it through tonight's game in one piece. And then..." I trail off.

"And then I'm coming over to my girlfriend's place and testing out that new mattress." I quirk a brow at his boldness, but he simply shrugs. "Let me taste you now, and I might consider letting you actually get a full night's rest tonight."

I continue to back up in the direction of my office as I shake my head. "No deal. Besides, I'm well acquainted with your midnight wakeup calls, and in case you haven't been paying attention, I'm a big fan of them."

"Oh, I pay attention plenty, Daze." He takes one step my way, but I lift my hand, halting his movements.

"Field, now. Play later."

"I want you in my office as soon as the game is over, Daisy. Don't make me have to chase you around this stadium." A slow smirk unfurls across his face. "Although now that I think about it..."

"Not at work." I fight to keep the sternness in my voice as I near the corner hallway that will lead to my office. "Have a good game. Love you." I smile and he instantly softens at my words.

"Dammit, woman. I love you too." A smile overtakes his face in a way that's becoming more common for Luke, and the thought alone almost has me running back into his arms. But then we'd have to start this whole song and dance again, and I really need to debrief with my friends.

But first I need to make a pit stop at my office to drop off my things and quickly check my email for pressing matters I may have forgotten.

Finally, I wave and turn, and a few moments later, I hear his boots walking farther away from me. I smile like a goof, imagining him standing there, waiting to see if I'd change my mind and run off into his office with him down by the clubhouse.

But that smile and any sense of levity drop like stones in the ocean the second I push open my office door.

Because there, sitting in my chair with a smug expression on his face, is my dear old dad.

"Ah, there she is. The prodigal daughter returns after all."

Chapter Thirty-Three

LUKE

This is ridiculous, but I'll play along.

Nick sits behind his executive desk with his elbows on his armrests and his fingers steepled, playing the world's most boring version of a staring contest.

Which is comical, because before this week, I could do this all day.

But knowing that Daisy is somewhere on this floor has me itching to get out of my seat and pull her into my arms one more time before I actually have to haul ass to the dugout.

Nick starts. "Okay, so this is how it's going to go—"

"I love her."

"You're going to—wait. What did you just say?"

"I love Daisy. And by some miracle, she loves me too. So I'll keep this real simple for you. If us working together is a problem for the Monarchs organization, then I quit, effective immediately. I won't take the Monarchs away from Daisy like her ex tried to. I love her too damn much to make her choose between the two. So if you're here to tell me you have some antiquated view of who your sister should or shouldn't date and are using your position as my boss to throw that weight around, then you can save it. Because Daisy's love and opinion are the only things that matter to me."

Nick stares at me harshly for a few moments before he breaks. "For fuck's sake. I get one chance to perform my brotherly duty to scare her new man shitless and what does he do? He falls on the proverbial sword for her." He scoffs, waving his hand my way. "Listen, man, I was well aware of your feelings for my sister long before you saved her from that wedding from hell. Which, by the way, I've yet to properly thank you for. I have a nice bottle of whiskey at my house with your name on it." He shifts forward, leaning on his desk. "And keep all that talk of resigning to yourself. I swear my wife has bat-like hearing, and if you're not careful, she'll barrel into my office offering you a raise to keep you," he grunts.

My lip twitches. "Well, I do have a woman who's awoken this newfound desire to spoil her rotten, so maybe a renegotiation wouldn't be a bad idea."

He looks at me, unimpressed. "Yeah, yeah. But if Luisa asks, I threatened you within an inch of your life and reminded you that if you ever were to hurt Daisy," he leans in even closer, "I know a guy." He lifts a brow, trying to drive his point home.

I lift from my chair and hold out my hand for him to shake. Even though this conversation was unnecessary, I actually have grown quite fond of Nick and his antics. And I know how much Daisy loves her brother, so that means I'll play nice.

"Thanks for the chat, but I've got a game to prepare for."

He shakes my hand. "Thanks again. My sister looked so different when she walked in. I barely even recognized her." He pauses. "Happy looks good on her."

I release him and make my way to the door, fully intending to leave, but not before I make one thing crystal clear.

I speak, my eyes never leaving his. "And for the record, Nick. You no longer need to 'know a guy.' Because if someone hurts Daisy, I'm the only guy you need to call."

Chapter Thirty-Four

DAISY

"What are you doing here?"

My father tsks. "Now, is that any way to greet your father? I see this rebellious streak still hasn't worked its way out of your system like I had hoped." He lifts from my chair and starts to round my desk.

I instinctively take a step back.

He tracks the motion and sighs, as if it deeply inconveniences him. "Daisy, come on now. What has gotten into you? First, you're nowhere to be found on your wedding day, leaving a smear of lipstick on a mirror as a sick form of joke. Then you block me from your phone, something my assistant had to explain to me after I couldn't get through to you. Do you know how embarrassing it is to have a member of your staff explain to you that your one and only daughter has decided to block her father after causing quite the scandal?"

I stiffen at his words.

Then I feel it. The old Daisy, discreetly trying to slip back into place. The version of myself that hates disappointing others and feels guilt for being an inconvenience.

But that's the thing about people pleasing. You become so accustomed to putting other people's needs before your own that standing up for yourself starts to feel like a radical form of resistance. Because in a way, it is.

I clear my throat, battling with the urge to start my sentence with an apology.

Because I'm not sorry. And if I were to apologize to anyone at this point, it would be the hundreds of guests who traveled from near and far for a wedding that never was.

And even then, I'm sure they flew in on private jets and were gifted free societal gossip to last them well into the holidays.

So instead, I steel my spine with the little strength I have left over from my week at the cabin and ask what I really need to know.

"Were you in on it?"

My father seems momentarily confused, but I'm not sure if it's because of my question or because I'm not cowering in a corner, begging for his forgiveness.

"I beg your pardon?"

"Damien told me everything. Or at least enough for me to know that our relationship was one big PR stunt. And from what I gather, you were in charge of making sure I always played my part. Is that true?"

My father grits his teeth as his jaw ticks to the side. That's more emotion than I've seen from him in years. He always seems so unflappable around me. "I have no idea what you're talking about. Are you sure you are well? You seem different. Maybe I should take you to see a doctor and get your head checked while we're there." He lifts his arm, aiming for the door, but I push it down, truly shocking him.

"I know about the other women. How he intended to use me for votes. And I know that you told him you would 'handle' me. Apparently after I was a no-show at the wedding, you got a demotion or something, because now he seems to be sending our stupid save the dates as some form of public statement. Care to comment on any of that?"

"Daisy," he starts with a patronizing tone. "You have much to learn about men in power and their pride. I don't know about all this nonsense you speak of, but if Damien said all this to you, surely it was coming from a place of hurt. The man was left at the altar and humiliated in front of his peers, during a campaign year no less, so you must be able to empathize that a hurt man will say awful things when he's down."

"I must empathize?" I repeat. "Either you're lying to cover for that man—for God knows what reason, since your loyalty should lie with me, your daughter—or you really are clueless about the snake I was engaged to and have still decided to turn a blind eye when confronted with the truth. So which one is it?"

My father takes a step back, looking me up and down as if he's seeing me for the very first time.

His face barely conceals his sneer as he asks, "Why are you dressed like that? I know you haven't been to your apartment since you up and vanished, but this is different. And your hair. You couldn't find a hairbrush in whatever hidey hole you ran off to?"

I suck in a shocked breath. I'm used to my father's microaggressions. To the point where I convince myself that some of them are potential terms of endearment. But having my white father criticize the hair I inherited from my Afro-Latina mother feels like a stab to the heart.

"Get out." I barely manage to whisper the words, not willing to let him see how deeply he cut me.

He looks bored, and by his tone, I'm doing a shit job of keeping my emotions under wraps. "Oh, come on now. I ask why you haven't gone to the hair salon, and I get kicked out?" He pinches the bridge of his nose.

Because of course my natural hair texture should be cause for an emergency appointment.

The same hair I constantly straightened because I knew he preferred it that way.

And unfortunately, somewhere along the way I must have taught myself that curly hair meant I hadn't tried hard enough to look presentable. Or that I couldn't go anywhere as I was.

That what I looked like naturally wasn't good enough.

But I've never felt prettier or more like myself than I have these last few days while running around up in the mountains with my hair flying wild and free.

And I think it has a lot to do with me learning to love myself a little better and caring a lot less about what my father thinks of me.

"I've been far too lenient with you. I knew that brother of yours would poison you against me, but now you're messing with Damien and his campaign, and this act of defiance needs to be dropped. Immediately."

To my horror, a tear slips free and slowly trails down my cheek.

My father freezes, shoulders tensing as his eyes zero in on the lone tear. He takes a step forward, instantly sending me one step back.

Raising his hands, he speaks to me in a tone you would reserve for a wounded animal you've stumbled upon in the woods. "Daisy, dear, I apologize for upsetting you. I think it's safe to say we're all a bit out of sorts, hmm? Please forgive me. Join me for dinner this week, and we can talk about everything he told you. I really want to get to the bottom of this massive miscommunication. And you're right. If Damien did say and mean all of those deplorable things, then it is without question that my loyalty and love lie with you, my sweet daughter." He places a cold hand on my cheek.

I don't move away from his touch immediately, even though it feels like I should.

Instead, a loud knock on my door has me stepping away. "Are you guys banging in there? Our men will be pissed if we see Coach Weston's di—" The door swings open to reveal a giggling Isabella with Luisa hot on her heels.

A flash of shock passes over my father's face as they step into my office.

Their mischievous smiles drop at the sight of him, then at whatever expression must be marring my face. "Daisy, are you okay?" Isa asks as she pulls me to her side, away from my father.

"How the fuck did you get access to this area, George?" Luisa sneers, since she has her own history with my father.

"Ah, if it isn't my lovely daughter-in-law. Crushed that I wasn't invited to your second wedding, by the way. Guess I can always hold out for the third one."

I don't know why my father insists on taunting Nick and Luisa.

I've always wondered why he couldn't put whatever feelings he has aside for the greater good of the family. It's what I've always done so I could continue having relationships with both men.

But I guess since I've always been the one sacrificing on the sidelines, he and his ego have gone unchecked for far too long.

But that ends now.

"Father, I think it best you leave now," I say calmly as he and Luisa stare each other down.

His head turns my way, and he nods. "I was thinking the same thing. But do me a favor before I leave and unblock me so I can at the very least take my daughter out to dinner and resolve this mess. One dinner, that's all I ask. After that, I promise you everything will be in its rightful place and we can finally move on from this disaster."

"You'll be communicating through our attorneys if you dare to set foot in this stadium again. After the last time you were here, my husband made it abundantly clear that you are not welcome."

My father keeps his pleading eyes on me, ignoring Luisa. "One dinner. At the very least give me the opportunity to clear up any misunderstandings. I've only heard Damien's side of things. I'm sorry for lashing out during a time of pure and utter confusion. Allow me to make amends."

I feel the girls' eyes on me widen as I offer a weak smile. "One dinner."

He nods as he runs a hand down his tie. "This week. I'll set it up." He squeezes my shoulder before sidestepping the ladies and walking out of my office.

I feel at war with my emotions as I lean against the closed door and slide down until my ass hits the floor.

Luisa and Isa each take a seat next to me, letting me settle in the silence before having to answer any of their questions.

I feel so vulnerable after that interaction. I'm usually the one trying to cheer others up while covertly hiding the skeletons in my own closet. And having my biggest one waltz out of here as if he were a business associate instead of a doting dad hurts.

"We don't have to talk about it. If you want to order all the sweets from the cafeteria, I can have them up here in the next five minutes," Luisa offers.

"Or we can talk about you and Luke," Isa tries instead.

"Isa," Luisa warns.

"What? We don't have to talk about the sex she's having with Coach Weston. Although I'm sure it was hot as hell, given how you look like you've had your back broken and put back together again."

I slap a hand over my forehead as an incredulous laugh escapes from deep in my chest.

"Maybe Daisy can tell us about life in the mountains. You know, about the landscapes and whatnot. That's what I was getting at," Isabella says innocently.

"Uh-huh. Sure you were." Luisa smirks.

I lean my head against the door, a small smile playing on my lips. "Want to hear about the time I found Luke in the backyard chopping wood while shirtless?"

By their ear-piercing screeches, I think that sounds like a resounding yes to me.

Chapter Thirty-Five

LUKE

I'm engulfed in a sweaty pile of bodies.

And I've got to admit, I kind of missed this.

The post-game high that comes after your guys completely obliterate the visiting team. This win was extra sweet for Mateo, since it was against the team we lost our World Series ticket to last season. Proving once and for all that we are the better team and would have gone all the way had he not decided to punch Isabella's ex in the middle of the game and get his ass ejected.

But we're past that now. Mostly.

And now the men, who sometimes act like overgrown children, cheer as they celebrate their seventeen-game winning streak.

"Looking good for a man who didn't know whether to use a bat or a racket, Vega," I yell out to him.

He places a hand over his sweaty bare chest. "Aw, you hear that Middlebrooks? He noticed me."

Ace Middlebrooks spreads his arms wide, his impressive tattoo collection on display. "Hey, what about me? That fucker may have sent the ball flying out of the stadium once or twice, but I prevented every player who dared run past third base from getting to home plate."

Children, I tell you.

"Yeah, yeah. Stop by my office if you want gold stars for doing your damn jobs." They laugh as I shake my head. "Now hit the showers. We're flying to Miami early in the morning and I don't want any of you out too late." I almost grunt the last part.

The idea of getting on a plane and putting distance between Daisy and myself almost makes me physically ill.

I've become so accustomed to having her within arm's reach that I hadn't really put thought into the fact that my job has me traveling more often than not for the better part of a year.

I look over at Mateo and wonder how the hell he does it, knowing how obsessed he is with his fiancée.

Maybe if I rush, I can get Daisy home in time for a late dinner before I eat her for dessert.

As if summoned to ruin the fun of my dirty thoughts, Nick comes through the clubhouse, hands in his pockets, his usually playful expression gone, offering nothing but stern nods to the players calling out to say hello.

Last time he was in here was to douse his now wife in buckets of sangria, but now he seems like a man on a mission, and I hope that this next pep talk doesn't take time away from the woman I haven't laid eyes on for the past three hours.

"Coach." He nods, moving us over to a quiet corner away from the guys in various stages of undress. "Since apparently you're the guy I'm supposed to call…"

I pause before leaping into action. "Where is she? Is she hurt? What happened?" I don't realize I've grabbed Nick by the forearm and basically dragged him toward the elevators that'll lead us to the executive offices until we're halfway down the hall.

He pushes me off discreetly while continuing to lead me to where I assume Daisy is. "She's fine. Fucking hell, you've got quite the grip strength. Were you a pitcher or catcher before coaching? I forget."

"Nick. What happened?" I punch the elevator button with more force than necessary.

"I said she's fine, Luke. Take a breather." He ushers me into the empty elevator, waiting for the doors to close before speaking. "My father was waiting for her in her office."

"How the hell—"

He lifts his hand. "I've already spoken to my head of security and settled it. He's been officially banned and is not allowed to set foot onto Monarchs property. But it seems with all the media frenzy surrounding Daisy, he was able to sweet talk his way inside, saying he was told to enter through the private entrance to meet her. It was an honest mistake, but one that I've made sure will never happen. Not on my watch."

"Or mine." I grab the elevator railing, guilt tearing me up inside. I should have walked her to her office instead of making filthy promises. We are no longer in our bubble up in the mountains, and I have to do a better job of protecting Daisy from not only the potential internet trolls, but the very real men in her life who will stop at nothing to tear her down.

"Twenty-five to life, Weston."

"What?"

"The mandatory sentencing for premeditated murder. Keep that in mind if you truly see a future with my sister. Because the way you're about two seconds from ripping that railing clean off the wall tells me you need the reminder. No worries. I've learned to recite that fun fact in my mind every time my father pulls a stunt like this. It gets easier to remember with time."

"Oh yeah? Then what do you suggest if another man blasted to the entire world that he still plans on marrying your girlfriend in two weeks' time, even though she left his sorry ass at the altar? What fun fact do you have left for that scenario?"

"Luke. We'll handle it. Leave that to me. In the meantime, your job is to make sure my sister isn't subjected to conjugal visits at Sing Sing Correctional Facility. Think you can do that for me?"

The elevator doors open and I burst through them before I start making promises I can't keep. And I don't stop until I'm pushing open Daisy's office door, allowing myself a moment to fully take in the scene.

Three grown women sit on the floor, long serving spoons in hand with multiple to-go containers filled with cake and ice cream.

"Hi." Daisy waves at me with her spoon, and the tightness in my chest loosens.

I keep walking until I'm stepping between containers and swooping down low to scoop her into my arms. I bring her to the small couch in her office and sit, placing her sideways on my lap so I can get a good look at her. My hands trace up and down her arms, searching for any physical signs of harm her father may have done to her, even though I'm well aware his preferred method of pain is emotional warfare.

"Nick told you, didn't he?" She sounds exhausted. It's the only reason I'm not saying that she should have been the one to tell me, regardless of whether I was on the field. Because when it comes to her, everything else is secondary.

"Are you okay? What did he say? Nick banned him from the stadium, and he doesn't know where you live now. And I know for a fact that your building is heavily secured, so you'll be safe there."

She groans as she leans into my chest, words muffled as she speaks. "Guys, he's not a hitman. Just your run-of-the-mill shitty father. I'm sure I'll survive."

I run a hand over her back in soothing circles, relishing the feel of her dropping more of her weight onto me. "You still haven't answered my question, Daisy girl."

"Daisy girl, swoon." Luisa elbows Isa.

I force my attention to stay on my Daisy, who is now sporting a dopey smile of her own. "Better now. How about we head out and check out my new place? I'm dying to see it and would love nothing more than to test out that massive bathtub that overlooks the city."

"Sounds like a perfect plan to me." I lean down and kiss her. I mean to keep it sweet, but at the taste of her lips, my body acts on instinct. I didn't have to censor myself while we were at the cabin, and it seems as though it's going to take a minute to train my body to react appropriately while we're out with our friends.

At the moment I realize we need to reel it in, Daisy wiggles her ass over my hard-on. Fuck, this is going to be awkward. There's no hiding the effect this woman has on me.

"Let's go before I have to bleach my eyeballs. Wife, come feel my forehead. I think I'm coming down with something." Nick fake coughs.

Luisa rolls her eyes as she helps Isa up. "I'm not falling for your fake illnesses anymore, big guy. You want some TLC, you're going to have to beg for it."

"*Okay*, I'm off to find my man because these damn Stonehaven siblings have an engaged woman feeling lonely as hell." Isa complains

"Who's lonely?" Mateo says, rounding out our group.

"Oh, thank God." Isa launches herself into his arms, and he catches her without missing a beat.

They all leave quickly, giving me my first moment alone with Daisy in what feels like an eternity.

"Hi, you." Her nose nudges mine.

"Hi, love." I nudge back.

She hums, her eyes closing as she smiles. "Ready to test out that bathtub?"

"Already had your shampoos and lotions couriered over to your place. Let's get out of here."

Chapter Thirty-Six

DAISY

SLEEPING IN A BED without Luke is highly overrated.

He's been gone for a day and I'm already dreading the fact that I'll have to sleep alone for another night before he flies back from Miami with the team.

After we came home two nights ago, he made it his personal mission to christen every surface of my new apartment before ending the night cleaning up and getting dirty all over again in the shower. The blush that overtook my face when I had to Windex the imprint of my ass cheeks off the living room window this morning could probably be seen from Mars.

But today is Sunday, and I have a full day planned with furniture shopping for my new place. After I was able to peel myself off Luke, we took a tour of my new home. Inspiration hit immediately, and I told him my dream vision.

He laughed when I said I needed a massive couch meant for movie nights with my six-four boyfriend, and scowled playfully when I mentioned wanting a dining table large enough to seat a handful of Monarchs players and their significant others. He also chuckled when I described every single kitchen gadget I'd need before inviting Luisa's family over.

His smile turned serene when I decided I wanted to cover the large wall by my front door in corkboard material so I can pin up Polaroids of the friends and family who come through my door. A permanent reminder that this space is mine and it's filled with an abundance of love.

I know I won't be able to get through most of my to-do list today, but I'm so excited to have something to focus on that doesn't involve the men who are hell-bent on causing me constant headaches.

I should be on cloud nine after landing my dream apartment, a place I can finally call my own, but I can't help but feel like I'm playing the waiting game. Anticipating the moment the other shoe drops.

The girls and I came up with a statement that I can put out today, but it doesn't feel right. To put these practiced words about my disaster of a personal life out there. Unlike my brother, I did not seek out a powerful position that would inevitably put me in the spotlight. I've always known that I'd be mentioned in the bylines due to my role as his sister and as a Stonehaven. But then I had to go and date a New York politician and really screw up any chance of keeping myself out of the line of fire.

My doorbell rings, snapping me out of my thoughts. My heart races at who it could be. I only have one neighbor on my floor, and I haven't heard a peep from them since I got here. And besides Luke, I haven't given out my address. Not even to the girls since we were knee-deep in cake and public statement jargon.

For a moment, I panic, thinking it might be Damien on the other side of that door. I'm not ready to face him, much less while being alone in my apartment, and especially not when Luke's at an away game.

I know Luke's trauma and potential triggers, and while it'll be a cold day in hell before I agree to meet up with my ex in person, I would still want Luke to be aware if there's a chance of our paths crossing at a charity event or party. I never want him to feel like I'm sneaking around behind his back. I know firsthand how easy it is to fall prey to our biggest fears, and I want to do everything in my power not to contribute to any potential fears he may have.

The doorbell rings once more, and I tiptoe to the door, silently raising to the peephole, and spot a delivery man holding up a large envelope. Maybe it's papers from my realtor?

I open the door, sign for the package, and lean against the kitchen counter as I rip it open. The second I do, my phone starts to ring. Seeing Luke's smiling face stare up at me has me dropping the package and scrambling to answer.

"Hi," I say breathily as his piercing blue eyes come into view.

"God, I miss you. Tell me again why I'm not allowed to quit?" He sits on his hotel bed, and my eyes drift down his bare and tatted chest.

I shake my head. "You know, I never figured you were one for the theatrics, Coach."

"Fine. Then you're traveling with me to every away game. It's settled."

"I don't like to fly often if I can avoid it."

"Why?"

"I hate turbulence."

"I'll punch the air for you."

I erupt into a fit of giggles, and his lip twitches, most likely from trying to keep his frown in place.

"I got an alert that you got my package."

Oh. "That was from you?" I bend over to pick up the envelope and pull out the contents inside.

"It's not as pretty as the one you grabbed up north, but I thought…" He shrugs, not finishing his thought.

I look down at the handful of postcards from Miami and smile brightly at the man who sent them. "You know." My voice takes a teasing tone. "This isn't how postcards are supposed to work. You need to write a message on the back and then send them in the mail without a fancy overnighted envelope." I raise a pointed brow.

He huffs. "Well, if you'd turn them around, you'd see that I did write on them. But I sure as hell wasn't letting anyone read the words that are meant for your eyes only. And I wanted you to get them while I'm still here, not when I'm already back and you're too busy to read them because my hands are all over your body."

A shiver runs down my spine, and he smirks at the knowledge of what his words do to me.

I quickly scan the back of the postcards, and sure enough, he did write a short but sweet message on each one. "When did you have the time to do this?"

The man has a jam-packed schedule, and I can't imagine him strolling down Miami Beach to collect these.

"I grabbed them at the airport when we landed and asked Middlebrooks to ship them for me when he went out to lunch with his mother yesterday."

I smile as I think of Ace, our resident playboy, having lunch at Versailles, the Cuban restaurant he always takes his mother to when he's in town. I love knowing that he's secretly a mama's boy and only speaks Spanish while he's in Miami because his mother doesn't speak much English. I wish he'd show more of that side of himself to the world, but he seems fine letting everyone think he's just another pretty face.

I reach the last postcard, and a loud laugh escapes my lips as I flip it over to read the message.

"I really didn't think I wrote anything that funny on any of those," Luke grumbles.

"Ace shipped these out for you?"

"Yeah, why?" Suspicion laces his tone.

"So I'm guessing this one didn't come from you?" I lift the card in question.

"I'm going to kill him."

I continue to laugh as I hold up the postcard with a near naked man covering his privates with his hands, the message across the top saying "Welcome to Miami. Donde todo es muy caliente." And the chicken scratch note on the back reads "In case you miss Coach too much. Hopefully this will hold you over!"

Luke's phone shakes as he types.

"What are you doing?" I wipe the tears that have formed around my lash line.

"Sending his ass to the weight room. I want him there from now until our game tonight. If he's able to lift his arm to throw the ball, then he hasn't pushed himself hard enough."

"Doesn't that defeat the purpose? If your player can no longer *play*?"

"Depends what you think my purpose is."

"Luke."

"Just a second, Daze."

"Be nice." I pause. "Please?"

He stops typing and looks back up at me and sighs. "You know I can't say no to you." He taps the screen a few more times. "I'll reel it in. Two hours with our trainers after the game."

I smile. "How lenient of you."

"I'm going soft."

I tap my chin. "Really? Because that's not how I remember it."

A wicked smile graces his lips and has my nipples tightening in response. But neither of us has time for this right now. "Oh no you don't. You've got a stadium to get to, and I've got so much to buy for this place, it's not even funny."

His smile is replaced with determination. "Give me a list to work from so I can take some things off your plate."

I shake my head. "I told you, I want to hand pick everything. Or at least all the important stuff."

He nods, deep in thought. "What about electronics? TVs, a sound system? Can I help you out with that?"

I brighten at the suggestion. "I actually could use a little help in that department. I usually get whatever the salesperson is trying to sell me on." I chuckle. "And I know there is a built-in sound system somewhere in here but have no clue how to connect it to my phone."

"Consider it done."

"Okay, but I need to give you my credit card number before you order anything."

He gives me a bored look. "I think I can swing it, Daisy."

I return the look. "I'm not about to have you bankroll this for me. I'm a big girl, and I can afford it on my own."

His jaw ticks before he sighs. "All right. How about I get what you need, then show you the bill? Then you can pay me back. Less back and forth that way, don't you agree?"

My eyes narrow, but I can't disagree with that logic. And the way he's getting worked up about wanting to take care of these tasks for me is getting me all hot and bothered, so I'm not going to fake being put out. "Fine."

"Good." He smirks a little too mischievously for my liking, but we both need to get on with our day, and I know I have to be the one to initiate getting off the phone since he has no problem threatening to quit every time he realizes he needs to hang up.

"Okay, now put a shirt on. Some of us have work to do."

He runs a hand down his chest until it's out of frame, and my eyes almost pop out of my head. "Have a good day, Daisy girl. I love you."

"Uh-huh. Yeah. Love you too."

I hang up and blow out a deep breath.

Then force myself to get ready and walk out the door.

Before I do something crazy like book a last-minute flight to Miami.

Chapter Thirty-Seven

LUKE

I silently curse the nail gun in my hand for not being quieter.

But this is the last thing I need to get done before Daisy wakes up. Then I can move on to making her breakfast.

When I got in, I soundlessly snuck into her room, thinking I'd wake her with some much-needed morning sex.

But given the condition of the apartment and how she was sprawled out on the bed, it was obvious she needed her rest.

I don't know how she did it, but the place looks fully furnished.

Gotta love living in New York City, because where the hell else would she have gotten same-day delivery for the deep brown leather couches, coffee table, and dining room table? I smile at how similar these couches look to the ones at our cabin.

She had artwork leaning against walls I assumed she wanted them hung on. The kitchen island was stacked high with empty cardboard boxes for every pot and pan imaginable. A light rug now runs through the kitchen and I'm currently nailing a large piece of rolled up corkboard material to the spot she pointed at when we walked through the place half naked a couple of nights ago.

I hear her shriek from her doorway and turn. She's wide-eyed, hair in a cute twist of curls at the top of her head, and she's wearing my hoodie.

I manage to turn off the nail gun and place it safely on the ground before she's running my way and leaping into my arms.

I bury my face in the crook of her neck and exhale deeply for the first time since I left her.

"What are you doing here? I thought the team wasn't getting in until this afternoon!" She wiggles in my arms, placing her hands on my cheeks, pulling me into the sweetest kiss known to man.

"They are. I got on a two-a.m. flight and landed around five. Been busy and trying to keep quiet so you can rest." I nod at her living room, and it's then that she finally takes in my handywork.

Her brand-new TV is mounted on the wall, her artwork is hung up, and the corkboard wall by her front door is secured. I walk her to the kitchen island and set her there, staying between her open legs as I reach over and pick up the small bright yellow Polaroid camera.

"I don't know if this is the right brand or kind you had in mind, but I thought it might be what you needed to take pictures of your friends and pin them to the entry wall. It had the best reviews, and the yellow reminded me of you."

She takes another slow perusal of her place, her eyes welling with tears. When they land on the camera, I think I may have severely overstepped. She's made it very clear that she wants a hand in everything she does with her apartment, and maybe in my haste to surprise her I went a little overboard.

"Luke."

"I'm sorry. I can take it all down if I got it wrong, and we can—"

"You got on a plane in the middle of the night instead of flying with the team so you could see me. You managed to put up a TV and a million other things while I slept. And you—" She hiccups, two tears streaming down her face. "And you put up my crazy wall idea and bought me the cutest camera I've ever laid eyes on. You—you listened. You know me. You..."

"I love you, Daisy. And if you'd let me, I'd love you for the rest of my life and consider it an honor."

I don't even realize I'm holding her left hand and stroking her bare ring finger until I hear a soft gasp escape her sweet lips.

In this moment, I realize what it looks like. All I need is a ring and to drop down to one knee. But the last thing I want to do is rush Daisy when she's rebuilding her life brick by brick. All that matters is that she knows how I feel and that I plan on sticking around.

Her forehead rests against my own. "I love you so much, Luke. To the point where sometimes... I don't think I deserve you."

I squeeze her hand, lowering my head until her eyes meet mine. "Please tell me that's some kind of sick joke."

She shakes her head softly. "You've lived a drama-free life these past few years. And here I come with the world's biggest baggage while you come to the rescue every single time, even when I don't realize I need it."

"Correction, Daze. I was practically the walking dead for five years. And you stepped into my life and made it worth living again. So if you think for one second that any of the turmoil you're experiencing right now is a deterrent for me, then I've done a shit job of proving otherwise." She bites her lip and I nudge her chin up higher. "If you'd let me, I'd tell the entire world that you're mine. Let them write a million articles until their fingers bleed. I don't give a damn. Because all that matters to me is that you feel safe and loved."

"I do," she says shakily. "With you, I do." She loops her arms around my neck and pulls me in for a kiss.

I wrap one arm around her hips, pulling her closer while sneakily grabbing her new camera with the other and lifting it up toward us. "Smile, Daisy."

And she does, while I place a kiss on her temple.

The photo slides out of the camera, and we watch the film come to life with our happy faces on it.

I scoop her off the counter and walk her over to her newly installed photo wall. "Care to do the honors?"

She takes out one of the colorful pins I added to the wall and sticks our picture in the very center. "Perfect." She sighs as she looks at what I know will be the first of many happy memories on her wall.

"I agree," I say as I keep my gaze firmly planted on the woman of my dreams.

Chapter Thirty-Eight

DAISY

THE MONARCHS CONTINUED THEIR unprecedented winning streak this afternoon when they beat the Miami Mavens 5-3 on our home field.

It was a daytime game, but Luke and the team are staying back a few extra hours to go over film and cool down with the strength and conditioning team. Therefore Luisa, Isabella, and I decided to head over to No Boys Allowed for a little girls' night out. I sent a last-minute text to Valentina, asking if she'd like to join us, and to my surprise, she accepted the invite immediately.

"So Luke has a hot sister," Luisa says before we've even settled into the reserved booth by the arched window looking out into the busy Manhattan streets.

"Let a girl look at the menu before you start in on her, sheesh." I pass a cocktail menu to Valentina and send her an apologetic smile.

She bats her eyelashes playfully as she takes it. "No, please. Carry on and tell me I'm cute. After a few drinks I'm sure I'll be giving your husband a run for his money, declaring my undying love for you."

We all laugh, the sound loosening the tension I was holding. I want Valentina to feel comfortable with our little group. She seemed so sweet and funny when I met her, but I could also sense she has a protective streak, like her brother. And now that I'm dating Luke, I fear I might make it my personal mission to make her my new bestie.

"Speaking of drinks, what are these?" Isabella's eyes widen as she takes in the updated cocktail list. "Strikeout margarita?" She coughs up a laugh as she reads on. "Our sweet and spicy margarita made with top-shelf tequila, a hint of jalapeño pepper with tajin seasoning, and a colorful sprinkle rim," she finishes with a knowing smirk.

Luisa shrugs. "I've changed this place up since Nick bought it for me, and I love the idea of it being a bar that caters to women who enjoy sports."

I smile, loving how Luisa has taken this outrageous gift from my brother—one inspired by unwarranted jealousy—and turned it into a real hotspot. Isabella continues reading. "Fair Trade martini. Vodka and fresh lemon juice, with sugar free simple syrup and orange liqueur. And absolutely no fruit."

Luisa nods. "It's my take on a lemon drop martini, except this one is almost sugar free, making it a PCOS-friendly cocktail."

My smile broadens. "God, Luisa, you're so incredible." I continue to read the list. "You've literally thought of everyth—wait. What is this?" I look up in time to see her do a terrible job of covering up her smirk as she looks over her shoulder to flag down a waiter.

"Hmm, are you referring to our newest cocktail, Home Runner?" Now she doesn't even bother hiding her devious smile.

"D-did you name it after Luke?"

Must be, since that's what broadcasters called him when he played.

"I'll let you be the judge of that. Read the description."

I look back down and do just that as I read out loud. "Our version of a rum runner. Dominican rum and blackberry and banana liqueurs with fresh pineapple and orange juice. Adorned with a fresh... daisy." I look up in astonishment as she smiles sweetly at me.

"Thought I'd have something sweet and not too strong on the menu for you. And the name was too good to pass up. Oh!" She turns in her seat and points. In the middle of the bar is what looks like a dugout, but instead of a long, deep bench, multiple short ones make up the shelves for the liquor bottles. And carved into the center is an old-school phone painted in Monarchs colors. "Almost forgot the best part." She nods at Valentina, and I know what she's about to say. "That's our bullpen phone. Only Nick has the number to it. When he calls, the whole bar lights up in navy, maroon, and white. And that's the signal that all the men are to leave the premises, their food and drink tab fully covered by Nick. Hence the name, No Boys Allowed." She beams.

Valentina laughs. "And the guys aren't pissed about being told to kick rocks?"

"Nope. Besides having their whole night comped, they love the anticipation of coming to the bar, not knowing whether they're going to drink for free. Social media has been buzzing about it. But people started to catch on that the phone only rings when I'm here, so now I have to remind Nick to call when I'm not in to keep the mystery alive."

"Should we expect him to call the line tonight?" Valentina asks.

I groan. "Of course he will. Mateo and Luke had to stay back for team business, but Nick was free, and I had to peel this one off him." I hitch a thumb at Luisa.

"Of course he'll call," Luisa laughs. "But I'm so excited for him to do it tonight since we're all together. The place goes absolutely mental, and if there aren't any baseball games currently playing live, the TVs switch to Bravo and whatever Real Housewives episode is due that night. I swear the women stay double the time and spend triple the money than the men would have anyway."

Valentina taps her phone to check the time. "The new episode of *The Real Housewives of Salt Lake City* is on in an hour. Any chance he'll call by then?"

She elegantly lifts her shoulders. "I can send him a steamy email. That usually gets him going."

"Home runner," I blurt to the waiter, who has come to stand by me. "Please," I add on. "And keep them coming." I'm going to need it if Luisa goes into detail again of how she and my brother like to send sexy emails to one another like the weird and horny executives they are.

The women laugh, Valentina chiming in first when they've all settled. "This is an amazing spot you've got for yourself, Luisa. I don't know how you manage to have a side gig and own an entire baseball team."

"She's still the general manager too," Isa adds proudly.

Luisa smiles as she looks around her establishment. "I call this place the baby before my baby." My eyes widen, but before my mind can form a single thought, Luisa beats me to it.

"We're not actively trying. Although we're not *not* trying." I groan, but she ignores me as she continues. "Nick and I are loving the phase of life we're in. And even though that man makes me want a million babies with him, there are still goals I want to reach in my career before we start adding members to our family. And it's nice to also know that it's okay to wait and enjoy our marriage. Especially since we started off... under unique circumstances."

"That's one way to put it." I smirk at the memory of how those two got together in the first place.

"And actually, Nick and I have been talking, and..."

I lean forward. "Go on. Don't leave us hanging like that."

"Well, nothing is set in stone, but we will be starting the adoption process soon. We want to get all the necessary approvals out of the way in case a child needs a home next season, or the one after that, we'll be ready. Nick and I feel very strongly about adoption, and not as a second choice or a failsafe." She faces me. "You and Nick had no one step forward when your mother passed, and we often talk about how different things may have been if there had been a loving family willing to take you in." My eyes immediately well as she reaches for me. "Please don't cry. I didn't mean to upset you."

"You didn't." I firmly tap a folded napkin against my lash line. "I just really want that for you guys. I know you're going to make the best parents someday."

"Thank you." Her watery gaze meets mine. "PCOS made me feel like motherhood was unattainable. Pregnancy announcements would come with a guilty pinch of jealousy. But now, they bring a smile to my face, because I know that Nick and I will move mountains to grow our family, however that may look, when the time is right." I chuckle because I know that to be true. "But tonight..." She straightens. "We drink and order every appetizer on the menu. Then we see how long it takes for the men to come barreling into this place like overeager puppies."

"Valentina, do you live in the city? I'm surprised I haven't seen you around the stadium," Isa says after her second cocktail. I'm still on my first and giggle, knowing that Luisa and Valentina are well onto their third.

"Mmm." Valentina continues to take a long pull of her martini as she nods. "Yeah, uh. I moved back recently. I was living in the Dominican Republic with my extended family for a while. I've always bounced between New York and DR. But I think I'm back for good now."

"What do you do, if you don't mind me asking?" Luisa takes a bite of a mozzarella stick.

"Freelance photographer." She lifts her glass to her lips as she murmurs, "Who seems to be more free than booked lately."

Luisa sits up straight, and I can already tell she's pulling on her general manager hat. She may be in charge of hiring and trading players for the team, but the woman has an eye for talent and can never pass up an opportunity to grow the Monarchs family. "What kind of photography?"

"Well, I started with street photography. Easiest way to practice when your test subjects are strangers running to catch the train. But that got old quickly, so I moved on to weddings to keep a steady stream of income while I shot what I really loved on the side."

"Which is?" I prompt.

She looks up from her martini, looking slightly panicked. "Oh, um. We don't have to keep talking about me. I'm pretty boring." We all keep our eyes on her until she tips her drink all the way back and answers quietly. "Sports photography."

Luisa's lips lift into a pleased smile. "You hear that, ladies? A sports photographer."

Valentina scrambles to cut in. "I-I mean I'm not even that good. Half the time I can't get the shot of the baseball flying out of the stadium, and that's the shot that everyone wants to—"

"A *baseball* photographer?" Isabella throws her hands up and leans against the cushioned booth. "You're on your own now, girl. I can already smell the Benjamins on the contract Luisa is drafting in her head."

"Isn't Tom retiring?" I lean forward, and I fear my smile must be matching Luisa's at this point.

I definitely want Valentina to feel comfortable around us, but I think I may want her to join the Monarchs family a tad bit more now that I'm in love with her brother and would adore the opportunity for all of us to work together.

We're deep in conversation about logistics with the team when a low murmur settles across the bar. For a moment I think the rum is getting to me, but then I hear it.

I hear *him*.

"There you are, love. Ready to call it a night?"

I'm too slow to react, frozen in place. Only when cold lips press against my cheek and bright flashes of light coming from the window blind me, do I finally jump into action.

"Damien, what the fuck are you doing here?" I hiss at the same time I hear Luisa shouting for security.

The bullpen phone rings, lighting up the bar and sending everyone around us into a fit of cheers.

With the crowd preoccupied with the mass exodus of men and some of their significant others, Damien moves in close, his hand wrapping around my upper arm and squeezing until I wince. "Let's go. Don't make a scene. And remember to smile for the cameras waiting outside. If you behave, I'll even let you pick out your own dress for our next wedding. But the new hairdo has got to go."

I manage to pull free right as a mean-looking security guard places a heavy hand on his shoulder. Damien looks up with his billion-dollar smile and nods at me. "Sorry about the confusion. I'm picking up my fiancée. Seems like she had a bit too many..." He lowers his voice so only I can hear the rest. "And has forgotten her place."

Valentina comes up from behind me and steps between us. We may be the same height, but her personality makes her seem ten feet tall. She looks back at me. "Do you want to call the cops? I saw him grab you."

Damien fake laughs. "Oh honey, please introduce me to your new friend. She seems very funny, although I fail to understand her attempt at a joke."

"I'm Valentina, and I'm pretty sure the woman you're calling *honey* is my future sister-in-law since I'm certain my brother is biding his time before he locks her down and marries her." She leans in closer, and I tug her arm back, but she's still hovering over him menacingly as she fumes. "He also owns land outside the city and is very well versed in the art of swinging an axe, so I suggest you don't take it as a *joke* when I tell you to fuck all the way off and never think about laying a finger, or better yet, your beady little eyes, on Daisy Stonehaven ever again."

Damien takes a step away from us and the bouncer. "Enjoy the rest of your night honey. See you at home," he yells over the crowd, keeping that creepy smile in place the entire time. He speed-walks out of the bar, probably so it doesn't seem like he's being escorted out.

"Are you okay?" all the girls ask at the same time as I absentmindedly rub a hand over my arm where he grabbed me.

"Yeah, I'm fine. But I need to get out of here. I want to get to Luke before Damien pulls another stunt."

"Good idea. I'd rather you be with him when he sees those photos," Valentina says as she pulls me through the crowd to the exit.

"What pho—" I say as we're met with flashes from outside. Knowing how Damien and his campaign work, that was probably a hired photographer from their team, tasked with getting a candid of us.

"I'm calling Nick. Isa, maybe check with Mateo. See if he's still with Coach. Need to gauge whether we're going to need to use him to hold back one furious boyfriend plus an unhinged brother."

I don't wait for them to coordinate. Only I know how deeply affected Luke was when he found out his ex-girlfriend cheated on him with his best friend. And while I know there was nothing I could do to stop Damien, I'm not going to be careless with Luke's feelings and allow even a shred of doubt to cross his mind by not giving him a heads up. I'm pretty sure I can talk him down from a blind rage, but I could not bear it if my silence caused him pain.

I click on his contact, and he answers on the second ring. "Thank God. Mateo was giving me shit for wanting to call and check in on you." I can hear Mateo shout something lighthearted in the background, letting me know they're still together.

"Are you guys almost done? Or will you—"

"Fuck yes. We're walking to our cars on our way to crash the place. Nick said he was gonna call the bullpen phone and clear out the men first."

"Oh, okay. Well, change of plans."

His tone goes serious. "What's wrong?" I hear his heavy footsteps pick up the pace.

"Nothing! Nothing is wrong, but, um—" I look at Luisa as she mouths "my place" and I nod. "We were thinking of heading to Luisa and Nick's place next, so maybe we can all meet there?"

"Okay... are you sure everything is all right?" I pause longer than he deems reasonable. "Daisy, are you still at the bar? I'm coming to you, and you're going to tell me—"

"Please drive safely. I'm fine, but Damien showed up. And there was a photographer outside the bar, most likely planted there by him, so you might see photos of him kissing my cheek and talking to me. The girls were with me the entire time and your sister told him off, but you never know with these pictures and how they get edited, and I need you to know that I had no idea—"

"Daisy, breathe, baby."

"No, not until you tell me you believe me and that you're on your way to Nick's place and not to hunt down Damien." I can hear a displeased sound coming from his chest at the mention of Damien. "Please, Luke? I need to see you."

"Daisy girl, of course I believe you. And I'm on my way. And not because you asked me to, but because I need to make sure for myself that you really are okay. I should be at Nick's place in ten minutes."

Luisa's private car pulls up to the curb and we start to pile in. "His place is at least twenty minutes away."

"I'll still be there in ten. I love you, Daisy."

"I love you too."

Chapter Thirty-Nine

LUKE

I PULL INTO THE private garage under Nick's brownstone and am out of my truck before the engine's fully turned off.

I curse his fancy elevator for taking an eternity, and when I finally enter the mahogany enclosure, I try to focus on my breathing instead of the need to break something with my bare hands.

Like Damien's neck.

The doors open and I'm out in a flash, walking toward the voices coming from the living room.

I know I won't be able to calm the fuck down until I have eyes on Daisy and can confirm for myself that she is unharmed and unaffected by whatever the hell Damien pulled tonight.

"I'm thinking a restraining order should do the trick," Nick says as I turn the corner and immediately lay eyes on Daisy, who's sitting on the oversized chair by the fireplace. I'm vaguely aware that my sister is here along with others, but I push that to the back of my mind as I head straight for my girl.

"Luke!" She stands quickly, but before she has the chance to take a step toward me, I'm on her, pulling her up into my arms. "I'm okay, I promise." Her hands wrap around me and slowly start to play with the hairs at the nape of my neck.

"Gimme a minute. I need to hold you for a minute longer to make sure."

"I'm okay, I promise. Hate that this happened. I don't want you to worry."

I ease back until I can stare into her beautiful brown eyes. "I'll always worry when it comes to you, Daisy." I straighten and run my hands up and down her arms, gently squeezing. She flinches slightly, leaning one arm out of my reach as discreetly as possible.

My eyes zero in on her arm and I'm two seconds away from pulling down her sleeve when she raises her hands and says, "It didn't bruise. I already checked."

My blood boils, and it's clear I'm not the only one who's irate.

"Say that again for me, sis? You're telling me this fucker put his hands on you?"

Luisa steps into Nick's arms, but his gaze is pinned on my girl, who's nervously biting her lip.

My sister claps her hands, forcing the attention away from Daisy momentarily. "Okay, fellas, this is how it's going to go. Daisy and the rest of us ladies will tell you everything that went down. And you're going to listen quietly. Without exerting any toxic, alpha-male energy that Daisy clearly doesn't need after running into what we can all agree is her massive asshole of an ex. So sit, have a glass of water or a horse tranquilizer for all I care, simmer the fuck down, and let Daisy process. Because from what I've seen, all she's worried about is not stressing you out." She points to Nick. "And making sure you knew that she didn't betray you." She points to me next and dread pools in my gut knowing that Daisy was more concerned about me and my feelings than whatever the hell that piece of shit just put her through. "Give the woman some breathing room and... and... Luisa, do you know how to make that Fair Trade martini from scratch by any chance? Because that douchebag interrupted right as I got my last drink, and it messed with the happy buzz I had going. It's been forever since I had a girls' night out and I'll be damned if it ends like this."

Nick grumbles. "So Coach, that's your sister?"

I nod. "The one and only."

He keeps his frown in place, looking between me and Val. "I think I like her. Though she does talk a lot more than you do."

I shrug, and Val and I say "adopted" at the same time.

Daisy slips from my side and pulls Val into a fierce hug, which my sister seems to return with equal vigor.

"Well, you heard the woman. A round of refreshments before we spill the shitty chisme," Luisa states as she starts to pull Nick toward the kitchen with her, Isa and Mateo trailing behind.

My heart still aches thinking of what Daisy must have gone through tonight. But my sister is right. My girl is a people pleaser through and through, and I need to be careful not to let my instinct to keep her safe cause her to doubt our relationship.

I love her for wanting to protect my heart from the ache it once felt, but what I feel for Daisy cannot be compared to my last relationship, not by a long shot. And I know my girl would rather swear off sweets for the rest of her life than cause me purposeful harm, so I'm going to have to have a little chat about her well-intentioned but unnecessary concerns.

Later, we all sit around the fireplace, listening intently as the girls recount the story. Of how he ambushed them, kissed Daisy's cheek, grabbed her arm, and tried to threaten her into coming home all while having a photographer outside taking photos.

I manage to keep my temper at bay and keep a soothing hand on Daisy's arm the entire time, tracing odd patterns, attempting to remove the feel of his touch.

But as Nick goes into media mogul mode about next steps, all I can do is stare at my knuckles, knowing I'm about to get them bloodied for her.

Because no one touches my girl and walks away unscathed.

Chapter Forty
DAISY

By the end of the night, I knew I had to get off the fence and make a statement.

A public one.

By morning, I'd published something short and to the point on my personal social media accounts and Nick's various magazine outlets.

@DaisyStonehaven While I wish it hadn't come to this, I fear I'm well overdue to address the media. As some of you may be aware, Damien and I did not follow through with our marriage. That decision was mine and mine alone. I wish nothing but the best for Damien and his campaign moving forward, but I would appreciate some much-needed space and privacy as I move in a different direction. I thank you all for your concern and well wishes and hope to see you at a Monarchs game soon.

Daisy Stonehaven

The post went viral immediately, especially since the photos of Damien kissing my cheek had gone live. The fact that my face was scrunched up and the women around me wore shocked expressions didn't help his narrative in the slightest.

But unlike last time, Damien and his team responded immediately with a statement of their own, painting him as the grieving groom who plans on taking a few days away from the spotlight to focus on his family. It was obviously a crock of bullshit, but part of me feels relieved to know that I can start putting that part of my life to bed and move forward.

All this back and forth means I've stuck mostly to hiding out in my apartment. I've continued to fuss around the place, trying to make it as homey as possible. Which means Luke's been by my side through it all.

I feel selfish keeping him here all the time, so I offered to stay at his place since I've yet to see where he lives. But he's adamant about helping me work on my apartment until it's perfect. And that's when a little idea for a secret party was planted in my mind. Which is why I'm currently standing in my apartment while my favorite people mill around.

"Hey, where did you put the sopita?" Valentina asks as she places the large bag of rice on the counter. She's been here all day helping me set up for my incognito mission.

"Oh shit. I knew I forgot something. The store didn't have the chicken bouillon I like, so I was supposed to stop at a different market after, but I must have forgotten. I can probably order it and have it delivered right away," I pick up my phone from the counter, but she waves me away.

"Don't worry about it. I'll run to the bodega down the street. I don't mind going to pick it up, especially because they sell the best Dominican chocolate for hot cocoa. I don't care if winter is long gone. I can always go for some good Dominican hot cocoa," she says dreamily.

I laugh. "Wow, do you know all the bodegas in the city and their inventory so well?"

She shakes her head while smiling. "No, but I'm here often because—"

"Did I hear you've got a bodega run to make, sis? Better get to it so my girl and I can start cooking up a storm for this crew." Luke wraps his arm around me from behind, and Valentina looks up at him, having a silent conversation I'm not privy too.

"Oh yeah. Right." She goes to turn but stops to face us again. "Anything else I should grab while I'm out? You said it's just us hanging out and no one else, right?" She looks out at my living room where Isabella is sitting with Mateo and his daughter Anna. Nick's on his phone showing Luisa pictures of their dog, Delilah. And Luisa's mother, along with Isabella's and Mateo's are sitting at the dining table sipping their coffee.

She's asked me the same question three times now, and I'm starting to wonder if there's a certain someone she's trying to avoid, but I can't imagine who, since she's new to the group and has never even set foot in the Monarchs Stadium.

I must do a shitty job of hiding my suspicion, because she rushes out, "I thought someone from your mom's side of the family might live in the city and show up. Wanted to make sure I bring enough of whatever you need."

Luke stiffens behind me, and Valentina's eyes widen.

"Luke, I swear to God if you're giving her a dirty look, you're gonna get another towel whipped at your nipple," I threaten.

He squeezes his arms around me. "You're vicious."

"Sorry," Valentina interrupts. "I didn't mean to overstep. I know your mother is no longer with us, but I didn't know if there was other family around. I shouldn't have said anything." She looks like she's about to melt in a puddle of mortification, and since I know the feeling far too well, I decide to pull her out of it quickly.

"My mom was an only child and her parents passed away before Nick or I were born. So I guess that's how that goes." I shrug, having come to terms with it long ago.

Her brows furrow. "Okay," she says tentatively.

"Drop it, Val," Luke says from above me, and I swat his hand on my stomach, warning him to cut it out.

She looks back up at him but rolls her eyes as she carries on. "I'm sorry, and please forgive me if this is intrusive, but did your grandparents not have siblings? Were there no, I don't know, family friends? Neighbors? The milk man who could potentially be your daddy and not that raggedy ass George Stonehaven guy?"

I bark out a laugh that has me slapping a hand over my mouth.

"Jesus fucking Christ, sis," Luke bemoans above me.

"What? A girl can dream, can't she?" she says far too innocently.

"Honestly? I wouldn't know. She died when I was a baby and Nick was eleven. Nick doesn't remember much from that time, since we lived in London before we were sent off to Connecticut to live at a boarding school, and whatever family connections we had would be in the Dominican Republic. It's not like there was social media back then, so whoever was in my mom's life would be hard to track down."

Valentina looks stricken by the information. "So growing up, there was no one from your mom's side?"

I muster up a pathetic smile. "I was lucky to have really nice Latina nannies. I've heard horror stories, so I guess I really can't complain."

She bites on her thumbnail, her mind seeming to run a mile a minute. "Okay, so..."

"Val," Luke warns.

"Hush. I'm having this conversation with Daisy, and you can try to talk her out of it during your pillow talk, but not now." He groans and she smiles victoriously. "Would you be okay if I poked around and looked into your mom's side of the family in the Dominican Republic? My whole family lives on the island, and trust me, we know a lot of people. Maybe it's a long shot, but who knows? Maybe I can find a long-lost cousin or high school friend."

My breath catches in my chest at the thought of meeting someone who knew my mother. Someone who could tell me about her. Nick has done his best over the years to give me as many details about her as possible, but he was only a child himself, and I worry that his memories are influenced by what he wants me to hear. "I-I would love that. You would do that for me?"

Her eyes soften as she places a hand over the one I have on Luke's arm. "Of course I would. Text me her full name and the address of the home where she grew up and I'll take it from there." She looks up at Luke, no playful defiance in her eyes this time. "I'd do anything for my family. You're stuck with me now."

I know she didn't mean to give me a gut punch, but that's exactly what it feels like. Like when Isabella and Luisa took me in as one of their own. That feeling of being chosen and accepted with no hidden agenda or transactional relationship in sight.

"I swear to God, Val. That was sweet as shit, but if you make Daisy cry at her own housewarming party…"

Valentina's eyes shimmer with mischief, and now it's my turn to fix her with a serious glare, which she responds to with an eye roll that is usually reserved for her brother.

Guess we really are family now.

"Oh, don't worry. I promise not to make her cry at her own *housewarming*, brother. So chill out. Relax and kick your feet up or something."

"Weren't you on your way to the bodega?" I shoot her another widened glance, and she must decide to take pity on me, because she grabs her phone, purse, and the spare keys I gave her off the counter and walks toward the front door.

"Toodaloo. Try not to miss me too much while I'm gone, losers."

Chapter Forty-One
LUKE

Daisy's acting off.

And it's not because of her ex. I've made sure to let her know she can always talk to me about him without worrying about how I may feel or react. And I'm proud of myself for not coming out of my skin every time I'm reminded that the fucker is walking around going unchecked by me.

For now.

No, something else is going on with Daisy. But she seems to be in a great mood, enjoying having a home filled with the people who truly love and care about her.

"Man, you've got it bad." Mateo chuckles beside me, handing me a cold beer.

I don't bother taking my eyes off her as she chats with the moms at the dining table, soaking up their attention like a sponge. "Yeah. And?"

He taps the neck of his beer with mine, forcing me to look his way, worried he'll spill it on Daisy's new carpet. "Trust me, I get it. Every morning I wake up with the desire to haul Isabella's ass to the courthouse, but she wants her small ceremony in La Romana, at Altos de Chavón, and I can't deny her anything she asks for." He sighs as he looks off to the side, watching Isa and his daughter Anna working hard at making friendship bracelets.

I was surprised earlier when Anna came up to me and offered me the first one she completed. And I was touched when I realized she spelled out BEST COACH EVER on it.

"Oh, I almost forgot." Mateo pulls two tickets out of his back pocket. "I got these a while back but won't be able to attend. Figured you could make use of them and take Daisy with you."

I take the tickets and stare down at them, my brows quickly lifting in surprise. "You had tickets to Bad Bunny's sold-out concert in *Madrid* just lying around?"

He lifts his shoulders nonchalantly. "I know you listen to his music. Figured you guys could make a trip out of it. It's during the offseason. I'm sure you can handle covering the flight since your girl's brother literally owns a private jet. But I also have a suite booked at the Four Seasons that you guys are free to use. I'll email over the details. It's booked in your name so you shouldn't have any issues."

My jaw unhinges, confused beyond belief. I look up at Daisy in time to see her darting her gaze away from mine. Is she up to something? Before I can give it much thought, the doorbell rings. That must be Val back from her bodega run.

I move to stand, but Nick's already at the door. "What are you two delinquents doing here?" Nick says with a laugh. I hear hard pats on the back and chuckles before Ace and Julian come into view.

"You didn't." Mateo laughs, then looks at me. "Ace texted, asking what I had planned today, and when I mentioned I was heading over here to hang with everyone, he practically threw a fit."

"So you gave him a pity invite to Daisy's housewarming?" I smirk at the idea of Ace having FOMO.

Ace breezes in, lifting Anna and spinning her in a circle, causing her to squeal before placing a big kiss on her cheek. "There's my favorite girl. Are you adding any new ones to my collection?" He raises his left wrist, showing off the collection of friendship bracelets that are intertwined with his diamond bracelets and exorbitantly expensive watch.

"On it now!" Anna's head tilts down, tongue poking out of her mouth in concentration as she doubles her speed.

I stand and meet him at the back of the couch to greet him but narrow my eyes at the massive Prada shopping bag in his hand. "That must be a large and expensive candle, because I know damn well you didn't buy my woman a pricey handbag or shoes for a housewarming gift."

Daisy slips into my side, laughing. "Ignore him, Ace. All gifts are welcome in this home." She giggles at my pinched face.

"You knew he was coming?" I ask.

Ace cuts in. "Mateo and I share locations." He winks at Mateo, then smiles at us.

Daisy shakes her head. "I got a call from security. He babbled about more Monarchs players waiting for access to my apartment before jumping into a cute spiel about how, even though these two are his favorite players, he still wouldn't let them up unless I gave the green light." She looks back at Ace. "I actually felt bad about not inviting you guys but since almost everyone's coupled up, I didn't want you guys to feel left out."

Ace looks behind us and smiles salaciously. "Well, I see three fine ladies sitting by their lonely selves at that dining table. I'm sure Julian and I can keep them company."

"Middlebrooks, you stay away from my mother," Mateo warns.

"Yeah, ours too," Luisa says as she comes to stand next to Isa.

"Speak for yourselves, youngins. Middlebrooks, Vega, get over here and serve us more coffee," Luisa's mother shouts.

"Your wish is my command." Ace winks in their direction, and I actually have to laugh at the guy. The playboy act never ends with this one, and I gotta say I appreciate the commitment to his craft, as outrageous as it may be. Julian makes his way to the dining table, leaving coffee duty solely to Ace, who says, "And for the record, this is for you, not your girl. It's a leather jacket so you can ditch the one that gives you lumberjack vibes." He chuckles. "And besides, I don't have a death wish. Why would I bring a gift for her to your birthday party?"

The room goes quiet. No one moves, as if they're all holding in a collective breath.

That is until Mateo breaks the silence. "You fucking idiot," he whispers over the couch so his daughter can't hear him curse.

Ace points at himself, then circles his finger around the room. "I'm missing something here, aren't I?" He smiles nervously, scratching the back of his neck. "You know what? I have a coffee to deliver, so if you don't mind..." He gives us a wide berth as he walks over to the kitchen and tinkers with the coffee machine as if he's been here countless times.

I feel Daisy shaking in my arms, and when I look down, I find her laughing silently. "Daze, what are you up to?"

She bites her lip. "Well." She waves around the room, all eyes on us. "Surprise? This was supposed to be your extremely low-key birthday party. So low-key you weren't even supposed to know it was happening." She whispers the last part.

"That would have been a great detail to fill me in on, Martinez," Ace yells from the kitchen as he glares at Mateo while stirring sugar into a comically small coffee cup.

"I would have, had you been invited," Mateo yells back.

I look around the room with new eyes. The bracelet on my wrist, the tickets to the concert in Spain, the home-cooked meal being prepped in the kitchen.

"I'm sorry if you hate it. But last year when we threw you a party at the stadium, you looked so uncomfortable with all the attention on you, and you bolted as soon as we sang 'Happy Birthday.' I know you don't like a big fuss being made over you, so I figured we'd celebrate it a week early and tell you it was my housewarming so you wouldn't catch on," she says all in one breath. "Are you mad?" She winces slightly.

My hands rest on her cheeks and I lean down until we're eye to eye. "Daisy fucking Stonehaven." I shake my head, at a loss for words. "I love you so much. This is perfect. You are perfect. Thank you so much for loving me like you do. This is the best birthday ever." I close the distance and press my lips to hers.

Our friends whoop and holler around us.

This woman knows me so well. Loves me in a way I never knew could be possible with a past like mine.

The only reason I peel myself off her is because we are in the presence of nosy mothers and a child. I'd love to send everyone packing, but that would mean all of Daisy's efforts would be in vain. So instead, I place one more chaste kiss on her lips and straighten. "Does that mean that there's Dominican cake somewhere in this house?" I rub my hands together deviously.

Daisy rolls her eyes. "Of course there is. What kind of heathen do you think I am?"

I love her fucking snark. Not too long ago she would have shied away from this fun and sassy side of herself. But knowing she's comfortable enough to push back has me grinning, and I don't even try to stop myself from hauling her back into my arms for another kiss, this one much more salacious.

"Best." *Kiss.* "Birthday." *Kiss.* "Ever." *Kiss.*

"Ew, can't you guys at least wait until we're all gone and talking about you behind your backs before you start mauling each other's faces again?" Val says as she walks toward the kitchen counter.

Halfway there, she stops short, face going unnaturally pale.

A crashing noise comes from the kitchen. The coffee mug is no longer in Ace's hand but in shattered pieces on the floor by his feet. His jeans and Timberland boots are splattered, but he doesn't seem to notice as his shocked eyes remain fixed on my sister.

I'm about to ask what the fuck is going on when Ace speaks up first. "Val-Valentina? Um, wow." He clears his throat, running a hand down his face before he points it at her. "It's nice to see you. You haven't changed at all. I-I mean y-you look, uh. You look well."

Questions arise quicker than I can keep track. He knows my sister? Why the hell is he acting this way? He's never been tongue-tied by a woman, and trust me, I've seen him with many.

And my sister and I verbally spar like it's our day job, but it's always in good fun, even when she's running me up a wall.

So when the icy tone drips from her lips, I'm instantly on high alert. "And you look like you haven't changed a bit either..." She looks down at the broken pieces of ceramic by his feet. "Leaving a mess wherever you go."

His face falls, confusion marring his features until they turn tight.

Val looks our way. "Hey, Daisy, I got everything you need. Keep the chocolate. I'm sure you'll love it." Her eyes meet mine. "Happy birthday, bro. Sorry I can't—."

"Bro? Coach is your *brother*?" Ace asks, dumbfounded for some reason I'm not privy to.

"Sorry I can't stay," Val continues, ignoring his comment. "Let's grab lunch this week and I'll make it up to you."

"What the hell is going—" I start before Ace interrupts.

He chuckles darkly. "Guess some things never change. Care to tell us where you're running off to now, or you just gonna keep me in the dark again?"

Again?

Val's mouth opens, a retort at the ready, when she suddenly looks like she's at a loss for words.

The moms quietly approach Ace with a broom and pan in hand. Their appearance seems to break whatever trance he and my sister were in, because he jumps into action, taking the broom from their hands and sweeping up the mess himself while one of the moms uses a large dish rag to wipe the spilled coffee from the lower cabinets and the floor.

And when Ace looks back up, his face falls again. Because Valentina is gone.

Chapter Forty-Two

LUKE

Things were tense at practice today, and everyone could tell.

Middlebrooks is usually the one you can count on to chat up the guys and keep them distracted from the grueling drills I send their way.

But he was radio silent, following my orders to a T while barely glancing in my direction.

I tried getting to the bottom of it with Val when we went out for lunch the day after my party, but she shut me down before we had our waters placed on the table. Told me to respect her privacy and to not go digging up her past.

Which means Ace is a part of the past. And now I'm trying to figure out how to be a respectful brother while also wondering if I'm going to have a problem with Middlebrooks from here on out.

Practice is over and everyone is heading to the showers when I call him into my office. He doesn't seem surprised when I do.

"Looking good out there today."

"Thanks, Coach." He nods respectfully, fully lacking that signature cocky smile as he takes a seat across from my desk.

I force myself to look more closely. I've battled with my demons long enough to know how to spot them on someone else.

And Ace? He looks fucking haunted.

I change tactics, putting my brother hat away and instead do what I know Daisy would do in my position. Offer to help and lead with grace. "I'm not going to beat around the bush, man. I know something happened between you and my sister—"

"I didn't know she was your sister. She never—" He lets out a humorless laugh. "Doesn't matter. It's all good, Coach. Promise. I'll keep my head in the game and leave all my high school bullshit in the past." His gaze falls to his tightly clenched hands.

I raise a brow at that. "High school?"

He sucks in a breath. "She never mentioned—" He shakes his head. "Like I said, it doesn't matter."

"Well, it does to me. I'm your coach and she's my little sister. Clearly something went on with you two, or neither of you would be acting so bent out of shape lately." I sigh at the reminder of Val's sunken eyes the last time I saw her. "I'm trying to figure out if I'm supposed to beat your ass for hurting her, or if she—"

"Hurting her?" His head snaps back up, and I see that his eyes are red, rimmed with tears.

I know I'm not a man of many words, but fuck me if I'm not stunned into silence. And I have no idea what to think.

He stands abruptly, making it to the door in a flash.

"Ace."

He shakes his head. "You don't have to worry about me. Like I said, I'll keep my head in the game. But when it comes to your sister, I'll make one thing clear. The last time I saw her was the first and last time I ever said 'I love you' to a woman I wasn't related to. She was my everything. My first love. First..." He clears his throat. "And then..."

I shift in my seat, trying not to look uncomfortable with the new information coming my way. "And then?"

His eyes meet mine and the pain laced in them is all too familiar.

"And then she was gone. Different school, different *country*. Without a single explanation. And even though I've stalked her online a few times in moments of weakness, I never saw her again, not until I saw her standing in Daisy's apartment. And she had the audacity to look at me like I was the enemy. Like I did something wrong. Like I ripped out her heart and broke it into a million pieces while I stand here as the physical embodiment of her handiwork from doing just that."

"Ace, fuck." I run a hand down my face. "I'm sorry, man. But there has to be an explanation for all of this."

"I'm sure there is, but I'm pretty sure it's too late."

"And why is that?"

"Because look at me." He smiles, eyes devoid of emotion. "I'm already the monster she made me out to be."

Chapter Forty-Three

DAISY

My long-awaited dinner with my father was scheduled for tonight, but Valentina begged me to cancel, or at the very least to move it to tomorrow. Which is something I never would have done a few weeks ago, but now had no qualms about.

First, because Valentina clearly needs me tonight, and I would never leave her hanging. And second, because I've spent far too long being at my father's beck and call. This time around, he can wait on me.

It's been two weeks since Luke's birthday party, and I've been slowly trying to coax her back into hanging out with us.

So when she told me she'd be waiting at home for me, I jumped at the chance to finally have that one-on-one time with her.

I try to ignore the fact that it's Mother's Day, the one holiday I've never been able to celebrate with my own mom, as I rush through the rest of my workload. Unfortunately, I get tied up with all the holiday festivities since we threw a private brunch for the players' wives and moms, and since I was already working on a Sunday, I decided to get a head start on prepping for the big game coming up this weekend.

That's why I'm arriving an hour later than intended. When I slip inside my apartment, I instantly bump into a wall of solid muscle. "Oh, hey. What are you doing here?"

Luke frowns before taking my purse from my hands and planting a quick kiss on my lips. "Aren't you supposed to say "honey I'm home" or "get naked immediately" when you greet me after a long day at work?"

I smirk as I lift up onto my tiptoes. "You were at work with me all day, even though it was your day off. Or have you forgotten that you're technically my coworker?"

"How could I forget? You won't let me fuck you in my office," he complains.

"Luke! Seriously? We have more important matters at hand." Valentina comes up from behind him and slaps him behind the head.

"Ouch. Stop eavesdropping on me and my girl."

"Ugh, men." She shakes her head, but when her eyes land on me, they shine with happiness. "Hey, Daisy. I'm sorry to spring this on you, but I didn't want to say anything in case it didn't pan out."

"What are you talking about?" I chuckle awkwardly, looking at Luke's anxious expression.

She takes my hand, and Luke places his warm one on my lower back, guiding me to the living room. "I think it's better if I show you."

I hear a low murmur of voices and halt when I see a group of strangers sitting on my couches, eyeing me nervously.

"Oh, we have guests," I say lamely.

"Daisy girl, Val and I have some people we'd like you to meet."

I plaster on a smile. "I see that. Um, hi I'm Daisy. Sorry I'm late. I didn't know we were throwing a party." I laugh timidly as one woman stands, eyes watering the closer she walks toward me.

I find myself inching backward, but Luke's steady hand on my back keeps me in place as the woman with curly gray hair comes to a stop before me. She shakes her head, eyes raking over my face in awe. "Hi, Daisy. My name is Carla. And I—" Her voice wobbles before she clears it. "I was your mother's best friend."

Luke's other hand is on my hip now. How he knew my knees were about to buckle is beyond me.

"You're... what did you say?" My voice barely registers to my own ears.

"Hi, Daisy," a dark-skinned man who looks to be in his fifties stands but stays by the couch as he speaks. "I'm Amaury, your mom's cousin. We grew up together in Jarabacoa," he says with a thick Dominican accent.

My head whips back and forth between the two strangers before a new voice pipes up.

"Daisy, yo soy Marlene. Yo era vecina de tus abuelos y mamá."

She was neighbors with my mother and grandparents, I translate easily in my head.

"Hello, Daisy, I'm Monica," a sharply dressed blond woman with an English accent says. "I studied and worked alongside Carmen in London."

I look up at Luke's watery gaze, one that must mirror my own. "Wh-what's happening right now?" I whisper.

"My sister." he answers shakily before clearing his throat. "She was able to track down Carla via a social media post memorializing the anniversary of your mother's death. Once they got into contact with one another, Carla introduced Val to everyone who's here today. These are only the ones I could convince to hop on a plane with twenty-four hours' notice. But there are more family, friends, and loved ones out there. People who never forgot about you and Nick and are waiting for us to video call them whenever you're ready. Many of them don't have visas to travel to the U.S., but I can talk to an immigration attorney and get the process started on that or we can fly down there and visit whenever you want." He turns me so I'm fully facing him, his soothing hands on my shoulders as a single tear slips down his cheek. "Your mother is here in this room with us, Daisy. In your heart, in the memories that are about to be shared. In your eyes and spirit. She's here. Always has been and always will be. So what do you say? Are you ready to be reintroduced to her? Because from the little I heard while we were waiting for you, she sounds just as incredible as the woman I've fallen madly and deeply in love with."

My head slumps against his chest as a sob breaks free.

It's slowly sinking in what Valentina and Luke have done for me. It's the most precious gift I've ever been given.

And in this moment, I feel her.

Luke was right. My mother is here with me tonight. And I can't wait a second longer to learn about the woman I've been daydreaming about my entire life.

I turn, facing the crowd with tentative smiles on their faces.

The first woman, Carla, speaks up again. "I brought pictures. Would you like to sit down and look at them with me?" Her hand reaches out slowly, and I take it in mine immediately, gripping stronger than appropriate for a first-time meeting, but I don't care.

Because if this woman was my mother's best friend, then that means my mother held these hands. Shared secrets and jokes with this woman. Which makes her an endless pool of invaluable knowledge to me.

I nod and walk over to my couch, greeting everyone as I go.

I settle, and when Carla sits next to me, I gently tap the free seat next to me for my mother's cousin, Amaury, to take. Luke gently squeezes my shoulders before quietly announcing that he and Valentina will be bringing out more drinks and snacks.

Everyone reintroduces themselves, most likely understanding that I needed a minute to really grasp their names and their relation to my mother.

I look back to thank the two people responsible for this miracle, only to catch Luke giving his sister a bear hug, his eyes shut tightly as he embraces her, his lips mouthing "thank you so much" repeatedly.

Carla squeezes my hand and pulls a thick photo album off my coffee table. "Are you ready, Daisy?" Her voice wobbles on my name, and I think I'm going to need an entire box of tissues to get through the night.

I nod. "I'm ready, but first I'm going to need to call my brother, Nick. He deserves to be here for this."

Everyone brightens and nods with enthusiasm.

After a tearful call I'm sure made absolutely no sense whatsoever, Nick bursts into my apartment with Luisa hot on his heels.

He looks perplexed as he takes in the scene before him. And this time, I get to be the person that helps another remain upright, with the help of Luke of course, after he was introduced to our guests.

He excuses himself before we get started, and when he walks back into the room with red, but smiling eyes, we all act as if we didn't hear the anguished cry coming from my guest bathroom.

Luke silently hands him a glass of the scotch I always keep on hand for him, and we all shuffle around so Nick and I are seated side by side, hands clasped tightly, when Carla opens the first photo album.

And finally, I'm introduced to my mom.

Chapter Forty-Four

DAISY

It's nearing midnight, and we can't stop laughing.

And no one's showing any signs of leaving.

The first hour was filled with more hugs and tears than I could count. But then the night took a turn for more lighthearted stories.

Like how Marlene, my mom's childhood neighbor, once caught her own daughter and my mother trying to sneak out early one Sunday morning to walk to the local bakery with large cups because apparently, they would get free frosting from the lady in charge of decorating the cakes if they came prepared with their own to-go containers.

Or how my mom and Monica, her old law school friend and coworker, once studied well into the night, only to pass out and end up locked inside their school library. Apparently, they had to wiggle out a tiny window on the second floor and landed on prickly bushes, almost breaking a limb each, though they were too deliriously tired to care.

"Damn, how was our mother way cooler than either of us?" Nick grouses from beside me as he picks up a photo of her in a cut-off grunge T-shirt and shorts.

"Seriously, like how badass was she?" I lift the photo in my hand, showing her zip-lining somewhere in the Dominican Republic as a teen.

"Well, actually, up until her parents passed away, she was mostly a people pleaser," Amaury, her cousin, says.

"What?" The cider in my hand almost slides out of my grip.

Carla nods. "It's true. She was definitely a daredevil." She nods at a photo of my mother swinging on a rope before jumping into the ocean from a dock. "But she had this constant worry about making sure everyone around her was happy. Bending over backward for random people in her life whenever she felt like she was letting them down. No matter how absurd the circumstances. It wasn't until her father passed that she changed into the fierce woman we all knew her to be as an adult. She was her mother's protector when vultures descended, trying to pressure her to sell her family home, since the property was quickly rising in value. But then her mother fell ill and passed away the same year her father died. Your mother ended up inheriting the home. Once her parents were gone, she decided it was her time to leave the nest and discover the world. She had a full ride scholarship to law school in London and took the opportunity without a second thought."

Monica cuts in. "Only when faced with protecting the ones she loved did her claws come out, and then she never put them away." She chuckles as she takes a sip of scotch. "And used that fire to become an incredible barrister who lived in the UK."

It looks like I do have things in common with my mother after all.

Nick clears his throat, wiping his hands of crumbs and failing to meet anyone's gaze as he asks, "Why didn't any of you come forward after she passed?" Silence falls upon the room. "Don't get me wrong, I'm thrilled to meet you all, and I won't hold what you say against you. I'm only curious."

His eyes lift and he doesn't bother hiding the vulnerability behind them.

Everyone seems to shift around us, eyes volleying between them all before Carla takes the lead. "We did," she says slowly. "We all did."

Both Nick and I lean back, but he speaks first. "What do you mean? There was no one at her service. No one called us or visited, even when we moved to the States, closer to the Dominican Republic." There's an edge to his voice, but he manages to reel it in at the end.

"Well, I won't pussyfoot around it," Monica states. "It was your bloody father. He never informed us of her funeral. I only found out about her passing three days after the fact when she didn't show up for work."

Carla bristles next to me as she turns to us, pure fury on her face. "She was my best friend. Our kids were supposed to be cousins. You guys were my niece and nephew in my heart. Back then, we were both single mothers struggling financially, getting our lives off the ground. But we spoke on the phone constantly. I helped her plan Nick's Pokémon-themed tenth birthday party and had a massive Pikachu shipped over, even though it cost almost as much as my rent in shipping alone. And I picked out the outfit Daisy wore home from the hospital the day after she was born. It was created by a local Dominican designer. During that last year, she was doing well at work and finally establishing herself. She was planning on flying down with you two to visit us. We had the entire itinerary planned for a whole month's stay. My best friend was finally coming back home and she was bringing the two little humans who had me wrapped around their pinky fingers. But when she passed away? Ripped away from us far too soon and unfairly? Your father decided to do the same with you two."

I swallow audibly, my skin vibrating with dread. "Explain."

Amaury speaks. "We called every single day. Begging him to send you to live with one of us. The entire town would have raised you as their own if necessary, but we needed you returned to your family. Your real family. Because we knew that the man who fathered you was never a part of your life, and now he held all the power with legal guardianship. The sick man never allowed us to speak on the phone or send letters. And when we threatened to fly over there ourselves, having scrounged up enough money for Carla to represent all of us, he told us that he'd already shipped you guys off to a different country. And reminded us that you were minors, and if we kept calling, he'd involve his attorneys and force legal action." He looks down, almost as if he's beating himself up. "You have to understand, we didn't have much money back then. Still don't. I was working on visas for my family to enter the US for better job opportunities. And this man was powerful. I knew I could not face off with him and win. And none of us were a sibling, aunt, or grandparent, so we were forced to... give up. I'm so sorry. I should have fought harder. It is a regret I live with every day of my life."

Carla grabs my hand and Nick's, eyes fierce. "My best friend died, but I mourned all three of you. Knowing I never got to meet you in person and protect you from the man who was so manipulative and careless with your mother's heart. And there hasn't been a single day that I haven't thought about you two and wished things could be different. I know I, we, can't change the past, but we'd all like to be a part of your lives now, if you'll allow it." She visibly holds her breath.

Nick and I look at one another. Gone is the self-assured CEO, and in his place is a sad and shattered eleven-year-old boy.

We were loved. We were wanted.

But we were exiled by our father.

A wave of sadness threatens to pull me under, but then a comforting hand curves around the back of my neck, the touch so uniquely Luke's. I see Luisa move and take a seat on Nick's lap, embracing him as his shoulders start to shake with furious tears.

But I remain perfectly calm, refusing to shed another tear.

Stock-still as all the pieces start to fall into place.

The parent I tried so desperately to placate and feel love from was the person responsible for causing pain in so many lives.

I spent years innocently breaking myself down to perfectly moldable little pieces that would be more appealing to him, and for what? Even if the man possessed a heart with the capability to show love for his children, it was never going to be enough.

I was never going to be enough.

But it wasn't because I'm unlovable. He just isn't capable of loving anyone but himself. And I truly think he sees absolutely nothing wrong with that.

And knowing this, I have zero doubts that he conspired with Damien behind my back, trading my submission, the kind I had given him my entire life, and used it as some form of sick political currency for his company's monetary gain.

I stand as I address the entire room. "We had no idea, and I'm sickened by the fact that we've lost all this time with one another, but we would love nothing more than to have you all join our little family from here on out. If you'll still have us."

Everyone stands in a rush, and hugs and kisses are exchanged.

When Valentina stands before me, I don't hesitate to pull her in for a tight hug. "Thank you so much. Thank you, thank you, thank you. You have no idea how much this means to Nick and me."

She wipes a tear as she chuckles. "By the way I've been secretly crying in the kitchen between food and drink refills. I'm pretty sure I got the gist of it."

I turn in search of Luke and find him releasing Nick from a hug. I take a step in their direction, catching the tail end of Nick's side of the conversation. "...and I swear to God, if you don't marry my sister after all of this, I'm calling that guy I know, and you'll be—"

I raise my brow at them, and they shamelessly shrug it off like it's no big deal.

I know I initially beat myself up for feeling as though I was falling for Luke far too quickly, being used to caring about public perception and appropriate timelines. But if he were to get down on one knee right now, I'd pull him back up and wake a judge and demand they marry us right this very second.

His eyes narrow, as if he's reading my mind, and now it's my turn to shrug.

"Thank you all for the hospitality, but it's late. We're all going to head out and let you digest everything you've heard tonight," Monica states as she lifts her purse over her shoulder.

"There is a private car outside that will take you back to your hotel. You will have the suites for a week. Longer if you wish to extend your trip. Just say the word," Luke offers.

They all nod appreciatively, and I smile widely, knowing that they'll be in town longer to spend time with us. I can mentally see Nick clearing his work schedule as Carla pulls him in for a goodbye hug. "Dios mío, Nicholas. You were Carmen's pride and joy. Her little man. She would be so insanely proud of you, I know it." She pats his cheek and then moves on to me. "And Daisy, her baby girl. She dreamed of you for years, thinking she would never have another child, secretly wishing for a baby girl, and then you came along, making her final dream come true." She kisses my cheek before she takes a step back. "If she saw you two working together…" She shakes her head. "Her legacy is alive and well in you both." Her eyes stay on me a moment longer before she chuckles. "I still can't believe she named you Daisy."

Luke comes to stand behind me, wrapping me in his warm arms, pulling me closer to his chest.

"Why is that?" I ask, looking around to see everyone giggling amongst themselves.

All my life I've assumed it was her favorite flower.

"I grew up hearing this story so many times." Carla smiles. "Your grandparents were next door neighbors growing up, and your grandfather fell in love with your grandmother when they were still in diapers. When they were teenagers, he asked her parents for permission to date her."

"And they said no, because they were too young," Marlene cuts in.

"But your grandfather was undeterred. He said he would win your grandmother's heart and prove to her parents that his love was true." Carla pauses.

I look between all their smiling faces. "So what happened next?" I ask eagerly.

Carla grins. "Your grandfather worked in landscaping after school. So he bought as many daisies as he could afford, and instead of simply giving her a bouquet of flowers that would die within a week, he planted them along the path from their house to their school. So your grandmother and her parents would walk by daisies, *her* favorite flower, every single day."

Luke stills behind me, and my nails dig into his forearms across my stomach.

"Your mother loved her parents' love story. So much that she named you Daisy. She never found a love like that but wished it for her baby girl so strongly. She named you after the one act that brought her parents together, which led to her, which led to you."

They all laugh at my shocked expression, not knowing that I'm reliving the visions of that moment in Luke's driveway. The thousands of daisies he planted himself. But instead of doing it with the intention of winning my heart, he did it thinking he would never have it. And now having heard this story, there is one thing I know for certain.

Luke is my soulmate.

And if I dare dream a little too hard, I'll allow myself to believe that maybe my mother hand picked him for me.

Chapter Forty-Five

DAISY

The last two days have been emotionally taxing.

While I've enjoyed getting to know my mother through the eyes of those who knew her best, I've also had to come to terms with the reality of who my father really is.

For so long I made excuses on his behalf.

I knew students at my boarding school who never spoke to their fathers or were disowned by their parents, and I told myself that I could have had it far worse. That at the very least, my dad made sure to set me up with a good education.

But that farce ended after our surprise guests left and an emotionally drained Nick informed me that all the funds that paid for our education and care came from my mother's life insurance policy. Her will demanded it.

I was already set to walk away from my father after finding out he'd kept my mother's loved ones away from us at a time we needed them most. But the fact that he spent my entire life boasting about providing financially for his children, as if he deserved some kind of medal for it, strengthened my resolve.

Our dinner is tonight, and I decided that I needed a final face-to-face conversation to end our relationship.

He picked an overpriced steakhouse in the heart of midtown, a place where people love to be seen, as the spot for us to have our long overdue heart to heart. Because of course he did.

Which is exactly why I washed and diffused my hair today, giving my long curls an extra bit of bounce, and threw on one of the coziest outfits Luke bought for me back when we were hiding up north. A cream cropped T-shirt and lounge pant set, oversized brown cardigan, and for sentimental value, my white Converses. Which Luke now lovingly refers to as my "runaway" shoes.

I do my makeup nicely, and while my clothes are cute and trendy, I am very much underdressed for this restaurant, which is exactly what I planned.

I beat the doorman to the door and salute him on my way in. I breeze by the hostess stand since I spotted my father as soon as I walked in. I honestly could have guessed that he'd pick the center table, knowing that the man loves an audience, which is exactly why this short but sweet meeting is going to be so satisfying.

"Oh, hey there, Dad." I plonk down into the chair across from him.

His jaw drops as he blinks repeatedly. Confusion quickly transforms into embarrassment. "For the love of God, Daisy. This is a fine establishment. What are you—"

"Hmm, it is nice. Maybe Nick will buy it for Luisa. Although I am much fonder of the last bar he bought for her."

His lip curls at the mention of my brother. He's never been able to hide his envy for his biological son and the way he has far surpassed him in wealth and success. Something I've always tiptoed around, wanting to keep the peace between the two men in my life.

Lovely how I won't have to do that anymore.

"Daisy, I don't know what has gotten into you lately, but luckily, there is still a chance for you to right your wrongs."

I wait for it. That twinge of guilt that'll send me backsliding into being my father's perfect little people pleaser.

And a wide grin overtakes my face when I realize... it's finally gone.

A waiter comes by our table, lifting the bottle of wine that's been decanting at my father's side to pour into my glass. My hand covers the wineglass before he has a chance to continue. "Actually, I'll have a Coke."

The waiter nods and scurries off.

"A-a Coke? Daisy, this is a two-hundred-dollar bottle of wine. Soda is for children with poor dental care. And you are a woman of societ—"

"Yeah, so I'm going to stop you before we go around in circles, because I have plans after this. So why exactly have you called for this dinner? I want to know right now what it is that you think we need to talk about."

It's too late. My mind is already made up about going no-contact with my father. But out of morbid curiosity, I'm dying to know if he'll play the act of an apologetic father or if he'll fess up to the lifetime of fuckery he's engaged in.

He takes a sip of his wine, pulling discreetly at his tie. "About you and Damien. I think things have gotten a bit out of hand."

And there's my answer, folks.

"He's very apologetic about how he spoke to you after you up and disappeared from your very own wedding, leaving the poor bloke reeling. But I assure you, he is still willing to carry on with your engagement and take the appropriate steps to setting your relationship back on track."

"Willing," I mouth to myself as a fresh Coke with lemon and ice is placed in front of me.

"Yes, we can carry on with the engagement and have you wed in the summer, I suppose. Right before the campaign kicks into high gear," he yammers on excitedly.

I nod. "Interesting. You're a part of the engagement? When are you and Damien going to go public with your relationship? I'm sure it would do wonders for his family values platform."

He snarls at me before forcing his face into a scary smile. "This is not the time for silly jokes, Daisy. You are a Stonehaven, and it's about time you start acting like it," he hisses through his teeth.

Having had enough of this, I wave him off and go for what I'm really after: the truth. "Were you ever going to tell me that my mother was the one who funded my education and my livelihood for the first eighteen years of my life, or were you going to ride that lie out until the wheels fell off?"

He goes still before pointing a finger in my direction. "Is that what your brother told you? He went digging around for all those wills your mother apparently kept behind my back, and now thinks he knows everything. But let me tell you, I still had responsibilities to follow through on, even if that absurd life insurance policy that she somehow paid for footed the bill for that boarding school. I am still your father, and that's all that matters."

"Hmm, and what about the family and friends who contacted you after Mom died, hoping to keep in touch with Nick and me?"

His eyes widen slightly before he's able to school his features again. "What? Someone on social media reaching out to you, trying to scam you or something? Don't believe everything you read, Daisy. You are far too innocent and naïve for this cruel world, which is why you're lucky to have Damien and me around to keep you in line."

I could barf over this table at the way he's speaking, but I need to clear up one last thing. "And after I fall back in line, is that when your hedge fund is going to take over Damien's family money, or do you have to wait until after I walk down the aisle? Just trying to get all my ducks in a row before I royally fuck you over, *Dad*."

He goes beet red.

Gotcha.

Before he's able to respond, his phone lights up with a message, changing his demeanor completely. "My apologies. I need to use the restroom. I'll only be a moment. Wait right here." He runs off with a smirk before I've had the chance to deliver the little speech I reserved for him.

Oh well. Looks like I'll have to go without it. Because I wasn't lying when I said I had plans after this.

Tonight's game is a monumental one for the Monarchs. If they win, they will have achieved the longest winning streak ever in MLB history. The fact that it's against the other iconic New York baseball team, another titan of the sport, makes this game extra exciting.

I lean down to grab my bag, but when I sit up, I have to bite my tongue to silence the scream I almost let out at the sight of Damien, who is now sitting confidently in the chair my father was previously occupying.

"Aren't you a slippery one to catch alone as of late?" He swirls the wine around in his glass, looking like an evil mastermind.

I move to stand but decide to make myself comfortable in my seat instead. Because it seems as though I'm about to have a two-for-one meeting with the men I'll never speak to again.

He smiles victoriously at me as he leans over the table, serving me that glass of wine I wasn't interested in to begin with. I stare at him, noting every inch of his face. The face I had somehow convinced myself I was in love with. Wanted to marry and have children with. How the hell did I miss the thinly veiled cruelty behind the mask? The same brand my father seems to brandish.

Goddamn, those daddy issues really screwed me there.

My instinct is to leave, not wanting Luke to have to witness yet another leaked photo of Damien and me. But last time I was ambushed, Luke made it clear the only thing I needed to worry about was him getting his hands on my ex, and not a miscommunication between the two of us.

And by the way Damien is taking in the eyes of everyone sneaking a peek at us, I can't really say I'm against a little bit of violence anymore.

Speaking into his swirling glass, he starts. "So this is how this is going to go. You are going to put on the ring I have in my suit jacket and we are going to walk out of here hand in hand. Apparently, people are eating up my whole redemption arc and are dying to see if I can get my girl back. Everyone loves a second-chance love story, and we're going to give it to them." He smiles wickedly. "And after my election win, I'll kick you to the curb and you'll be free to date that unkempt man who works for that sports team you're so fond of."

I stiffen at the way he speaks of Luke. "How did you—"

"Please, Daisy. I have resources and I am prudent at using them. When your little pit bull of a friend came at me at that grimy bar, it was easy to put the pieces together." He leans in farther, as if we're sharing a salacious secret. "Although I must say, my risk-averse fiancée, how daring of you to go for a man whose last partner is currently six feet under after giving drunk road head. Never knew you had that in you."

The only reason I'm not throwing my untouched glass of wine in his face is because while he was spewing his vile words, I noticed his tiny pupils and the continuous flow of sweat curling around his hairline.

Looks like the women he sleeps with aren't the only ones who dabble in drugs.

He's clearly high and desperate. And while I would love nothing more than to publicly humiliate this man and shred any chance he has of being on the ballot this fall, I am also well-versed in true crime and do not need to be looking over my shoulder for the foreseeable future, waiting for him to jump out from every corner.

Instead, I level him with a glare that should set him on fire as I speak calmly. "Now that you're done rambling, allow me to inform you of how"—I point between the two of us—"this is going to go."

His eyes narrow, but I carry on. "You are going to leave me, and the ones I love, alone. You will keep my name out of your mouth and try to salvage whatever votes you think you may have after making a total ass of yourself by publicly declaring that we were still engaged, and in return, I will make sure my brother doesn't bury you in legal fees and my man doesn't get his hands around your neck. Sound like a deal?" I add cheerily before standing up and walking straight to the exit.

To no one's surprise, there is a small crowd of paparazzi waiting out front. God, this is getting old.

And like the show pony he is, Damien steps out right behind me, smiling for the cameras as if we're walking out together. The camera flashes are incessant, and working in media for the Monarchs, I know how easily it could be to misinterpret a moment captured on film alone. It's why I love working the Hot Mic'd segment, because it gives my players a chance to show off their personalities and who they really are behind the jerseys.

Which is why I risk my chances at being featured on a murder podcast and take the opportunity that Damien has given me. While he has his back turned to me and is chatting it up with one photographer about wedding plans with "his lady," I smile at the cameras myself.

As I lift both of my middle fingers and aim them his way.

Chapter Forty-Six

LUKE

Fuck, my woman is hot when she's riled up.

I should be fuming at the picture on my phone, a clear sign that Daisy's ex ambushed her once again at a dinner that was meant for her to say goodbye to her father once and for all.

But I can't control the twitch in my pants when I see her petty smile while she flips the bird to that weasel.

I'm still staring at the picture, standing near Daisy's office waiting for her, when our friends approach me cautiously.

"Okay, so maybe he hasn't seen it yet?" Nick whispers.

"He has a small smile. Maybe the body is already in his trunk?" Mateo adds.

"I can hear you guys," I say as I continue to zoom in on Daisy's smile.

"He seems fine, guys. We've all got a job to do, and I need you on the field in thirty, Martinez. You too, Coach," Luisa says as Isabella giggles beside her.

Daisy interrupts whatever I was about to say as she bulldozes straight into my arms. She backs away before I'm able to wrap myself around her and ask her if she's okay.

"I know you all saw the photos. Can you believe that I was engaged to that guy? Like seriously." She fake gags and we all widen our eyes. "Could none of you have staged an intervention or something? I probably would have provided the snacks myself."

"Well," Nick hedges. "Some may say we did try to warn you."

She raises her hand to stop him. "No one likes an 'I told you so', bro. So save it."

"Whoa," Luisa and Isa say in unison as Mateo stares in astonishment.

"Daisy girl, you good?" I ask in a teasing tone.

Her eyes glare subtly. "Oh yeah, fine and dandy. Anyone else want to ask any more dumb questions, or just my insanely hot boyfriend over here?"

"Uh, Daisy. Maybe we should go up to the suites and cool down for a bit," Isabella suggests.

But I have other thoughts in mind. Filthy ones, in fact.

"Actually, Daze. Come to think of it, I probably should mention that I forgot to bring the cookies you baked for the players last night. You know, the ones you reminded me repeatedly not to leave behind before I left? Yeah, those."

She turns slowly in my direction. And if I weren't so turned on by her attitude, I would be terrified by the look she gives me before she stands face-to-chest with me. "Are you kidding me? Luke! I told you no less than a hundred times that those were my 'good luck' cookies for the team. You know how Vega needs his sugar fix before a game to really get him going. Ugh!"

"Okay, Daisy, maybe we should—" I interrupt Luisa because I am far from done with my girl.

"Well, in all honesty, I probably ate most of them before leaving the house. That seems about right. But it's no big deal.

It's not like baseball players are superstitious about these kinds of things during big games or whatever."

I swear her head almost spins as she lays into me. I nod seriously, taking the verbal ass beating as our friends stare on in horror. When Daisy looks down to pull her phone out of her purse—to see if she can get freshly baked cookies delivered to the team in time—I meet their worried gazes and wink while keeping my serious expression.

They all muffle their laughter as they slowly walk away.

Because now they're well aware, as I stand before my gorgeous five-foot-five Dominican girlfriend, getting read to absolute filth, that I'm exactly where I want to be.

Chapter Forty-Seven
LUKE

"Wait, so the cookies were in your office all along?"

Daisy steps behind my desk, unknowingly sealing her fate.

"Daisy, you made quite a scene out there, laying into me in front of all our friends," I drawl lazily, causing her to whip her head in my direction and drop the cookies back onto the bookshelf where she found them.

"B-but you were egging me on. You knew you had the cookies and you—"

I tsk. "Excuses, excuses. I have a big game tonight, Daze. And I have to keep my head screwed on straight. But now I can't do that. You know why? Because all I can think about is bending you over my desk and giving you a railing in return for how you behaved upstairs."

Her eyes widen as they look down at the erection straining my pants, then back up to my devious face.

She clears her throat. "You're a big boy. I'm sure you can multitask. I mean, I do every time you're on the field and I need to be focused on my own work. Because it's downright pornographic when you lean against the dugout ledge, with your ass in those baseball pants on full display. Or how you flip your baseball hat backward and set my ovaries on fire. God, even when you spit, I envy the ground it lands on." She finishes on a pant, and I know I've got her.

I round my desk, caging her in. "Envy, huh? Then let's rectify that right now."

Her eyes are hooded, lust bleeding out of her pores. "Oh yeah? And how do you suggest we do that?"

I smile wickedly as I respond. "On your knees."

Her eyes nervously dart around the room, fully aware that we are in my office and that a player might knock on my door at any moment.

My locked door, but she doesn't know that.

Which makes the sight of her slowly dropping to her knees before me almost buckle my own.

I take a seat in my oversized chair, like a king on a throne, as my queen holds me captive. She wordlessly unbuttons and unzips my pants, releasing my hard cock so it bobs heavily before her face.

She places her hands on my thighs, waiting for further instruction, as if the precum leaking out of my tip wasn't a big enough hint. She smirks, seeing the look of desperation on my face.

How sad I'll have to wipe it clean off her face as I take over and finally give in to what she's been asking me for since the first time I laid my hands on her body.

"You think you're cute right now, with this little innocent act?" I laugh deviously as I take her mane of curls and wrap it around my fist twice, tilting her head back when I'm satisfied with my grip. I give it a little tug and relish the small moan she rewards me with. "Remember all the times you've begged me to fuck you like I planned on breaking you?" She bites her lip as she nods, eyes so wide she won't miss the promise in my words. "Keep that in mind during the next few minutes when you're choking on my cock as I fuck your face. Now go ahead, show me how much you love sucking my dick, Daisy girl."

For a split second I worry that I've taken our little game too far with my words.

But as she attempts to take all of me into her mouth, I'm assured that this is exactly what my girl is after. She runs her tongue over the thick vein on the side of my cock before twirling her tongue over the tip of my dick and sucking. Hard. I use my grip on her and push her down my lap, causing us both to moan.

"That's it. Just like that."

She hums as she continues to bob up and down my dick. But I said I wasn't going to be gentle, and I always keep my promises.

I push her farther down and keep her there for a few seconds before bringing her back up. Then do it again.

"You can take more of me, Daisy. Breathe through your nose and open the back of your throat. Yes, you're doing so good," I hiss. "You're such a quick learner. I know you can deep throat me. Take a little bit more. Here, I'll even help you out," I lift my hips upward as my hand pushes her down and she gags, the feeling sending a zap down my spine as my balls tighten. Fuck, I'm not going to last much longer.

I keep a steady pace, her nose almost brushing my pelvis when I bring her down. And this time, when I do, I give her further instructions. "Keep breathing, baby. Relax your throat, just like that," I wait as she follows my directions beautifully. "Now swallow," she does, and I lift my hips up an extra inch until she's taken my entire cock. Fuck. I'm going to come, but I need her to follow one more instruction before I do. "I'm going to come, and you're not going to swallow." Her tear-stricken eyes look up at me in confusion as I continue. "I want you to keep it in your mouth and show it to me like a good girl, got it?"

She nods faintly, and I can no longer hold off. My release pulses into her mouth mercilessly. She uses her hands until she milks me dry and I collapse back into the chair.

And although I just had the best blow job of my entire life, I have a job to do myself and can't linger in my blissed-out state.

While keeping my grip in her hair, I order, "Open your mouth and show me."

She opens her mouth slowly, trying to keep my release from spilling over her lips.

"Wider," I demand.

She opens up more, and the sight has my dick jolting back to life.

I lean over her, tilting her head back as I rasp, "This what you were after? Then here you go."

I don't give her a chance to respond as I pucker my lips and spit into her open, cum soaked mouth.

Her eyes flare with a mixture of arousal and surprise. I use my free hand to close her jaw, then wrap it around her delicate neck. "Now. Swallow me. Every last drop."

And she does, like the good girl I know her to be.

Chapter Forty-Eight

DAISY

Holy Fuck.

That is the hottest thing I have ever experienced in my life.

And I've been fucking Luke Weston for over a month, so that says a lot.

He continues to tower over me, hand in my hair, as I wipe the corners of my mouth clean.

I love when he praises me.

But this? I think I just discovered I have a degradation kink too. Because fuck, he has me wanting to act like his little whore until the end of time.

While he was the one in the chair, looking down on me as he pushed me to the limits I never knew existed, I was the one who felt empowered, knowing how affected he was by me, knowing I had the power to completely undo him.

And by the look of awe on his face, I did.

This is exactly what I've been asking for. To be pushed out of my comfort zone so I can explore my sexual desires thoroughly. I've read enough romance books to know that there is so much I haven't dabbled in, and while some things are a clear no-go for me, there are many fantasies that I have yet to try but can only do them if Luke feels comfortable enough to fuck me like he disrespects me.

I wiggle on my knees, searching to ease the ache he's put there, when Luke tsks from above me. "And here I thought I'd fucked the brat out of you. What is it, Daisy? Did deep-throating my cock and swallowing my cum and spit make you wet?"

I sigh and shrug, because if he wants a brat, I'll show him a brat. "Don't be lazy about it, Coach. Why don't you come and see for yourself if you wanna know so bad?"

Oh shit. Maybe I should have thought that through.

His chair falls behind him as he stands, hauling me up with him by my armpits. Then I'm spun around and bent over his desk quicker than humanly possible.

But Luke is far more animal than human right now, so I guess that tracks.

My pants are ripped down my legs. His cleated shoes kick between my feet, forcing me to widen my very exposed stance.

Yes, I think to myself. I love it when Luke eats me from behind. It feels much more forbidden when he does it this way. Especially when he runs his tongue up my tight back hole, creating an incredible sensation I pretend to be surprised by every time he does.

But instead of his skillful tongue running down my slit, I feel a brisk gust of wind before his hand smacks down on my ass.

Chapter Forty-Nine
LUKE

"Ow!"

"That wasn't hard, Daisy. But this one will be." I smack her other cheek, and I wasn't lying when I said this one would sting more. Yet she's moaning and tilting her ass up higher for me.

My heart rattles at the idea of potentially harming Daisy. But if this is what she wants, then you bet your ass I'm going to give it to her while enjoying every fucking second of it.

I chuckle darkly behind her. "You've gotta be fucking kidding me. This is supposed to be your punishment, Daze. Yet you're begging for more, aren't you?"

"Yes," she says needily, and I reward her with two more spanks.

I hum. "But you do have a point. How careless of me not to check for myself how wet you are."

With that, my thumbs spread her open, smearing her wetness from her opening to her clit and back. "You're fucking soaked. Is that from choking on my cock and swallowing my cum and spit, or me reddening your ass, Daisy girl?"

"All of it." She wiggles her ass in my hands, hoping I take pity on her and relieve that ache that must be driving her wild.

I growl behind her. "And would you look at that?" One thumb circles her clit firmly. "Your clit is so fucking needy and swollen, Daze. Is this where it aches? Need me to take care of this little problem for you? Or should I pull your pants back up and leave you how I found you? Bratty and unsatisfied."

"Please, Luke. I-I'm sorry. I won't be a brat again. I'll be a very, very good girl," she pleads, but I lean to my side and spot the smirk on her face as she pants on my desk. She catches me watching her. "Well, maybe I'll try? That's the best I can offer." She winks at me, and I spring into action.

"You don't deserve this, but you're dripping all over my desk, causing such an inconvenience. I have no choice but to…"

"*Fuck.*" She bucks as my hands keep her ass cheeks in place and I start to tongue fuck her from behind.

I continue my assault, breaking momentarily to taunt her. "Next time you make a mess like this, you're licking your cum off my desk yourself. Especially since you did such a good job swallowing mine. Sound fair, Daze?" I don't let her answer as I thrust two fingers into her tight pussy. They tighten around me, threatening to pull me in.

Fuck that.

My cock has been hard as a rock and ready to go again since the second I had her bent over my desk bare.

She whines as I stand and take a look at my handiwork. Daisy bent over and spread open for me on my desk, her hair wildly tossed over her shoulder as she looks back at me, eyes pleading for mercy.

I don't wait another second.

My hands are on her hips, not having to line up my cock because it knows exactly where to go the second my tip slides along her entrance. With one hard thrust, I push in to the hilt, hitting that spot that has her pussy pulsing around my cock.

"Luke!" She screams my name. Long gone is the Daisy who would be mortified if anyone knew what we were up to in my office, and in her place is the woman who can't think beyond her next orgasm.

I set a punishing pace, railing into her, giving her that cock she was so hell-bent on having. My girl wanted it rough, and that's exactly how I'm giving it to her. I will be providing an absurd amount of aftercare later, but right now my only goal is to fuck my girl exactly how she wants it. If she isn't walking funny by the time I'm done with her, then I haven't done my job properly.

With that in mind, I push even harder, the legs of my desk scraping along the floor each time I do.

"Oh my fucking God, Luke. Yes, yes, right there. Don't stop. Please don't—"

I barely have enough time to bend over her body and clasp my hand over her screaming mouth before she comes. In this position, I'm seated even deeper, enjoying the way her plump ass bounces against my brutal thrusts. Her orgasm continues to pummel over her, and her pussy squeezes me so tight I don't stand a chance.

I come inside her on a roar that I have to muffle by biting the crook of her neck.

She screams when I do and continues to squeeze my cock as she milks me dry.

I pant as my tongue lashes out softly, running over my teeth marks, and send a silent thank you to the universe that I didn't break her skin.

I stand and slowly pull out of her, causing us both to wince.

"Are you okay?" I ask quickly, stepping to the side as I brush some loose strands out of her face.

She takes a few deep breaths, but I'm already relaxing at the sight of her blissed-out face. "Oh, I'm more than all right. I think I'm finally on board with you quitting your job if it means we can stay at my place and do that all day long."

I chuckle as I lean back and take her in.

Fuck, I'm going to need her to cover up soon or I'm really going to have to come up with an excuse to miss our big game.

"You sure you're not sore?" I ask as my fingers circle around the hole that has my cum slowly leaking out of it.

She tenses, then laughs. "Oh, I'm fucking sore all right. Even athletes need rest days, right, Coach? But then I'll be back at it. Mark my words." She ends her statement with a low moan as I slowly continue to use my cum to play with her clit.

"Is that right?" It's not lost on me that she came from penetrative sex alone. Something she swore her body was incapable of doing until I got my hands on her. And somehow it leaves me feeling like her clit deserves a little TLC.

"L-Luke."

"Sorry, I'm busy. Like you said, athletes need rest days, but their coaches also know when to push them further, to achieve their full potential, isn't that right?"

My two fingers easily slip into her cum-soaked pussy and rub back over her clit at a torturously slow pace.

"O-oh. That feels, so, so, so good."

"Hmm, you mean this?" I press down on her clit, rubbing tight, firm circles, causing her to clench and spill more of our cum onto my desk.

"Luke, fuck, yes. Ohmygod. Don't stop. Yes, yes, yes!" I bend over and swallow her screams with a kiss, then feel her unravel beneath my fingers and tongue, savoring every little breath that comes out of her sweet mouth.

"That's my girl," I breathe over her lips before I kiss her gently once more.

Then I straighten, finally tucking my semi hard cock back into my pants, and take a seat in my chair while I catch my breath.

Daisy pushes to stand and turns to me with a dopey smile, her pants still tugged down around her ankles.

"Now that... was something."

I smile. "You liked that, huh."

She bites her lip and nods, staring back at the desk, her cheeks flushing with color at the sight of the mess we made.

"Good," I answer, my smile turning cocky. "Because we both have to get back to our day jobs, but we seemed to have made a mess there." I raise a brow at her shy expression. Too late for that now, sweetheart. I nod my head forward as I lean back and enjoy the sight before me thoroughly. "Now come here and let me clean your pussy with my tongue, then you can show me how well you can clean up my desk with yours."

Chapter Fifty

DAISY

I can't look anyone in the eye.

If I did, I swear they'd know.

Before I left his office, and after I licked our mess off his desk while holding eye contact with the growing bulge in Luke's pants, we cleaned up and brushed our teeth in his en-suite bathroom. It was stocked with travel size options of all of my favorite products. Seems like he knew he would eventually get his way with me and stocked up appropriately.

My nipples wouldn't get the memo that sexy time was over and looked like they could poke an eye out through my top. Luckily Luke had another hoodie, one he had to buy since I officially stole his old one, and put it on me before leaving his office.

I swear he was speaking to my chest instead of me when he grumbled a "see you later." Then he pressed a quick kiss to my forehead and rearranged himself in his pants.

I asked the new intern to mic up the players for me tonight, not wanting to face anyone or get close to Luke while he's in his dugout. I swear that in the condition I'm in, I wouldn't be surprised if my body bent over the second I saw him next. Because what we just did... wow.

But I actually do have a job to do, and I need to start acting like it.

I go up to my office after checking in with my staff.

Tonight, Martinez, Middlebrooks, and Vega will be participating in Hot Mic'd. This will be a special episode because if the first few innings go well, our streaming channel, Monarchs Live, has given us the go-ahead to broadcast the visual and audio recordings of our players in real time. This way, those at home can enjoy their side banter during commercial breaks, and fans in the stands can listen in via our mobile app.

Luke will also be mic'd tonight, but as usual, I'm the only one who will have access to his channel.

The guys will be instructed to switch their mic packs to Monarchs one if we've been green lit to go live by the network. Until then, they all have their own channels that my team and I can jump between, picking out the funniest snippets to put up on our social media pages.

I look out of my office window and down to the stadium. It's our first warm night game and I can feel that summer is just around the corner.

The retractable stadium ceiling is officially open, the bright lights shining beneath the dark sky and the seats are already filling with the rowdiest baseball fans New York has to offer.

My cell phone vibrates on my desk and a notification appears.

ISABELLA:

> Coach is on the field, which means you're done boning, so get down to the suite immediately so we can watch our team make history tonight!

LUISA:

> Yes please. Someone needs to drink these ciders Coach insisted we stock in here, so hurry along before I start offering them up to the fans below us to make room for the Presidente beer YOUR tio Javier somehow snuck in… even though we have our own *facepalm emoji*

I laugh to myself as she refers to her dad as my uncle, something he and the rest of the parents of the group have come to expect from Isa and me as well. Tiás and tíos, little cousins, and family friends. I marvel at the little family I've been able to find here within the Monarchs organization.

It makes the hurt of letting go of the family I thought I was supposed to have sting a little bit less, and makes it easier to leave them in the past, where they belong.

ME:

> I'll be right down. Let's go cheer on our guys!

I pull the hoodie in closer, enveloping myself in Luke's delicious scent once more before I grab my phone and headset and head out to enjoy the night with my real family.

Chapter Fifty-One

LUKE

"Where's Daisy?"

The poor intern before me almost flies out of his shoes at my rough tone.

"Sh-she sent me down here to mic you guys up. Said she'd be supervising from one of the suites?" he rambles.

I nod, but before he tries to put his hand under my shirt, I take the microphone wire from him and set myself up quickly. It's second nature by now. It's usually Daisy's hands skimming down my collar and back, but it seems like the little minx has gone into hiding after our little sexcapades. Smart girl.

I look above the dugout to the suite that belongs to Nick and Luisa and spot her immediately. Waving her dainty fingers my way with a secret smile. I narrow my eyes slightly, letting her know I would have preferred to have her down here setting me up. It was probably the right call, however, given how I can't shake the visual of her spread over my desk and need to focus on the game.

Though I must say I'm shocked mostly by the person standing next to her, sipping on a beer.

My sister.

I never thought I'd see the day. I have too many questions I want to ask her, but the new guy before me seems to need my attention again.

"Channel one is Monarchs Live. The players are to switch to that one only if Daisy makes the call. They all know what channels to stay on in the meantime, and you're channel seven."

"And only Daisy has access to that channel, correct?"

He nods profusely. "Yes, sir. I mean Coach."

I glance back up at Daisy with an unimpressed look, and I can't tell from all the way down here, but I swear I see her mouth "be nice."

I shake my head and say a quick thank you to the intern before sending him on his way.

I take a look out at the field. My guys are out there wrapping up their stretches, trying to contain that excited energy that comes along with games like this. We may be barely into the first half of the season, but it feels like a championship game given what's on the line. A chance to make history.

The crowds are eager and ready for a good game, talking trash among their seat neighbors while eating supersized snacks.

The energy is tangible, and I allow myself a moment to close my eyes and thank the universe for allowing me to find my way back to the sport I've loved since I was a child. To be able to play and manage a team at this level is nothing short of a blessing. Just like the woman who keeps dancing along to the Aventura song while wearing my hoodie as if she wasn't the one putting in requests to the DJ responsible for our game tunes.

Her hair flies around her, only keeping out of her face due to the headset placed over her wild curls, smile wide and hips shaking.

My Daisy is free, and I'm itching for our next batch of off days so I can take her back up to the cabin so we can continue what we started up there. And I can show her the ideas that have been taking root in my mind. I just hope it doesn't scare her off.

"Big game today. Promised my wife if I get a shot of you smiling, I'll retire early." Our team photographer, Tom, comes to stand by me, wiggling his camera by his side.

I chuckle to myself. The guy never gives up hope.

Luisa and Daisy have mentioned wanting Valentina to join the Monarchs staff as our new photographer, but I never gave it any thought. Now seeing her here, standing in the stadium I swore I'd never see her in, has me thinking Tom's days may be numbered.

I tap him on the shoulder, then steady him when it seems like he might fall over. "Easy there, Tom. Wouldn't want your wife to be mad at me for not letting you go home in one piece. Especially after you tell her you can retire after tonight."

"Wait, what? Seriously? You're going to give me the shot everyone's been clamoring for?" His body shakes with excitement.

I'm called onto the field for the national anthem and simply nod as I pass him. "I'll signal you when it's time to come over. Hopefully it's when our team takes the win." I wink then turn back to line up with my team.

The anthems are sung, and before I know it, I'm back in my spot in the dugout. I'm busy talking to the pitching coach when an announcement snaps my attention back to the field, and I see red.

"And as a surprise to the Monarchs family, New York Senator Damien Fischer is here to throw the ceremonial first pitch."

Chapter Fifty-Two

DAISY

"You can all stop looking at me weird. I'm fine."

Luisa, Isa, and I exchange looks of concern, but Valentina carries on as if we're not deliberately staring at her.

While I was on my way down to the suite, I got a text from Valentina asking if it was too late to snag an invite to the game. I was surprised to hear that she wanted to come after Luke told me she had turned down every invite he'd sent her way. Even more so when she told me she was standing outside the stadium gates.

I had security track her down and send her my way immediately.

She looked more than a little rattled when she entered the suite with me, but I guess there's nothing that a stadium hot dog and a cold beer can't fix.

"I think I want another hot dog. Is it just me, or does free food taste better?" she asks as she stands to make her way to the catering station that's been laid out for us.

"No, you're onto something. No offense to the staff that cook for us, but why else would I be downing this much food if it weren't for the fact that I knew it'd be going to waste otherwise?" Isa states as she balances three snacks on her thighs.

Luisa shakes her head. "We stagger out the plates in batches, and whatever isn't consumed by the suite guests at the end of the night, the kitchen packages up and sends over to the local homeless shelter. It's impossible to have no waste with over seventy thousand consumers a game, but we try our best to not go overboard and make sure to feed those in need no matter what."

I sigh. "My hero."

Luisa rolls her eyes but knocks shoulders with me as she does.

"So you saw your ex tonight. How did my brother take that?" Valentina says salaciously, taking a bite of her hotdog.

I laugh nervously, cheeks reddening at the memory of what I experienced at the hands of her brother.

"Ew, never mind. I don't wanna know. To think I thought you had rolled your ankle or something because you were walking funny." Valentina shudders.

"*Anyway*, I think I need to focus on the voices in my head." I point to my headset as I blush from head to toe.

"Is that why you made me get up and get you a cider instead of getting it for yourself?" Isa cackles from where she sits behind me, and I shake my head.

"Well, at least there's no misunderstandings after you gave your ex the one finger salute. With two hands. A classy touch if you ask me," Valentina says before taking another large bite.

"I'm glad I finally put that behind me, and that I'll never have to see him again."

My team starts talking over themselves at a rapid pace, and I wince, lowering my headset volume. "Guys, settle down. I can't hear you all at once."

Valentina starts to choke next to me, eyes wide as she stares down at the field.

I start smacking her back, trying to remember if I know the right way to do the Heimlich, when she swats my hand away and forces herself to swallow. "Daisy, what the fuck is your ex doing down there?" She points down at the field.

My girls and I stand, snacks and drinks discarded at our feet as I stare down in horror at the sight before me.

Damien's jogging up to the pitcher's mound, waving at the crowd with a wide smile on his face and a mic in hand.

"How the hell did he get on my damn field?" My brother bursts into the suite, but I pay him no mind as he and Luisa take off with security in tow.

Oh God. Luke is also down there. Fuck.

He's standing by the dugout. His back is to me, but the way Mateo and Ace are each holding on to his shoulders, tells me he must be raging.

God, if we have another fight on this field, I swear the baseball commissioner is going to take action against us. We survived the scandal with Mateo and Isa's ex, but players get into scuffles all the time. Luke is an employee representing the Monarchs organization, and I don't think they'd take too kindly to broadcasting him wringing a senator's neck on live TV.

I jolt when I realize I don't have to wonder what they're talking about. I switch over to Luke's channel and hear Mateo yelling exactly that into his ear. Next thing I know, they're easing him back down into the dugout and out of my sight.

But I still have ears on him.

LUKE: I swear to God. If that man tries to get anywhere near Daisy, I will end him with my bare hands.

ACE: And we'll help you hide the body. But right now, we need you to keep your hands clean and trust that the big boss is handling it. I don't think Nick is exactly thrilled that his little sister's ex is in his stadium, uninvited.

MATEO: Exactly. And trust me, Coach, men like that are dying to find a reason for you to swing on them so they can sue you to kingdom come. Think of what that process will do to your woman. He'll get pity from the public and end up being our goddamn governor, while you're blacklisted in this industry. Nah, forget that. Instead, you've gotta play this smart. Hit him where it hurts.

LUKE: Kidney shot or are we talking straight to his tiny cock?

MATEO: His ego. Think about it. Daisy bruised his ego hard with what she did earlier. He's here trying to save face. But he's on our home turf. This is our field and we aren't going to let him skate by.

ACE: Yeah! Wait, so do we have a plan, or do we still have a game to play? I'm fine either way, just need to know where we're going with this.

SILENCE.

ACE: No, I still ride at dawn for you guys, but I'm... you know what? You guys come up with the plan, and I'll slide myself in wherever you need me, cool?

LUKE: Oh, I got a plan, all right. But for this, I'm going to need my girl. Daisy, I know you're listening. Stop freaking out. I know exactly what I'm about to do and you're going to help me do it. So get your sweet ass down to my dugout. Now.

Chapter Fifty-Three

LUKE

I'm pacing back and forth like a caged animal.

Tightening the bill of my baseball hat so my hands have something to do.

This is the first time I've been close to Damien since I helped Daisy run away from her wedding, and the knowledge that he is within reach is testing my restraints on civility.

He's talking with the intern I saw earlier. And I can tell from here that the poor kid is in way over his head. He's clutching a handheld microphone in his hands like his life depends on it. But Damien manages to slip it out of his hold with a flourish and a smile.

"Good evening, New York City! What an honor to be in your presence tonight."

The crowd cheers. I imagine because New Yorkers are naturally inclined to clap whenever their city is celebrated and not because they give a damn about this idiot.

I look up at the crowd and can see looks of confusion mixed with shocked smiles. I'm sure many of them have seen the photos of him and Daisy and those that haven't are about to be shown by their seat neighbor.

"I know this may come as a surprise to most, seeing me here tonight, especially if you've seen a colorful photo that's been floating around social media for the past few hours." He chuckles, but his eyes lack sincerity. "But I'm not here tonight as the man who is in the running to become the next governor of the greatest state in America. No, tonight I am here as a man who is trying his damnedest to get his woman back. A woman who is an integral part of the Monarchs family. My Daisy." He places a hand across his chest.

Daisy barrels into the dugout, eyes searching for me, and I'm on her in an instant. "Are you okay? Did he try to find you first? What do you need—"

"I need Martinez to throw a ninety-nine-mile-per-hour fastball at his head. Maybe then he'll get it through his thick skull that I'm done playing his games."

"That's a plan I can get behind. Just say the word, Coach." Mateo sidles up next to me, eyes fixed on the field.

Damien is still yapping, earning a few *aww*s from the crowd. The fucker thinks he's got everyone fooled.

But his first mistake was thinking he could play with Daisy's heart.

His second was fucking with what's mine.

And I think it's about damn time he gets what's coming to him.

I turn to Daisy, careful to keep an appropriate distance in case she's not ready for another headline, this time with me being added to the mix. "Daisy, do you trust me?"

Her eyes soften as she places a hand on my chest, knowing full well that there are cameras on her, trying to capture her reaction to Damien. "With my life. So what do you have cooking in that mind of yours, Coach?" She smirks, and the sight has me dying to pull her into my arms and lay one on her.

Just not yet.

I wink down at her before I speak loud enough for my guys to hear. "This is a ball game, after all, and I think it's about time we all have a little fun. What do you say, boys?" I shout the last part.

A chorus of *fuck yeah*s vibrate inside the dugout, causing more than a few heads to look our way. Damien's head turns as well, eyes locking on Daisy as he continues to spew more nonsense that eats up airtime when we still have a game to play.

I look at my team and shout out orders. "Martinez, get that man a ball. If he's so hell-bent on throwing the first pitch, let's give him what he wants."

He rubs his hands together. "Yo, Torres, get your ass over here," he calls out to our catcher. "What do you think about fucking with that asshole over there?"

Torres comes to stand by us. "About fucking time. I was going gray waiting for you guys to make a damn move."

"Daisy, last chance." I look down at her excited eyes. "I can end this once and for all, but I gotta warn ya. Life is gonna get a little crazier after what I have planned."

She steps closer, unwittingly close to unraveling my plans with the eager smile on her face. A smile I want to press my lips against. "If it's a life with you, then I'm all for it."

That's all the confirmation I need to move forward.

There's only one thing left to do before we kick off what I hope to be the demise of Senator Damien Fischer.

"Martinez, Vega, and Middlebrooks." I meet Daisy's trusting eyes and smile as I shout, "Move over to channel one, we're going live."

Chapter Fifty-Four

DAISY

I'M LIKE A KID on Christmas morning.

I should be mortified that Luke and the guys moved over to live streaming their conversation. Should be digging a hole to hide after he told Tom to have a camera on him at all times, along with the other mic'd players.

But if this all goes to hell after Luke is done with whatever devious plans he's concocted in his head, it'll be worth it.

Because the sight before me is one that will be cemented in my mind, and on the internet, for all of time.

Mateo steps up to the pitcher's mound. *His* pitcher's mound.

Interrupting Damien's ramblings that have honestly gone off the rails at this point. Even if Mateo hadn't interrupted him, I'm sure there are some people scratching their heads, wondering what the hell he is up to.

I quickly texted Luisa and Nick to stand down and let this play out, that Luke had it handled.

Nick's question about whether EMTs should be sent down to the field almost made me chuckle, but my eyes are fixed on my ex, who's starting to break a sweat as Mateo towers over him.

Mateo smiles and holds out a baseball, and Damien releases a deep sigh and returns the smile.

But as he goes to reach for it, Mateo drops it and mouths "oops" as he shrugs and smiles up at the laughing crowd. He returns to the dugout without a backward glance.

Damien's smile falters, and his eyes find mine in the dugout, hardening momentarily before fixing his mask back into place.

If he thought he could fuck with the Monarchs family, the one he so dismissively spoke about in my presence during our relationship, then he's about to become a case study for "fuck around and find out."

He bends over quickly, scowling over his shoulder as Tom flashes his camera at the unflattering angle of him bent over and straightens.

Torres punches inside his mitt, signaling where Damien needs to throw the ball. Before Damien can take his stance, Torres starts to fuck with him, by walking closer and closer to him, miming where he should stand, assuming Damien can't throw the ball far.

The crowd erupts into laughter as he continues to do this for far longer than socially appropriate.

Behind me, Vega and Middlebrooks hold court with the rest of the players. Talking about things they've heard about Damien. Things I've shared with Ace and have given him the go-ahead to speak on. After emphasizing to death that he needs to say the word "allegedly" to make sure he doesn't land himself in hot water.

Apparently, he took that advice to heart, because I can hear him talking, "So, allegedly, and this is what the streets are saying, so if I'm off base here, y'all take it up with the streets, okay? But yeah. So allegedly, that Damien dude was cheating on Daisy the entire time they were together. Can you believe he would dog on our sweet little Daisy like that? Anyway, that's not even all. Apparently, I mean, allegedly, this dude got a thing for nose candy." He sniffs as he rubs his nose, acting as though there isn't a camera pointed one foot away from him. "And, uh, let's just say that allegedly, all those family values he drones on about are a cover for his real lifestyle. But that's just what I've heard." He raises his hands up innocently. "And the streets don't lie. Allegedly." He discreetly sends a smile my way.

"Nah, I've heard that too. Allegedly," Vega starts, and it takes everything in me to not fall over laughing.

Torres finally stops torturing Damien and squats down to take position to catch the ball. Damien looks flushed at this point, probably dying to get off the field and reevaluate his strategy.

He throws the ball, with terrible form if I may say so, and as it approaches Torres, he stands quickly and ducks to the side while exaggerating a yawn. Throwing the crowd into another fit of cheers.

I knew the showmen in these boys had no bounds, but damn are they good at fucking with my ex.

Luke turns my way. He's been standing in front of the dugout this whole time, baseball hat pulled low, eyes on his prey. And if I weren't so damn turned on at the sight of Luke's broad shoulders and the arms crossed over his chest, I might find it in myself to be terrified for Damien.

His piercing blue eyes find mine, and he calls me over silently.

The players go quiet behind me as I make my way toward Luke, the crowd shouting my name, staring back between Damien and me.

If they think they're about to get a *Never Been Kissed* movie moment with my ex, they are sorely mistaken.

"You ready?" Luke asks lowly.

I nod, even though I have no clue what I'm supposed to do next.

"Tom," he shouts and our team photographer jogs over. I swear the man has hearts in his eyes. Me too, buddy. Me too. "We're about to make your wife very happy. Now you keep your camera at the ready and on me."

Tom nods eagerly. "You got it! I'm ready to go. I can't believe I'm going to capture your first smile at Monarchs stadium."

He gets up close to Luke, causing Luke to put a hand on his shoulder to keep him in place. "Trust me, Tom, you're going to get more than a smile." Luke looks at me briefly before he's back talking to Tom. "Just keep a little distance, yeah? Think you can do that for me?"

Tom takes two large steps back. "Yeah. Yes. Of course. You got it."

Luke shakes his head, and then those eyes are back on me.

He slips a hand into his back pocket and pulls out two daisies.

I grin like a fool. "You had those in your back pocket this whole time, Coach?"

"Brought a bouquet for you but got distracted earlier." I blush as he steps forward, tucking my hair behind my ear and sliding one daisy there before placing the other in my hand. He leans forward, whispering in my ear. "I'm really going to enjoy what comes next. Hope you're not feeling too shy, because the spotlight is about to come your way, Daze."

My eyes widen as my stomach drops. Oh, fuck. What have I just agreed to?

Chapter Fifty-Five

LUKE

Sporting a glare that could kill, I readjust my hat as I make my way to the man who's lucky he's about to walk out of here on his own two legs.

He sees me coming and staggers back. Until he realizes that all eyes are on us and that he's safe. Mostly. Then he smiles smugly.

This fucker.

I don't stop for pleasantries as I smoothly take the mic out of his hand and smack his back hard enough to send him flying forward a few steps before he gets his footing.

"Well, that was sure... Something," I say into the mic. From this angle I can see that half the crowd is staring at their phones, most likely tuning into our live broadcast.

Who knew that Middlebrooks's and Vega's chisme sessions that usually have them looking like two cackling hens would actually come in handy some day?

"David, why don't you stand to the side over here and watch how it's done?" My hand guides him harshly off the mound.

"It's Damien," he mutters as Martinez and Torres silently act as bodyguards, walking him to the opposite side of our dugout, at a safe distance from Daisy.

I turn my attention back to the packed stadium. "I think we can do better than that last pitch, don't you?" I aim the mic at the crowd, and they scream their agreement.

I nod. "All right, then. Good thing I have someone in mind." My eyes twinkle with mischief as they meet Daisy's and her jaw drops. "Daisy girl, why don't you come up here and show that sorry excuse of an ex of yours how it's done?" I lift a teasing brow, and the crowd goes mental at my dig.

Daisy starts to walk over, and she seems genuinely shocked at the response she garners from the fans. They're cheering her name, waving wildly, trying to get her to look their way. And I get it, because I know how it feels to want Daisy's attention.

I force myself to take a few steps to the side as Middlebrooks catches up to Daisy and hands her a ball.

I know how nerve-racking it can be to stand in a stadium with thousands of eyes on you, but my girl's got this in the bag. She's been down here plenty during practice with the guys, and I've seen her curveball. It's solid.

Torres takes his place not too far away but close enough to make the throw impressive. He's definitely farther back than he was for dickface who's looking up at us with barely restrained anger.

"All right, Daze. Show them what you got," I say into the microphone.

She sends a soft smile my way, then she gets her head in the game. Placing her feet in a perfect pitcher's stance, she narrows her eyes at Torres. God, she's so fucking adorable. It's taking everything in me to stay put and wait until she's done with her pitch.

She gives Tom a little wink, which, of course, he captures effortlessly, then winds her arm back and sends the ball flying. It lands with a satisfying *umph* in Torres's mitt, and he makes a show of pulling it off and shaking out his hand.

This is the part when the catcher is supposed to run up and hand the ceremonial ball over to our guest. But Torres is a smart man and stays put when he sees me making my way toward my girl.

She's smiling from ear to ear, happiness radiating from her as she blooms under the attention.

She hasn't noticed me closing in on her yet, so I take advantage and yell out to Tom. "You ready?"

He responds by bringing his camera to his face at lightning speed.

I know I promised him a smile, but I guess he's going to have to settle for me claiming my girl in front of the entire world.

"Damn, my girlfriend looks good on my field," I say clearly into the mic in my hand as I reach her. She spins in my hold, that smile unwavering. "Here, now you're a real Monarch." I take my hat off and comb my other hand through my unruly strands, then flip the cap over and place it on her head.

She beams up at me, and I can't wait another second.

So I don't.

And for the first time, it feels as though she can read *my* thoughts. She seamlessly wraps her arms around my neck at the same time I circle my arms around her waist. I pull her into me, eyes searching hers, before she closes them.

And I lean down and kiss her.

The noise level reaches a fever pitch before it all seems to melt away, and all I can focus on is Daisy's lips on mine. Her body melding against my own until it feels like we're one.

She breaks our kiss when she starts to giggle nervously, seemingly more aware of our surroundings than I am capable of at a time like this.

It's satisfying to lift my gaze and see Damien being escorted off the field by a team of security guards. It may be a bit overkill, but my face must match Nick's satisfied look as Daisy's ex is being manhandled off the field, accompanied by the roar of cheers from the crowd.

I toss the handheld mic onto the ground, no longer needing the stadium's attention, and cradle Daisy's face in my hands after straightening the flower so it's still safely tucked behind her ear.

"I love you, Daisy. Every part of me belongs to you and I don't care who knows it."

She pointedly looks at the small mic still clipped onto me, as if I don't know that I'm still live streaming. So I look down at it and repeat it one more time.

She nods thoughtfully, biting her bottom lip. "People are gonna think you're obsessed with me or something."

"Good. So when I show up with your name tatted on my ring finger, I suppose they won't bat an eye."

"Wh-what?"

"You heard me. Hell, the whole nation heard me." I chuckle as I kiss the surprised look off her face. "Don't worry, it goes both ways. Because I'll tatt your name, but you'll be changing yours. I do like the ring of Daisy Weston, but all in due time."

"Y-you—Did you ju—Did we... Wow, words. Can I remember how to use them?" She laughs to herself.

I hum, pointedly ignoring her mini freak-out session. Because if it wasn't apparent before just how serious I am about her, this should leave no doubt. "You think anyone is listening to the live stream?" I ask as I quickly glance out to the stands.

She rolls her eyes playfully as she leans into the mic inside my jersey and speaks. "Are you guys ready to get this game started and get our boys on the field?"

Two seconds later, the crowd starts chanting "yes."

She laughs. "Looks like we got your answer, Coach." She raises onto her tiptoes and presses a kiss to my cheek. My smile is immediate, and when I lift my gaze, it lands right on a flashing camera.

Looks like Tom did get that smile shot after all.

Chapter Fifty-Six
DAISY

We barely make it through the front door of my apartment in one piece.

The Monarchs won, forever cementing their place in MLB history.

And while I'm thrilled for the team, truly over the moon for them, my mind couldn't focus on anything but getting my man back to my place as soon as possible.

The way he reclaimed his place on the field after all these years with a smile on his face and me in his arms had me counting down the seconds until I could get him behind closed doors, having had enough camera time to last a lifetime.

He lowers me to stand on my own two feet so he can take his hoodie off me, my shirt quickly meeting the same fate.

I laugh at his look of determination. "You know, one of these days, you're going to have to take me to your lair. I'm in so deep, I think I might be okay with you having a murder room."

He releases his hold on the edge of my pants and tilts his head before nodding. "All right, let's go."

He bends, and before I know it, I'm being thrown over his shoulder. "Luke! Put me down. Where do you think we're going in my bra?" I slap his solid back.

I'm stuck somewhere between amusement and dire concern for his mental well-being if he's contemplating putting me in his truck half naked.

My door closes in front of my face, and he shuffles for a few steps, but for the most part stays put. "Luke, seriously, I was joking about a murder room. I'm sure it's probably a little butterfly collection you're a little shy about. Maybe a hundred collectible Beanie Babies? If so, you must be really loaded, because those must be worth a fortune now—"

We move, but not in the direction I was expecting. Another door closes in my face, and I realize that Luke has walked into the apartment across from mine. I must be getting lightheaded, because that can't be right.

I'm suddenly seated on a kitchen island, Luke's cautious smile on display. "Surprise?"

I shift so I can see around him and almost fall over when I see the duffel bag he uses for away games by the front door. Along with his boots and sneakers. I continue my exploration and spot a Polaroid picture of us on his refrigerator.

"Luke, how? What... When did you...?"

"I own the entire floor," he says slowly.

It takes my brain a few seconds to make sense of his words, and then they hit me like a freight train. "You're my landlord? You owned the listing?"

"No, I mean, yes. It was an old listing. I still had it in my email from when I purchased this apartment. I bought the place next door to ensure privacy. When I accepted a job with the Monarchs, I knew that meant I needed a new place to live. And in this city, it was safe to assume I wouldn't have the same kind of freedom I had grown accustomed to living up in the mountains. So I bought out the whole floor, never intending to do anything with the unit next door. Until you needed a place to live."

My mind is sluggish. Unable to decide whether I should be upset he kept this from me or kiss him silly for providing a safe haven, a place I've been able to make my own.

I realize that I'm more surprised than anything. Doesn't mean I'm going to let him off the hook so easily.

"So you already owned the entire floor when you reached out to your realtor. All you did was, what? Ask him to give me this unit with no fuss?" He hesitates, and I straighten. "Spit it out, Luke."

"That was the plan. Initially."

"Initially?"

He sighs. "Yes, but then he told me the floor below me went on the market, so…"

"Luke Weston. You did not—"

"I bought the entire floor below us."

My jaw threatens to hit the ground. "What on earth would possess you to buy two floors of some of New York's most expensive real estate?"

"Long answer? I loved hearing you talk about all your ideas for your new place, and I knew that a two-bedroom apartment wasn't going to cut it. We can turn these four units into a two-story home." My eyes widen, but he continues. "You wanted a kitchen with enough burners to cook up a Dominican feast, a dining room big enough to hold an entire baseball team, and a living area where you and your friends could hang out and talk shit about the men in your lives." He smirks, then his smile turns gentle. "You can have your own office so you can work from home when the weather is unbearable. A library to hold all of your favorite romance novels and all the covers that Isabella designs. And now that you've connected with all these people from your mom's life, I think it's a good idea to have extra guest rooms. That way, we can host them here instead of sending them off to a hotel every time they're in town."

I sniff, hoping my watery eyes don't betray me. "Could have warned me that the long answer was devastatingly sweet."

His nose brushes mine. "Wanna hear the short answer then?"

I nod as I lean more into his touch. His soft beard grazes my cheek as he whispers in my ear. "Didn't want the neighbors to hear how nicely I can make you come."

Chapter Fifty-Seven

LUKE

We're all gathered at Nick and Luisa's home for a farewell party.

Today we're saying goodbye to our guests who have come from the UK and Dominican Republic to visit Daisy and Nick.

It's been a couple of days since Daisy and I went public, and the media attention has been intense, as expected, but it's nothing we can't handle.

Her ex, on the other hand, didn't fare as well after our impromptu live stream made headlines.

In less than twenty-four hours, a flurry of stories were leaked to the media, from women who had the displeasure of sleeping with Damien while he was engaged to Daisy and the men who swore he owed them money after running up massive bills at clubs. The kind of clubs that are known for drug activity.

Needless to say, he was forced to step down. Then his name was swiftly taken off the ballot after an internal investigation was opened into how he managed his campaign funds.

Pictures of him sweaty and disheveled at Monarchs Stadium will surely haunt him for the rest of his days, and I have made peace with the fact that I may not have put him in his place physically, but I'm sure someone will when he undoubtedly ends up behind bars.

I turn to the scene before me and wonder if it's ever going to feel normal having Daisy's adoring gaze on me. She's in the kitchen, surrounded by women who are the age her mother would be if she were still around. No longer shy in their presence, she moves around the home like she owns the place and offers Luisa's mom a sample of the rice that's cooking on the stove.

They've been in the kitchen whipping up a storm all morning, even though they swore this would be casual lunch. By the look of the cluttered counter spaces, this feast could easily pass for a holiday dinner.

"Her mother would approve of you, you know," Carla says, as she comes to stand by me. When I simply stare into her knowing gaze, she carries on. "She never had any luck in the love department. Even after she got pregnant with Daisy, she knew deep down it wasn't going to work out with George." She sneers at the mention of his name. "But when it came to her children, she wanted them to find deep, pure love. She knew it would be tough for Nick, given that he grew up without a good example of what a healthy relationship should look like. Still, she hoped he would find it in him to be vulnerable and caring, and I'm glad to see that he did." She nods to Nick as he places a gentle kiss against his wife's temple. "But Daisy? She named her after the woman who starred in the biggest love story she'd ever witnessed. She prayed for her children to experience a love so grand it would stand the test of time."

She pulls out a little velvet pouch and sends a funny smile my way. "I wanted you to be here when I showed this to Daisy. Just in case."

"Just in case what?"

"Daisy, I have something for you," she says loud enough to get my girl's attention.

"What is it?" she says, wiping her hands on the cute little apron wrapped around her waist.

Carla motions for Daisy to open up her hands and turns the pouch over so the contents trickle out.

There's a tangled-up necklace that has seen better days. A small pair of simple gold hoop earrings. And a thick high school graduation ring.

"These belonged to your mother. She unknowingly left them behind when she moved to London. She told me to hold on to them for when she came back. And now, well... I think these belong to you."

Daisy's eyes well as one finger traces reverently over the ring, then the earrings. "My mother wore these?"

Carla nods. "Oh yes. All the time. I tried to get the necklace fixed after she passed, but the chain is broken in multiple places, and the locket was cracked open long ago, leaving one side scratched and unusable. But I was thinking, maybe you could..."

"I could repurpose it," Daisy says quickly, her eyes darting between Carla and me. "I've seen videos where old jewelry has been melted down and turned into something new and beautiful. Giving the piece of jewelry another chance to shine." Her eyes are back on the priceless gold in her hands as my eyes meet Carla's knowing ones.

I'm going to have to thank her for that later. But for now, I simply say, "I know a jeweler. I can have him clean up the ring and earrings and see what he can offer when it comes to the necklace. That sound okay with you?" Daisy seems hesitant to hand them over when I open my hand for them. "It's okay if you need time to hold on to them first. Get acquainted with the pieces before handing them off to be cleaned and altered."

She releases a deep breath. "Yeah, maybe give me a couple of days to... I don't know, stare at them?" She chuckles. "But I would love to get them cleaned up so I can wear them as soon as possible. Nick should have the graduation ring, and I'll keep the earrings. And maybe we could have something created out of this poor old piece."

"Whenever you're ready." I lean down to meet her eyes, then kiss her forehead.

Because that's what the rest of our future depends on. Daisy's readiness for the next steps.

I excuse myself to use the bathroom, mostly for a moment of solitude. I've been seeing my therapist more often since Daisy and I got together, and the sessions have forced me to face the fears that I do an exceptional job at ignoring.

I close the door behind me and stare at my reflection in the ornate bathroom mirror as I rest my hands against the marble counter.

Every time I tell her how locked-in I am with us, with our future, I worry that I'm rushing her. Threatening to tattoo her name on me and change her last name to mine in front of a stadium full of baseball fans.

Jesus fucking Christ. I lost the plot with that one.

I actually said it out loud. Because I definitely meant it and those things are on my to-do list.

Daisy swears it's romantic, even though I sometimes think I'm operating like a lunatic.

I'm concerned I might be smothering her. Which is why I packed an overnight bag and planned on driving up to the cabin for a night or two alone so Daisy can have the chance to say goodbye to the people who have become family for her over the past few days.

I know my girl, and I don't want her to feel obligated to stay by my side when she should be enjoying these new relationships she's been gifted. It's my attempt at proving to myself that I can be a selfless, good boyfriend to Daisy, even when the thought of purposefully spending the night away from her feels like leaving a piece of my soul behind, the soul that I now believe is in fact worthy of her love.

But I already know I hit the jackpot with Daisy, and I don't want to fuck it up. I already felt like a creeper when I revealed that I owned two floors in our building, including her current apartment.

And as I saw her standing among the crowd that so naturally gravitates toward her, it struck me that the people in this very home could one day be my family as well. I still struggle to let people in, but the ones standing outside this door? They somehow snuck up on me and claimed me as one of their own long before I ever realized it was happening. No number of blunt words or brush-offs could keep them away.

They're here, and I hope to hell I can keep a tight hold on them like I do with Daisy.

With that invigorating thought, I solidify my resolve. I know better than anyone the importance of taking space for one's well-being. And if Daisy is too nice to ask for it, I'll offer it before she can feel guilty about wanting to enjoy her life with wonderful people who are ready to love on her.

Chapter Fifty-Eight
LUKE

The drive seems to drag on longer than usual.

Not even playing our favorite podcasts was enough to pass the time.

When I finally pull into my driveway, I groan at the memory of Daisy's reaction a few hours ago. The look on her face when I told her I was taking off early so she could enjoy her family almost had me eating my words and apologizing for causing that cute crease in her forehead.

But I stayed strong. I must have had a good reason to come up here by myself. Can't necessarily recall it now as I trudge up my front steps and open my front door, but I'm sure they were good. Decent, even? Somewhat logical?

Nope, still can't recall.

I'm deep in thought, moving mindlessly for so long that it takes a while to register that there are candles lit in the living room. And jazz music playing from the speakers. And it smells like... a home cooked meal.

What the hell did I just walk into?

"Oh good, you're finally home." Daisy pops into my line of sight, and I stagger back a step.

Her hair is bundled on top of her head in a loose bun, and she has a cider in hand. She's wearing nothing but one of my T-shirts and a dark pair of wool socks.

"Want to eat first or shower? I'm sure it was a long drive. Here, I'll grab your bag for you."

She moves toward my bag, but I drop it and pull her by the waist into my side, causing her to yelp. "Am I... hallucinating?"

She smiles as she pulls me down gently and places a quick kiss on my lips.

And I finally exhale. She's here. She's really here.

But this doesn't make any sense.

"H-how are you here? I left you at your brother's... and now?" I point over my shoulder, as if I've nailed the general direction of Manhattan behind me.

She tsks as she steps out of my hold, bringing the bottle of cider to her lips. "I must say, I am disappointed that you don't immediately know. I mean, c'mon. How many times did we watch *The Parent Trap* together in this very home?" She smirks before taking a long sip.

My jaw unhinges. I'm unable to form a sentence, so she carries on. "Oh, you know how it goes. The person with the faster mode of transportation beats the person who is dealing with self-doubt when it comes to the love of their life, yada yada." She waves her hand up and down at me teasingly.

"Yada yada?" I brush a hand over my mouth, the bristles of my beard keeping my hand from reaching for her until I get this straight. "You got on Nick's plane. Alone?" I ask, astonished.

She places her bottle on the kitchen island before walking over to me, nodding with an exaggerated pout. "Yes. And there was turbulence. And you weren't there to punch the air for me." She tenderly punches my pec.

I pull her into my arms, needing to touch her. Her arms wrap around my back, her nails scratching through my shirt in a way that makes me want to curl into her. "I can't believe you did that."

She burrows into my chest, humming. "You have no problem making grand gestures, and neither do I. Not when it comes to you." She places a kiss to the center of my chest before giggling and meeting my stunned eyes. "Besides, five minutes after you left, all the tías were shooing me out of the house with their tea towels, asking me what the hell I was doing not chasing after my, and I quote, 'hunk of a man.'" She grins. "By the time I got my shoes on, enough food to last us a week had been packed up and was being pushed into my arms. And don't worry about our visitors. Nick had already extended Carla's trip, and her kids are on a flight with her new husband as we speak so they can visit New York City for the first time. All expenses paid by my brother, of course. I think he was feeling a little left out on the spoiling when you footed the bill for everyone to come up. So he had to try and one-up you."

I huff. "I knew he wouldn't let that slide." I run my hands up and down her back, relishing her warmth. "Are you sure you're not missing out by being up here with me? There's so much time to make up for with your guests, and I've been monopolizing a lot of your time. I promise to learn how to chill out and let you have a life outside of our relationship. Eventually."

She nuzzles into my hold, eyes closed as she speaks. "You're cute. But you're also an idiot." I pull back to see the amused look on her face. "Luke, I spent most of my life alone. Nick is ten years older, so we've always been in different phases of life. If I wasn't in a classroom, I was by myself. Walking through life with people who were paid to be by my side or others who wanted something from my last name. Being wanted by you and the new people in my life is a privilege. Being overwhelmed with attention is not a hardship, but an answered prayer. I mean, sure, I might mess up here and there and overcommit myself to social gatherings until I learn how to balance it all. But I promise, if I need space, I'll let you know. You're going to have to trust that I can speak up for myself now. Just like I know you might not voice your concerns right off the bat."

I hold her tighter, not knowing what to say, besides the obvious. "You're right. I should have talked to you instead of assuming you couldn't speak up for yourself. Hell, I experienced life on the receiving end of your wrath when you thought I'd forgotten to bring your cookies to the stadium."

She glares up at me. "Yeah, some lines, we don't cross with me. Specifically, if it involves delicious baked sweets." I swat her ass, and she rolls her eyes. "C'mon, let's get you fed before we end up naked."

My stomach growls right on cue and she shakes her head as she steps out of my hold and toward the kitchen. I start walking to the bathroom as I say, "I'll wash up real quick, then we'll eat. But after, I have something I want to show you."

Chapter Fifty-Nine

DAISY

We're in Luke's truck, bouncing down an unpaved road on his property.

The sun is beginning to set, casting us in a beautiful afterglow.

"I hope you're not bringing me all the way out here to have sex when we have a perfectly good bed back at the cabin," I say as I cross my arms over my chest.

Luke pierces me with a heated look as he continues to drive effortlessly, balancing his left wrist against the steering wheel. His right hand reaches out to grab mine and places it firmly on his thigh. "Get your head out of the gutter, Daze."

I exhale loudly. "Oh yeah, sure. Eye fuck me and then send me on my merry way."

He chuckles. "Almost there. In fact, we can stop right here." He parks the car and hops out. Before I get the chance to take in the view, my door pops open and Luke is scooping me out of my seat.

"I can walk, you know," I weakly protest, because I do love being in Luke's arms.

"You're capable of anything, Daisy. I'm just a selfish bastard who can't get enough of you. Please bear with me."

I sigh loudly. "If I must."

He carries me bridal style up a hill. It's criminal that this man is somehow not out of breath by the time we reach the top.

He places me on my feet, then walks around until he's holding me from behind. I close my eyes as I let my head fall back against his broad chest, enjoying the sense of safety I feel when he's near.

His beard tickles my ear as he leans down. "Open your eyes, Daisy. This is kind of important."

My heart kickstarts, foolishly thinking that all those promises of forever are about to begin right now. In this moment, I know deep in my heart that it's not too soon. I don't need to wait for any archaic timeline most likely determined by a patriarchal society that places value on a woman based on her association to a man.

I just wish I'd worn a bra for this.

"Easy, Daisy girl. That's coming, just not right now." I can hear the smile in his voice and tilt my head down in embarrassment. "Oh no, none of that. I've got plans for us. You're going to have to be patient for a little longer. In the meantime, I need to hear your thoughts."

I clear my throat as I shyly meet his eyes. "On what?"

His eyes stay locked on mine as he nods before us. "On whether or not this view is nice enough for our bedroom in our new home." His hand gently moves my chin so I'm facing forward, and the air is sucked out of my lungs.

Before me is the most beautiful sunset I've ever seen, dipping low between the green mountains, shining pinks, purples and oranges over the lake way down below.

Oak trees surround us, standing tall over the untamed wildflowers that claim the land as far as the eye can see.

"Oh my God, Luke! This is beautiful."

His lips skim my neck. "Hmm, I agree." I face him, our lips brushing faintly as he keeps his eyes trained on me. "But you still haven't answered my question."

"There was a question? I mean seriously, look at this insane view." I turn back in time to see the wind pick up and send leaves flying whimsically over the ground.

"I was thinking bedroom, but I guess we can also design the home so we share this view with the living room as well." He turns me in his hold, breaking my trance and tuning me into what he's saying.

"Huh? You want to build another cabin up here?"

He shakes his head. "No, I want to build our new home up here."

"Our new home?" I parrot, eyes wide.

His hand reaches out, tucking a loose curl behind my ear before cradling my cheek. "We'll always have our place in the city, and our little cabin will always be our secret hiding spot. But here? I was thinking this could be the place where we can recharge. Come back to nature. Host barbecues with friends, go swimming in the lake in the summer, and skate in the winter when it freezes over. A place that is uniquely ours, with pictures of our loved ones on a massive wall by the entrance and a media room to watch all your favorite movies." He leans closer, his eyes shining with love and vulnerability. "And when you're ready, a place where you walk down the aisle… to me. Where our children can run wild and free, exactly like their mother has taught me to do. A home that started the moment I convinced you to run away with me and never look back. That's what I want to build."

My heart rate from before has nothing against the galloping beat in my chest now. "Y-you want all that." I swallow. "*All of that?*" My eyelashes clump with unshed tears.

Our noses brush as he nods. "All of that and more. Much, much more. With you." His lips don't wait another second to claim mine.

He pours every bit of himself into his kiss as I cling to him.

He reaches down and picks me up by the back of my thighs without breaking our connection, and I wrap my arms around him, allowing myself to fantasize about the life Luke has so beautifully depicted. My mind snags on his mention of us having children together, and I pull myself back before I start attempting those baby making plans immediately.

He places his forehead against mine, breathing heavily before he asks, "So what do you say, Daisy girl? Sound like a plan to you?"

I look back out to the view. He takes advantage and kisses my neck.

"Well..." I pause.

He stops his ministrations on my neck. "Well?" His arms tighten around me.

I sigh dramatically. "Does this mean I'll have to get a matching ring finger tattoo? I am a bit adverse to needles, so I need to know what's in the fine print before I agree to anything." I play with his hair as I look at him pensively.

His eyes flash before he nips the spot right under my ear. "Don't play with me, Daze. You know I'll get down on one knee right now if that's what it takes."

I wiggle in his hold, unable to hold in my laughter. "Okay, okay, yes! Let's build a home. Let's do all of it."

He stops, his face going serious. "Yeah?" He searches my eyes. "All of it?"

I nod. "All of it."

"Good." He heaves out a breath. "That's good."

I giggle as I nod at his truck. "Let's go find that bed I'm so fond of before you go off and make that tattoo appointment."

Chapter Sixty

LUKE

SUMMER

"I STILL CAN'T BELIEVE how much you cried at Mateo and Isabella's wedding." Daisy smiles down at her phone, no doubt looking at all the photos we took at their wedding this weekend.

It was a quick forty-eight-hour affair, since they're planning a bigger wedding in the off season, but it was beautiful. They lit up the entire Altos de Chavón amphitheater with candles, and we watched them get married under the stars, alongside their family and friends.

The only thing that broke my concentration during the vows was the less than covert way Middlebrooks was staring at my sister, who did her very best to keep her distance from him. I really hoped things would have smoothed over by now, especially since she's the new team photographer and travels with us to away games. Sooner or later, they're going to have to leave the high school drama behind them and play nice.

Daisy and I decided to stay an extra two days at the house in Jarabacoa that she inherited from her mother. The same house Nick and Luisa got married in a few months ago. This place holds a lot of happy memories for my Daisy girl, and today I hope to add another to the list.

"I wasn't crying, I was stoically weeping. At least that's how Nick put it."

"Ugh, I can't believe you guys are such besties now. I think he took more pictures with you at the wedding than with Luisa."

"That's because midway through, he snuck off with her behind the restaurant and I caught them—"

"Never mind, you were a stoic, burly manly man who released axe-wielding tears. There, is that better?"

I pounce without warning. Over the past few months, she's developed quite the mouth on her, and I've loved seeing her new sense of self flourish beautifully. I love punishing her in bed for it too.

"Get off. Your beard is tickling me," she squeals.

I lift my head from where I was nipping under her jaw. "I thought you liked it when my beard tickled you." I raise both brows playfully and I let her escape my hold. For now.

"I can't believe I took such a long nap after breakfast. Those tres golpes really took me out."

I smile. "A breakfast of mashed plantains, fried cheese, and salami will do that to you, I suppose."

"Oh yeah, and you eating me out after as dessert didn't do a single thing to send me into that coma whatsoever."

I shrug unapologetically as I watch her reach over to the nightstand for her laptop. Looks like it's almost time. Hope I don't fuck this up.

I try to nonchalantly come to sit by her and lean against the headboard. It's convenient since what I need is hidden under this very pillow.

"Oh no you don't." She tries to shoo me away. "I've got work to do, and if we're in bed together long enough, you know exactly what's going to happen."

I don't budge. Instead, I play my role as best as I can while racked with nerves. "First of all, you're not supposed to be working on our vacation."

"The intern said he needs help finalizing the clips to use for this week's segment of Hot Mic. It shouldn't take me more than ten minutes. Twenty tops," she promises.

I sigh. "All right, then maybe I can help you so we can get back to our vacation festivities."

She quirks a brow my way but doesn't insist on me moving. Thank God.

"Hmm, that's weird," she says as she types.

"What is?" I'm scared she might be able to hear my heart attempting to beat out of my chest.

"The attachment. It's usually a couple audio clips I can play right from the email, but instead it's a link to open a much larger file."

I stay quiet, not trusting my acting skills at the moment.

Her face is set in concentration as she continues to type on her keyboard. Then she presses play.

"Raise the volume," I all but shout before clearing my throat. "So I can hear and help you out."

She doesn't pay any mind to my sudden outburst as she does as I ask, and we wait in silence for a few moments.

"This must be wrong. I don't hear anything—wait, there's live transcripts on these?"

```
AUDIO RECORDING #1

"Testing, testing. One, two, three."

"Thank you so much for doing this, Luke. You really
didn't have to, but I very much appreciate it."
```

Her head tilts. "Wait, is that us? Why did they send me—"

"Keep listening, Daze." My stare must communicate more than I intended, because she goes stock still before maxing out the volume.

```
"So how does this work again, Daisy?"

"Only I will have access to your broadcast. Today is
just to see if the equipment is all good to go
before presenting it to the social media team and
having them sign off on mic'ing our players. So no
pressure. Go along as you normally would."

"Do I have to talk to you through here?"

"I'm sorry, I didn't mean to laugh. Everyone just
jokes that you're not much of a talker, so I don't
want to scare you into thinking that you're doing a
Ted Talk or anything. Like I said, go on how you
usually would and ignore that I'm listening."

"Hmm, right."
```

"Since you're my first test subject, you can pick what channel you want to be on. Give me a number one through ten."

"Oh. Um, what's your favorite number?"

"Mine? Uh, I guess I'll have to go with lucky number seven."

"Really?"

"Yeah, why?"

"That was my jersey number."

"Was it now? I might have seen or heard that around here."

"Daisy…"

"Okay, so I guess that's all. Have a good game, and thanks again!"

AUDIO RECORDING #2

"You really don't have to do this again, Luke. I don't want you to feel like you have to do this every game."

"Did you get what you needed from my recording?"

"Y-yeah I did, thanks. Also discovered what I should tweak for this go around. I'm mic'ing two players today, and we'll see if we can get enough to convince the team that we should go full steam ahead with this segment."

"I'm sure they will."

"Thank you."

"You already thanked me."

"Not for this. But for believing in me."

"Daisy…"

"Sorry, don't know why I got weepy all of a sudden. Promise you I'm not a basket case. Mostly."

"Hey, before you go. Want to eat lunch at my office, or yours tomorrow? And uh, you can tell me more about the segment, and maybe I can help coach the guys on what they should or shouldn't do while mic'd, to help your chances of getting picked up?"

"Oh, wow. Yeah, I mean yes. That'd be great! See you tomorrow."

"See ya, Daisy."

AUDIO RECORDING #17

"So at this point, I've gathered that you've given up on listening to my recordings past the first few innings, isn't that right, Daisy? I tested my theory during the last two recordings, when I made a joke about your brother, then repeated it to you a few days later and you showed no signs of recognition. God, it feels like I'm talking to myself like a weirdo, but I guess this is where I'm at. Talking to a mic instead of the girl I had no business falling for."

AUDIO RECORDING #37

"You know, for a minute there I thought I was being reckless. Thinking you'd figure out that I only speak directly to you, into this tiny mic, during the seventh inning. At first it was just a dumb thought. Playing on the idea of seven being your favorite number, and my jersey number… Although sometimes I wonder, is it really your favorite number or did it have anything to do with me? I'm not an idiot. I know you're engaged. Even speaking these thoughts out loud should make me feel like a terrible man, but it doesn't. Instead, maybe I should ask you if you really do listen to my recordings past the first few innings. And if you do, beg that you put me out of my misery."

AUDIO RECORDING #57

"He's an asshole and he doesn't deserve you. There, I said it. Not directly to you, but close enough. I saw how he treated you in front of your friends and how he took away your cake as if you were a child on the verge of a tantrum and not a grown-ass woman capable of making her own damn decisions. God, Daisy. What the hell do you see in him?"

AUDIO RECORDING #77

"I can't believe I did it, but I told you to your face. Not my truth, but what I pray is yours. You don't love him. But you're still going to marry him. And I'm still going to be there, because you asked me to. But I can't fault you for standing by your convictions. If I did, I'd be a hypocrite. You won't admit that you don't love him, and I won't confess that I love you. Now isn't that something?"

AUDIO RECORDING #97

"Three days. One hour. And five minutes. That's how much time is left before you walk down the aisle to another man. And it's slowly killing me, Daisy. With each second that passes, I feel you slipping through my fingers. Which is ridiculous, because I never really had you. Not in the way I desperately want to. But now it's too late. You're actually gonna go through with it. Like you said you would. I think I'm going to have to take some time off. I'll most likely be heading to a home I own up north. Would have loved to take you there. And show you the field of daisies I've spent almost a year planting. Although now that I say that out loud, I think the sight might have you running for the hills, so maybe it's best you don't find out about my little gardening hobby… But I guess that's something I really don't need to worry about now. Because you're marrying him, and there's nothing I can do about it. Fuck."

AUDIO RECORDING #98

"Well, this feels silly to do now. Especially since we've just come back from a week at my cabin. Our cabin, actually. Yeah, I like the way that sounds better. God, Daisy. I don't know how the hell I managed to pull this off, but I'm not going to question it. Because the second you told me you loved me is the moment I started putting our future into motion. I know I should be telling you this and not a mini microphone in my jacket, but I'm deathly afraid of losing you now that I finally know what it is to have you. But I'll always fight for us, our future. I'll always put you first and never allow you a second of doubt when it comes to my love for you."

AUDIO RECORDING #117

"My little Houdini. Can't believe you hopped on a jet and beat me to the cabin. I'll admit, I let my fears get the best of me and lived up to that Home Runner nickname. But I've got plans for you, future Mrs. Daisy Weston, and I promise the only place I'll ever be running to from here on out, is back home to you."

AUDIO RECORDING #147

"This recording is going to be a little different, so I need you to listen closely, Daze. I'm not in the dugout, and this isn't the seventh inning. Instead, I'm in our cabin up in the mountains, sitting up in bed, frozen in place by the sight of you sitting out back with a cup of coffee in hand and your face tilting up to the sky. I've thought of so many ways to do this with you, many of them you know of since I've not so subtly told you that you're marrying me no matter what, but I think I've finally got it all figured out. Because I don't want to just tell you that I love you more than anything on this heavenly planet. Or make promises about what I can give you throughout our lives. Although I know I won't be able to help myself and will continue to do both of those things until my dying breath. But no, I want you to be so sure, know so deeply in your bones how far gone I am for you, that I want to take it all the way back to the very beginning. Long before I threw your veil out of my truck window and somehow convinced you to run away with me. Which is why I had all those prior recordings included before this one. Fair warning, there are more of them if you want to have a listen, but please know I tried to pick the least pathetic ones for my sake. Okay, now back to why I'm really recording on my phone on this fine morning. In a few days, we head down to the Dominican Republic.

> Initially I thought that this cabin would be the perfect place to ask you, officially, to be my wife. But then I remembered that I needed to ask your mother's blessing for your hand first. And what better place to do that than at the house where she grew up? The place littered with evidence of her heart and emotional fingerprints. One of her children got married there, and the other hopefully, will get engaged. What better way to honor your mother than to live out her greatest hope for her children? To embrace her dream that they live a big life filled with the love she could only ever fantasize about. So if you look over to me now, you'll probably see me looking like a poor sap trying to keep it together and failing miserably. By now I should be taking out the ring I had specially made for you."

I pull the ring box out from under my pillow and slide off the bed. Bringing myself down to one knee, I open it. My recording continues to play as Daisy places both hands on her cheeks.

> "It's made with the recycled material from your mother's gold necklace. The jeweler was able to create a simple but sturdy band. One that curves and intertwines within itself, creating the look of a vine. The three smaller diamonds on each side of the three-carat center diamond create the illusion of a flower. A wildflower. Just like my girl. And now I think I'll hand it over… to myself. In person."

Tears silently stream down her face as she stares at me, then the ring, in awe. "Luke, is this really happening right now?"

I nod. "Yes, and surprisingly enough, I still have more to say."

We both laugh, breaking the tension that built while we listened intently to my mic recordings. She scoots down the bed, sitting on the edge where I'm currently waiting for her on bended knee.

I take the ring out of the box and take her left hand in mine. "For so long, I battled with the fact that I no longer wanted to be *just* your friend." She smiles. "When in reality, I wanted to be your very *best* one."

She sniffles as I continue. "The person you walk down the aisle to and raise children with. The one to hold your hand when life undoubtedly throws us a few curveballs. Instead of friendship bracelets, we'll have rings... or tattoos." I smirk as she shakes her head. "We'll share secrets and a last name. Our life will be one everlasting sleepover. And when the real world gets too crazy, we can run away together to our secret haven. The place where the rest of the world ceases to exist."

She hiccups and giggles through her tears. I need to wrap this up before we're both in the same boat. "Daisy, not only do I want to be your forever best friend," I lean down and kiss her bare ring finger, "but I want to be your husband. I want to be your family. So, I'll ask you today, like I ask you every day. What do you want, Daisy? Think you wanna do forever with a grizzly grump like me?" I blink away the tears so I don't miss the beautiful sight before me.

She wipes her cheeks with her free hand and takes a deep breath. "I want to be your wife, Luke. I want to be the mother of your children, and I want to see you become the best father on the planet. I want a small wedding with our closest friends and family. And I want to start forever as soon as possible with you as my husband."

I slip the ring onto her finger before my trembling fingers dare drop it, and we both stare at how right it looks on her hand. Then I haul her onto my bent knee and kiss her deeply.

"I love you. Can't believe you're wearing my ring on your finger." I kiss her smiling lips.

"I love you. So freaking much. I can't believe you pulled that off! That must have been so hard to do, pulling all those recordings, getting the transcripts, working with someone from my team—"

She's rambling, listing off a few of the many steps I had to take to get this done right. Of course she'd be concerned about the logistics when she's usually the one taking care of everyone else. But she's going to have to get used to it, because I plan on spending the rest of my life taking care of her.

I hold her face in my hands and gently pull her focus away from the laptop on her bed as she continues to rattle off the details of my proposal. "Hard? Daisy, I'm only going to say this once, so pay attention." She straightens on my lap. "There are things we can't control in life. We will be tested in more ways than one. Whether it has to do with work, our past traumas, or simply our day-to-day life." I scan her face and look deeply into the eyes I get to call my home for the rest of eternity. "Being away from you is hard. Talking about my past is painful. But loving you? It's the easiest thing I've ever had the privilege of doing. And it's been an honor to stand by your side as your boyfriend. But as your husband? Just you wait and see what life has in store for us, because something tells me that it's gonna be good."

EPILOGUE
DAISY

FALL
MY WEDDING DAY... AGAIN

I'VE ALWAYS DREAMED OF my wedding day.

Not so much the decor or guest list, but rather the quiet moments in between the madness with my new husband.

And luckily, I won't have to dream about it much longer.

Luke and I are meeting our friends and family at the private airstrip and boarding Nick's plane. Then we're heading to our brand new home in the Adirondacks Mountains. I don't know how the hell Luke got our massive home completed so quickly. Maybe throwing mind-numbing amounts of money and sending burly growls at our contractor did the trick.

Because today at sunset, I'll be marrying the man of my dreams in our living room. The one with sixty-foot ceilings and equally large glass windows that overlook the breathtaking landscape.

The fact that everyone will be staying on our property makes it feel like I'm finally getting a long overdue big family sleepover.

Luke has taken me by surprise, being more involved in the wedding planning process than I anticipated. He almost sent me into cardiac arrest when he reenacted his shirtless axe-swinging performance, this time to build a wedding arch for us. If there hadn't been contractors on the property hustling to get our house done in time, I would have been on my man in an instant. But like the good little fiancée I am, I sat and watched as my future husband hand crafted an incredible piece of woodwork. One that will be decorated with wildflowers and white daisies. Like the ones in front of our little cabin, the one that is meant only for the two of us.

I should have known he'd be this way about our wedding day. I knew that man was itching to run down the aisle. That point was evident when he got my name tattooed on his ring finger a few days after we got engaged.

Though I thought he would scrap our plans all together when I surprised him with a matching tattoo of an L on my ring finger, with vines that were a perfect replica to the ones on my engagement ring.

He almost had us reciting our vows right then and there. He also promised to get the daisy tattoo that he's apparently been planning for a very long time.

But now, with the way he's fussing over me, the real feat will be leaving the apartment on time. Concerned that we're breaking all the rules by seeing one another on our wedding morning, long before I'm due to slip into my beautiful and very comfortable white dress.

Aside from being tailor made for me, it's flowy and whimsical, and best of all, it has pockets. Although I am a bit partial to my second dress. The one I'll be wearing tonight.

The one meant for dancing and eating our Dominican feast. It's a short little white number, with detachable see-through sleeves that run up my arms up until my neckline. The best part? It poofs around my hips, exaggerating my curves instead of trying to hide them. My wedding stylist paired it with a beautiful pair of broken-in white heels. I'll wear them for a few photos, but Luke's already packed my white Converses, my lucky runaway shoes, for me to wear as I dance the night away.

Luke walks into the apartment looking flushed. "Okay, the car taking us to the airport is all packed. Am I forgetting anything? Shoes? Dress? Veil?" He pats his jacket and jeans pockets as if he'd find those objects there.

Usually, I would tease him mercilessly about being so flustered. But I can't, because it seems as though I'm in the same boat with him today, but for a completely different reason.

"Everything is all set. But we're forgetting one thing."

He straightens, scanning my apartment, the one we're living in while we make plans for the renovations that we'll take on next year. I couldn't imagine managing two active home construction sites, especially now that the team is only one month away from potentially playing in the World Series.

"What are we missing?" he asks nervously when I don't come right out with it.

I lift my yellow Polaroid camera from the entry table. "We need one last picture of you and me for the wall. Our last photo before we're officially husband and wife."

His shoulders relax, and I finally get that sweet smile that's been buried under his worries all morning. The smile he saves just for me.

He tries to take the camera from my hands—I usually defer all picture-taking to him since he towers over me—but this picture is one I'm going to need to take the lead on. "I got it. I need the right angle. It's an important shot, you know."

His brows rise playfully. "Where do you want me, wife?"

I tap my chin, feigning concentration. "Unfortunately, we don't have time for that specific position, but I guess this will have to do." I walk him backward, careful to have him facing the exact position I need him in for our photo. "Right by our photo wall. The one filled with the people we love and all of our happy memories."

The wall has become a ridiculous art project. A road map of our happiness. It is overflowing with postcards, Polaroids, and wedding invitations, to name a few things. It's so full that two or three things share pins now. Which means it's easy to miss the item I put up five minutes ago.

I step into Luke's arms, the ones that circle around me without hesitation, point the small camera at us, and smile. The delicate flash goes off, then the photo slowly slips out. I hold it by the corner gently, knowing that the next sixty seconds might be the longest of my life.

"Okay, let's pin it and get to the car. Nick is already on the plane, and I don't want anyone touching your ciders."

I chuckle. "I'm sure that on a plane with fancy champagne and expensive bottles of liquor, my adult apple juice will be safe. Besides, I won't be drinking on the plane."

He nods, kissing my temple. "Yeah, I'm not drinking either. I want to be sharp during our vows and need to make sure my breath is minty fresh for our first kiss." His knuckles tip my chin up, his lips taking mine in a slow dance that is so effortlessly us.

He pulls back, eyes shining with happiness, then whispers, "Let's go get married."

I look down quickly at the developed Polaroid in my hand, then meet his gaze with a watery smile of my own. "Let's go get married. But first, we need to put this on the wall. How do you think it turned out?"

He takes it from my fingers, and I find myself holding my breath. Until his laugh breaks me out of my nerves. "Daze, you might have to leave the picture-taking to me, you and I are barely in it. It's mostly our faces close up, and that huge chunk of wall behind us."

"You sure? I think I see the three of us in that photo."

His face scrunches in confusion as he looks for the mystery person I speak of. I know the moment he sees it, because he spins around, wide-eyed, hands hovering over the most important picture on our wall, as if he's trying to figure out if it's okay to touch it.

The sonogram picture of our baby.

His head whips in my direction. "Is this... are we... I mean you, are you—"

"Pregnant." I bite my lip, tears starting to run down my cheeks. "We're pregnant."

He drops down to his knees, hands on my still flat stomach, and leans forward to place a kiss there. "Our baby is in there?" he whispers.

I nod, wiping away my happy tears. "Looks like we brought a plus-one to our own wedding." I laugh shakily.

"Our baby. You're pregnant with... our baby. God, Daisy," he says in wonder.

"I went in yesterday for my annual checkup with my gynecologist. When my doctor walked into the room, she asked me how my first trimester symptoms were treating me. I had no idea the urine sample I'd given before I walked into the room would test positive for pregnancy. I haven't been puking, which is the only symptom I generally relate to pregnancy. And my birth control allows me to skip my periods, so not having one is normal for me. Hence, how I missed all the signs."

"But you've been tired—no, exhausted." He shoots back up to his feet and places his large hands on my cheek. "Are you okay? Is that normal?"

I smile. "Yes, it's very normal. I thought it was all the extra hours I was putting in at work after Hot Mic went viral. Turns out, I was actually a tired mama-to-be. I'm perfectly fine, and so is our baby. We hit the twelve-week mark two days ago."

"Okay, that's good. I have no idea what it means, but I'm assuming it's good. Right? Shit, I need... books. And to take a class. Twelve weeks, so we have what, six months left. All right, we can do this. But we need to baby-proof this place first." He points erratically at the living room. "That coffee table has pointy edges, so that's got to go. And, uh, plugs. Damn, I've never realized how many plugs we have in this house. We need—"

"To go get married. Or have I so quickly become chopped liver?" I sigh while holding in a chuckle.

"My Daisy girl." He leans down and kisses me thoroughly. "You're marrying me today."

"That's the plan."

"And our baby will be there." He smiles widely.

"And our families. Blood related and otherwise. The family and the love I've always dreamed of."

He nods. "I've always dreamed of you. And now you've given me permission to dream for more. For our little family."

I huff out a breath. "Okay it's my wedding day and I'm pregnant, so take it easy on my emotions, will ya?"

He laughs as he takes my hands and leads me out the door, but not before pinning our photo and bringing the sonogram image with us.

We say I do as the sun sets over the mountains, casting us in a kaleidoscope of vibrant colors.

I make funny faces while Luke whispers inappropriate jokes in my ear as we're taking our professional photos, causing me to belly-laugh throughout the whole thing.

We sneak kisses during the speeches and roll our eyes playfully when it's Nick turn on the mic and Luisa has to pry it out of his hands.

And when we've eaten more than we can handle, danced until we've lost track of our shoes, and cried more tears of happiness after announcing our pregnancy to the room brimming with love, we start to make our grand exit.

Luke loosens his tie as he smiles down at me.

I hop in his truck and wave at our guests who will be staying at the main house for the rest of the weekend.

"You ready to go home, wife?"

I wrap my ring-clad hand behind his neck. "If you're driving the getaway car? Always."

And off we go down the smoothly paved road leading back down to the bottom of the mountain.

Where he'll carry me over the threshold once again.

To our secret hideaway. The one that finally has an address.

On 7 Daisy Lane.

SURPRISE CHAPTER
VALENTINA

I can do this.

I'm a professional, after all.

All I have to do is get on that field and not punch my lying ex-boyfriend in his stupidly handsome face.

Because of course life couldn't do me a solid and make the man who shattered my heart into a million pieces hideous with age.

Nope. The fucker apparently had to go on and continue to use that panty-dropping smile as a weapon and become a household name.

You'd think that after ten years, I wouldn't be as affected as I am. But I guess I should have known that wouldn't be true, given that he's the reason I've refused to attend any MLB games for the last decade.

And it's kinda hard being a baseball photographer who refuses to step foot on a baseball field.

But today is my first official day on the job.

I have to come to terms with the fact that I'm going to be working with my ex and flying with his team all around the country too.

Maybe I'll use my flash to blind him when he gets within range or accidentally bring my camera lens out of focus when it's time to take his shots.

I shake the petty thoughts away.

I'm working for the New York Monarchs. With my brother's team and a whole crew of his friends that seemed to have welcomed me into the fold.

This is a very big deal and the best gig I could ever dream of.

So when it comes to Ace Middlebrooks, I'll have to stick to using my imaginary voodoo doll when times get tough, I suppose.

I giggle as I make my way toward Luke's office. I'm sure he wants to give me a "good luck" pep talk before I photograph my first game with the team. This place is massive, and I'm pretty sure I've taken a wrong turn once or twice, but I must be close to the clubhouse because I can hear the rowdy players the farther I walk down this narrow hallway.

I turn the corner and crash into a solid wall of muscle. I'm about to apologize when my eyes meet the ones my young and naïve heart once foolishly fell in love with.

"You," I accuse.

"You," he seethes right back.

I take a step to move around him. My brain cannot come up with a better comeback at the moment, and I'll be damned if I give this man the upper hand in wittiness. That title firmly belongs to me.

But when I move, so does he. And before I know it, he's pulling us through a side door I didn't see.

"Get your dirty paws off me. I'm not one of your groupies you can manhandle," I say as he closes the door to what I assume is a utility closet.

"Relax. I took you by the hand, like a true gentleman." He takes his baseball hat off and flips it backward.

My eyes narrow at the practiced movement. "Well, we'll have to agree to disagree on the gentleman claim, but since I have no desire to be alone in a room—closet—with you, I'll be going now. Shoo, pest." I wave my hands in his direction, hoping he disperses like a cloud of smoke.

His jaw ticks as he shakes his head. "It's the middle of the season. And this year, we're making it to the World Series. Therefore, you and I are going to have to address our past so we can move on from it and work together. Peacefully."

I chuckle darkly, offering him my fakest smile as I take a step toward him. "Do I look like the kind of woman who brings a man peace?" I bat my eyelashes.

His eyes quickly dart down my body and back up to my eyes. And I fucking hate that I felt every inch where his gaze lingered. "No, Valentina. You look like the kind of woman who could bring a man to his knees." He takes a step closer as I grimace.

"Really? Dropping a line on me? In a closet full of towels and cleaning detergents? I must say, I'm unimpressed with your new moves. Thought they would have been a bit better with how often you have a new girl on your arm."

His eyebrows raise as he takes another step. "Keeping tabs on me? Aw, you shouldn't have."

"I wasn't," I say defensively. "If you haven't noticed, you work with my brother, and it's kinda hard to scrub your face off every TV screen I pass by. Trust me, I've asked around. Would cost a pretty penny."

I swear his lip twitches before he crosses his arms over his chest. "Let's get back to the part where we get to the bottom of what happened between the two of us so we can both move on." He takes one more step, and this time, I take one back.

"Moving on didn't seem to be a problem for you then, so why should it be now?" My words come out harsh, and I wish it didn't make it seem like I still cared. Because I don't. Obviously.

His eyes zero in on mine, and now he's closing the distance between us. He doesn't stop until my back hits the towel-stacked shelves, his hands coming to rest on either side of my head on the shelf above me.

"You know what, Valentina? I've had a long time to think about you—I mean us and your little disappearing act. And seeing you at your brother's birthday party, that anger... disgust... yeah, that didn't exactly come from nowhere, did it?" His eyes sear into mine, searching for answers he should already know. "I'm guessing, somewhere along the line, you and I got something very, very wrong. And I say we should have a sit-down and put it all on the table and clear up this decade-old misunderstanding. What do you say?" He aims his wicked smile my way, the one he must use on countless unsuspecting women. The one he used on me before I knew better.

And even though I'm certain his cologne is working some weird spell on me, I have enough wits about myself to put him back in his place, where he belongs.

"Hmm, mansplaining my own lived experiences." I smile. "That's a good one, Middlebrooks. But I have a job to do, and beyond their better judgment, you have fans waiting for a second of your attention. So I'll tell you how this," I try to point back and forth within the minuscule space he's left between us, "is going to go. I'm going to do my job and you're going to stay out of my way."

"Is that so?" he challenges.

"Yep. But—" I sigh dramatically.

"What is it?" he asks far too eagerly.

"I am going to have to ask you for one pesky little favor." I pout as I bring my hands up and start playing with the buttons of his jersey.

He goes rigid beneath my touch. "What's that?" He clears his throat.

I smile deviously as I grab a strong hold on his jersey. "Stop. Thinking. About. Me."

I didn't mean to pull him closer as I spoke each word.

Didn't mean to lift up higher on my tiptoes, bringing our lips dangerously close.

But as Ace's chest vibrates with a low growl, his nose brushing against mine, I know he means the next two words he says with every fiber of his being.

"You. First."

THE END

**Untitled
Coming 2026**

ACKNOWLEDGMENTS

I'm so happy Luke and Daisy's story is finally out! This book has been floating in my mind ever since the idea of the New York Monarchs was planted in my brain. And thanks to my husband for holding down the fort, I was finally able to put it all down on paper.

A special thanks to my PA Anlly, who (lovingly) bullies me into getting things done on time so my readers can get these stories in their hands as soon as possible. Thank you for not putting a restraining order on me after constantly cold calling you on facetime, just to share my random plot ideas and unrelated streams of consciousness, you're a real one!

My beta readers, the people who champion my characters and make sure we are doing them justice, Anlly, Ariadna, Esther, Carla, Lela, and Ayushi. Thank you for being so helpful, and completely unhinged in the google doc. It's truly one of my favorite parts of releasing a new book.

This book would not be legible if it weren't for my incredible editor Beth, and my proofreader Nyla. Thank you both so much for taking care of Luke and Daisy and making sure they shine to their fullest potential.

My author pals who have been put through the ringer with the number of times I've asked for their advice on cover changes, plot points, and slutty little tattoos. Thank you so much for hanging in there and not kicking me out of the group chats, you know who you are.

And most importantly, to my readers. Thank you so much for reading my stories and showing me that Latine love is something worth celebrating out loud. Your DM's and tags bring the biggest smiles to my face, and I don't know what I did to deserve your overwhelming support in this lifetime but promise to always try to do right by you. Maybe a little surprise release to show my undying gratitude perhaps? Until next time!

www.ingramcontent.com/pod-product-compliance
Lightning Source LLC
LaVergne TN
LVHW091652070526
838199LV00050B/2159